THREE CHORDS & THE TRUTH

ALSO BY CRAIG MCDONALD

The Hector Lassiter Series
One True Sentence
Forever's Just Pretend
Toros & Torsos
The Great Pretender
Roll the Credits
The Running Kind
Head Games
Print the Legend
Death in the Face
Write from Wrong (The Hector Lassiter Short Stories)

Standalones
El Gavilan

The Chris Lyon Series
Parts Unknown
Carnival Noir
Cabal
Angels of Darkness
The Daughters of Others
Watch Her Disappear

Nonfiction
Art in the Blood
Rogue Males

THREE CHORDS & THE TRUTH

A Hector Lassiter novel

CRAIG MCDONALD

BETIMES BOOKS

First published in the English language worldwide by Betimes Books
2016

www.betimesbooks.com

Print ISBN: 978-0-9934331-1-5

Three Chords & The Truth is a work of fiction. Names, characters,
places, and incidents are either the product of the author's
imagination or are used fictitiously. Any resemblance to actual
persons, living or dead, or locales is entirely coincidental.

Cover design by JT Lindroos

For Svetlana Pironko,
for everything

PRAISE

"[The Lassiter novels] are compelling, thrilling and darkly humorous. Lassiter is a brilliant creation—a crime writer who learned his trade with Ernest Hemingway and the Lost Generation in Paris in the 1920s. He is also a man who seems dangerously prone to violent intrigue, doomed love affairs, tragic marriages and military campaigns (he's a veteran of the Punitive Expedition, World War One, the Spanish Civil War and World War Two). Lassiter witnesses history unfolding and, occasionally, has a role in shaping its course. With *Three Chords and the Truth*, Craig McDonald has crafted a remarkable coda to the series."

—Steve Powell, *The Venetian Vase*

"With each of his Hector Lassiter novels, Craig McDonald has stretched his canvas wider and unfurled tales of increasingly greater resonance."

—Megan Abbott

"Reading a Hector Lassiter novel is like having a great uncle pull you aside, pour you a tumbler of rye, and tell you a story about how the 20th century 'really' went down."

—Duane Swierczynski

"What critics might call eclectic, and Eastern folks quirky, we Southerners call cussedness—and it's the cornerstone of the American genius. As in: "There's a right way, a wrong way, and my way." You want to see how that looks on the page, pick up any of Craig McDonald's novels. He's built him a nice little shack out there way off all the reg'lar roads, and he's brewing some fine, heady stuff. Leave your money under the rock and come back in an hour."

—James Sallis

"Craig McDonald is wily, talented and—rarest of the rare—a true original. He writes melancholy poetry that actually has melancholy poets wandering around, but don't turn your backs on them, either."

—Laura Lippman

"Experiencing the work of Craig McDonald is akin to experiencing a painting by Picasso, a dance by Baryshnikov, music by Tchaikovsky. No two people will experience it exactly the same, but everyone who does experience it will walk away richer."

—Jen Forbus, *Jen's Book Thoughts*

"James Ellroy + Kerouac + Coen brothers + Tarantino = Craig McDonald"

—Amazon.fr

*I wish I could be
who I was before
I was me.*

—Screamin' Jay Hawkins

BROKEN ARROW
(FEBRUARY 5, 1958)

I

Howard Richardson didn't wake up planning to dump a hydrogen bomb off the coast of South Carolina.

But sometime after midnight, Howard indeed slung an H-bomb into the shallow waters near Tybee Island. He *deliberately* turned loose that shiny tube of several tons of explosives—twelve feet and thousands of pounds of potential mass murder.

It was a snap decision—a necessary choice, he'd forever argue—and one that would haunt Howard for the rest of his life.

It started in the late-evening hours of February 4th: a simple training mission. A "milk run" the planners said.

But with the Cold War careening at fever pitch, some wrong-headed upper-brass member insisted on *really* testing the protocols, so he quietly had a fully operational bomb stowed on board Howard's craft, a fact not shared with the bomber's crew, or even with her captain.

The device was a state-of-the-art MK 15, whose incalculable lethality dwarfed the A-bombs dropped on the Japanese thirteen years before.

Howard and company departed Florida's Homestead Air Force Base just as they would if they were ordered to dump their payload for real, on the Reds.

Everything was textbook in the early going.

But somewhere high above the invisible border between Carolina and Georgia, at a cruising height of thirty-eight thousand feet, something slammed into the B-47.

There was a god-awful noise and a bone-jarring jerk.

This glow suddenly out there to his right—*Jesus!* Howard Richardson could see the flames guttering on the glass: His stomach dropped. They were on *fire.*

It's an engine, he'd later remember thinking.

For just an instant, Howard thought maybe they'd been struck by a chunk of meteor or similar outer-space debris. At this altitude, what the hell else could it be?

Then Howard knew: it had to have been another aircraft.

Jesus Christ, he thought, tugging hard at the wheel, *Jesus F. Christ!*

They had collided with an F-86 Sabre fighter jet as they would learn much later.

The tiny, transonic craft had scalloped away a hunk of the much bigger bomber's wing and nearly sheared off one of the B-47's engines. What remained of the ruined engine was left trembling at a near impossible angle and spitting flame.

The Sabre's pilot immediately ejected, leaving his crippled craft to crash. He prayed it would do so somewhere at sea.

Even as Howard registered the collision—correctly guessed its likely cause and the possible toll on his bird—he struggled to regain control of the big, steeply diving bomber.

Crew members were already preparing to eject themselves from the damaged B-47.

But Howard couldn't bear quickly jumping to personal safety and leaving his crippled bird and dummy payload to slam into some unknown part of the densely populated eastern seaboard.

Though it was his understanding the bomb they carried lacked its nuclear trigger—a capsule of enriched uranium—it still packed four-hundred pounds of conventional explosives used to initiate the plutonic reaction.

He snarled, "No," to his crew as they scrambled to abandon ship.

Howard hollered, "*No ejections, dammit!* Let me see if I can maybe still fly this bird!"

They plunged nearly eighteen thousand stomach-dropping feet before she at last began to respond.

At twenty-thousand feet, Howard finally succeeded in smoothing out her flight.

He'd gotten his girl level, but she was shaking something fierce. Her pilot had her flying now, had his craft under at least nominal control, but he didn't know what was left of her.

In particular, Howard didn't know how much damage might have been done to her *underside*. Her ability to put down safely might be critically compromised.

Still, Howard meant to try and bring her in for an emergency landing. Deprived the weight of the bomb, their chances for a survivable landing would increase exponentially.

But there was that bigger issue: the terrible possibility the B-47 might still go to pieces over a populated area as it made its final approach.

It was unthinkable to risk *that*.

Even absent the bomb, the plane itself slamming into a neighborhood would be a slaughter.

Howard turned to his copilot, briefly locking eyes.

They didn't need to talk it out or thrash it around much at all. They were both professionals. They had trained endlessly for every conceivable scenario.

Strategic Air Command tactical doctrine endowed them with the authority to dump a *dummy* bomb in order to preserve the lives and safety of their crew and those on the ground.

He saw it in his co-pilot's frightened eyes: *Let's do it, skipper.*

Howard estimated their distance from the coast of Savannah to be no more than two remaining miles.

No time left, not with a bum wing and a dangling engine that might make another circling turn same as suicide.

So he got her low and dropped the bomb over the water.

As he felt her go, he held his breath, waiting for a feared explosion that never came.

Thank God!

Skirting the shallows, Dusty Beller wandered in the early morning fog with his gimpy old coon dog, Clayton.

Dusty had been fighting some kind of infernal insomnia, going on a full week now. He thought maybe some cool, clean early morning air would soothe his mind. He figured the hike might at least make him tired enough to at last sleep.

But something up there in the sky caught his attention, a trace of light Dusty first thought to be a falling star. Thinking he'd wish himself some shut-eye, he watched it tearing across the sky in silence for a moment.

Then he saw it was veering a bit, left to right. That didn't seem right. That was when Dusty realized it was a plane in trouble.

A low but increasingly shrill whistle grew louder, grew *closer*.

Something slammed into the Atlantic. A light-catching plume of spray rose high above the treetops, then doused Dusty in a cascade of falling water.

Drenched, trembling Clayton began a frantic barking jag.

Living close by an air base for as long as he had, Dusty had come to know all manner of military craft. He could usually identify them by simple shape and engine noise.

But this one sounded like nothing he'd ever heard, and certainly was not the kind of aircraft he was used to seeing overhead.

Miles away, Howard at last brought his crippled bomber in safely at Hunter Army Airfield in Savannah.

It was a masterful feat of flying under extreme duress: everyone assured him that was so. He reveled in the back claps and hearty handshakes from peers who could best appreciate his achievement under the most horrific conditions.

In the immediate afterglow, once he let himself think about what he'd done, Howard was equally proud of his performance—impressed by his own display of grace under the most extreme form of pressure.

His commanders awarded him the Distinguished Flying Cross for his cool handling of what could easily have become an unprecedented catastrophe.

That should have been the story, Howard thought. *That* should have been the stuff of all the resulting headlines.

A professional had come through in the worst of clinches. He'd saved his crew and saved the lives of unknown numbers on the ground.

But that's *not* how the rest of the world saw it. It all became about the bomb.

Howard was reviled by horrified Carolinians as a self-centered coward.

To many of those who lived along the shores where the bomb was dropped, the pilot was a conscienceless villain. Hell, a yellow *monster*.

That was all very bad, of course. But then it got *worse*.

It was made more terrible because *nobody could seem to find the goddamn bomb*. The so-called "Broken Arrow"— military jargon for a lost atomic weapon—was still missing.

Then the unthinkable somehow became even *more* nightmarish: Stories began to circulate that contrary to everything Howard had been told, the dumped bomb was in fact secretly carrying its plutonic trigger.

Opinions on the validity of that wild and chilling claim were evenly divided within the Air Force's own hierarchy.

That official uncertainty about the state of the bomb they'd carried was horrifying in a whole different direction, of course.

Despite assurances to the contrary, South Carolinians railed against the fools who'd seemingly put a working hydrogen bomb on a plane for a simple training mission: A bomb these same civilians believed to be rusting and festering in the quicksand and corrosive water somewhere off South Carolina's coast.

Somewhere in all that muck loomed a massive, canister of death capable of annihilating most of the southeastern seaboard.

It couldn't just safely sit there for all time, could it?

Someday, maybe a decade or two down the road, it had to blow, didn't it?

THE MAN IN BLACK
(FEBRUARY 7, 1958)

Poseur tough guy.

A dime-store jailbird.

That's what Frank Robbins thought of Mister Johnny Cash.

The pill-popping rockabilly crooner had performed his first jailhouse concert in Huntsville State Prison in fifty-seven. That was the closest the singer-songwriter had ever come to prison time himself, Frank had heard.

Oh, Cash had been held overnight in Podunk jails for being drunk or disorderly, or for perceived bouts of vagrancy. But that was the extent of Cash' personal lock-up experience. Cash wasn't truly stir-savvy. Nah, it was all for Mickey Mouse stuff.

After the Huntsville concert, Cash had decided to make a habit of playing to convicts here and there as he rambled the countryside, venue to venue.

Cash claimed he did his prison gigs for the sake of the inmates, but Frank figured the singer cynically undertook those concerts to burnish his reputation as a perceived badass.

In the commissary, a few days after Cash's Quentin concert, sharing his dark suspicions about the singer's personal motives, Frank quickly sussed to the fact he was of minority opinion on that score.

Merle, the wannabe country singer from Bakersfield, early started the tide turning against Frank.

Merle had drawled, "Christ, ease up, won't ya? Johnny was here on New Year's Day, for Christ's sake. The world was looking any-fucking-where but here, Frank. It wasn't a publicity stunt. Jesus, get a grip."

Maybe, Merle.

Maybe not.

And either way, the black-clad singer and Cash's friendly treatment of the dark-skinned segment of the prison population during that New Year's Day concert went far beyond the pale.

Frank laughed at his inadvertent color joke: Words were surely funny things.

Words were also powerful things. Weapons, in their own way.

Take that writer who'd come to Quentin along with Cash.

Hec was a novelist who'd ended up agreeing to run a little impromptu writing seminar for poetry- or fiction-writing disposed shitbirds.

This author had told Frank Robbins with a straight face words could actually change the world.

The novelist, this tall and charismatic Texan named Hec Lassiter, vowed writing had certainly changed his own life.

The craft of fiction writing had earned the fifty-something Lassiter a good and steady living; nice threads, pretty women and a chance to roam *widely*: to see a bigger world than he would ever have glimpsed working some nine-to-five, wage-slave day job in his native Southern Texas.

That's what Lassiter confided to the convict, anyway. He'd seemed sincere enough in the moment.

That lanky and dapper novelist, Hec, he'd said Frank showed promise as a writer in his own right.

Frank still believed old Hec meant every praising word.

Now, sitting in his cell with a notepad and crayon, Frank tried his best to shut out the sound from his cell-mate's nine-volt radio—more of that damned Johnny Cash singing his goddamn faker song, *Folsom Prison Blues.*

Hell, not only was Cash a huckster pretending to be a hard con, but Frank had a suspicion that Cash's signature song wasn't even entirely his *own.*

Cash's most famous tune was powerfully reminiscent—in some places, *line-for-line*—with Gordon Jenkins' earlier but obscure *Crescent City Blues.*

When Frank shared this theory with Lassiter during their brief writing recitation, the novelist shook his head. Hec said in that baritone drawl of his, "That's as low as a writer can go, stealing another writer's words, pal. God, I'd hate to think that could be true of old J.R. Cash."

Well, it *was* damn well true; Frank was sure of that. And he could tell he'd greatly upset Hec with his theory.

Shooting a man simply to watch him die?

That probably sounded plenty tough and cold to a faker like the so-called "Man in Black" who'd lift the line for his own.

But in the real world, you didn't kill a man simply for kicks. Not unless you were some kind of brain-addled rabid dog, frothing at the mouth and snapping your chain for no good goddamn reason.

The stakes and penalties for that kind of mayhem were far too high.

No.

Fact was, you killed for money, or maybe even for politics or religion.

You killed for drugs or drink.

Or you killed because some son of a bitch was putting it to your woman.

Frank stared at the blank page of his notepad, trying to think of the precisely right sentence to open his prison novel.

He had a black crayon gripped tight between his fingers. They wouldn't permit him pencils or pens in his cell, because those writing tools might be turned into weapons.

Drive a pen or pencil into a man's throat *just so* and you could bleed that son of a bitch out, fast.

But a child's crayon? Where was the danger in *that?*

If the goddamn screws only knew.

And, hell, it made his writing seem somehow rustic, putting it down there in fuzzy, waxen colors.

He actually kind of *liked* that: Frank thought it gave his prose on the page a flavor of raw realism.

And so-called "truth" was the vital thing in writing, after all.

Frank had already intuitively grasped that, and much of what Hec Lassiter impromptu lectured on had confirmed Frank's earlier, fumbling epiphanies.

It was all about the *telling detail,* as Hec had put it. The right and crisp putting down of a perfectly crafted line or phrase, making it rest there on the page, *just so.*

One true sentence.

That's what Hec called it. He said it was every honest writer's "Holy Grail."

Frank wanted that *real thing* for his prison novel: no faking, no *posturing*.

One true sentence, then another and another after that. A train of those suckers, falling all along the way to the perfect and stark, "The End."

As he sat there brooding, Frank stared across the cell-block at one Robert Breen, sitting there, dark-skinned and scowling.

Bobby Breen was a 24-year-old Angelino who'd raped a white woman and consequently faced a fifty-to-life term for his terrible crime.

The Brotherhood had decided to commute Bobby Breen's sentence in black top dance.

But that *commutation* surely wouldn't change Bobby's "lifer" status in any good way for old Bob. It would be a "back door parole," as the saying went.

That squirrely bastard Bobby quickly averted his eyes when he saw Frank staring at him.

Yep, boy rightly sensed his sorry days were numbered.

Frank knew the precise sum of that stingy number.

So did all those in the Brotherhood, as they'd picked their judgment day by *committee*.

Frank put crayon to paper and wrote:

It rained hard in the yard the afternoon Bobby Breen faced true *justice.*

Nah, that didn't work, not even *close*.

And "hard" and "yard" made it sound like nursery rhyme.

It still needed much tweaking. And it couldn't be written before the fact: not without putting Frank at risk for a further stretch than he already faced.

Well, Frank surely had time for that writing of it all *after the fact*.

A wide smile: Hell, *he* had all the time Bobby Breen so sorely lacked.

LIVING LEGEND
(DECEMBER, 1958)

(Excerpt from a radio interview with Hector Lassiter, broadcast by WPAR, in Parkersburg, West Virginia)

"Hey, cats and kittens your old buddy Gaylord Layton! I'm sittin' here gassin' with legendary crime novelist and screenwriter, Hector Lassiter. Hec's the *très* cool cat they call the 'man who lives what he writes and writes what he lives.' The one they call 'the last man standing of the Lost Generation.'

"My new best buddy, Hec, he's one colorful, large-living dude, babies. Hec was born in 1900 in Galveston, Texas and survived the killer 1900 hurricane there. Old Hec chased The Mexican bandit Pancho Villa with Black Jack Pershing. Hec fought in the Great War, then fished and boxed with Papa Hemingway in Key West. They say Hec organized his own guerilla outfits to help liberate Paris during World War II. For sure, Hec's written many of our best-remembered and best-selling crime novels of the last thirty years. And he's penned more movie scripts than even he can remember.

"For the past year or so, Hec's been moving through the country music world, touring with Johnny Cash and other hillbilly singers to gather material for a new book he's writin'. It's a novel about country music entitled, *Three Chords and the Truth*. So let's say a big 'howdy-do' to Mr. Hector Mason Lassiter."

APOCALYPSE

1

Basil Sloan was eight feet of mayhem tamped down into six feet of muscle and beer gut.

His knuckles were tattooed with "pain" and "loss" and his forearm read, "The only hell Mama raised."

In Basil's case, I tended to believe there was truth in advertising.

Logan, evidently sensing trouble too, said, "Here, Hec', best take the *big* stick."

See old pal, it's all about heft. Me? I prefer a long, thick heavy shaft.

We're talking pool cues, here, partner. I opt for 21-ouncers because they're best for breaking balls of any kind. They're also less apt to splinter swung up against some uppity cocksucker's nose or teeth.

I stole another gander at Basil, then accepted the heavier cue stick; bent low over the table, robin's egg blue eyes deciding on a six-two ball combination.

Easing up on the *in media res* presentation, you see, for three weeks, I'd been playing wheelman to singer-songwriter Logan "Buddy" Loy Burke.

Logan was touring in support of a first, long-playing album. The independent (translation: *un-agented*) troubadour's "tour" consisted of dive-bars and taverns in countless water-tank towns strung out all along old Route 23.

We'd started in northern Michigan, then meandered southerly on down through Ohio and at last made our way this night into chilly-ass Kentucky.

Yes, tonight we were courting trouble in a roadhouse along the Tennessee-Virginia border.

Logan had wrapped up his last set, then challenged a couple of mouth-breathing knuckle draggers with suspiciously far-apart eyes to a few racks of eight ball.

Bets for beer soon enough ratcheted up to wagering dead presidents when the locals got a look at Logan and I and our feigned ineptitude with the pool cues.

But the last two racks had somehow witnessed a marked improvement in our game.

The dim boys with eyes near-on-the-sides-of-their-heads were getting increasingly *surly*. Basil, who I took to be a key stakeholder in our opponents' game, was looking still more dangerous. Big fella had a quiet and unsettling seethe on.

A song I'd dropped quarters for finally got its turn on the jukebox: Marty Robbins' *The Story of My Life*.

Logan, chalking his cue, said sadly, "Christ, I just don't know why I even try anymore, Hec. Music business is in damn disarray. Presley getting his ass drafted? Jerry Lee tying the knot with his jailbait blood? *Great Balls of Fire*, indeed. And you know, Cash still has everyone mad at him for playing that concert for the San Quentin inmates that you went along for."

"Well, you were never part of that screwed-up Sun Record combine, anyway," I said. "Count yourself lucky. Those suckers are all on a bad public relations roll, kiddo."

One of our pool competitors, some endomorphic truck driver-type named *Connie*, said to Logan, "What, you're some kind of country singer?"

"*He* is," I said, stroking my cue and sighting in on the combination shot. "Reckon you must have wandered in after Logan's show. Logan was on stage better than a couple hours. He owned this joint, did it with just his voice and a guitar."

I decided to muff the shot, but played a safety, wedging the cue ball between the rail and eight ball.

I slipped off my still relatively new spectacles and tucked them in my sports jacket's interior pocket, in case things went decidedly south.

Old Basil just didn't strike me as the sort to have qualms about swinging on a four-eyes.

Connie looked at my leave, then sighed *deeply*.

Nodding my way, he said, "And *you*? Some kind of god-damn pool hustler, ain'tcha?"

"Oh, Christ no," I said. "I write books. Novels. Some screenplays. Seen *Rooster of Heaven*? That was one of mine."

Connie walked around the table, checking angles. I'd left him nothing. He said, "I'm a night-hauler, hardly ever make it to the drive-in picture show."

Drive-in. Hm.

I briefly gnawed on that reference. Yep, in these environs, they weren't likely to have a proper *cinema*. Hell, they didn't have a single traffic light as I'd seen.

Connie's partner, an unsettling enigma whose nickname seemed to be "Shiv," crouched low over the table, squinting one eye. He left open the eye with the tattooed tears: three splashes of sorry and blurry cellblock ink stained that cheek.

Shiv was so skinny I figured it for a contest as to which was scrawnier—Shiv's neck or the butt of his cue stick. Yet, given that nickname and those jailhouse tattoos, I figured he might be second only to Basil for potential to inflict damage. Hell, Shiv might be even *more* dangerous than Basil since he'd clearly missed evading incarceration at least three times.

Shiv said, "Con', you do anything but go to the rail, you're gonna drop that eight ball in the side pocket. Best you just try and hit one of ours and risk the ball-in-hand. Expect we're gonna lose anyhow, now that these boys ain't layin' back on us no more."

Real acid there. Yes sir, this was going to end with fists flying. It was clear these backwoods types would settle for no less.

I sidled up next to Logan. The crooner was twenty-four, six-one and just under two hundred pounds. In theory, a good buck to have by your side in a roadhouse brawl. I shook out a little talc and stroked the tapering end of my cue. Logan said softly, "Please tell me you're carrying your Colt, Hec."

I shot him a look. "Are you insane? I figured we'd maybe get in a bind like this one and didn't want to kill anyone. Not around these sorry parts. Even if we were in the right, they'd throw away the keys on us, kid." I shrugged. "Peacemaker's in the glove compartment."

Logan wasn't pleased to hear it. He said, "Then since we both make our livings with our hands, I *gotta* insist we take a powder, Hec. I'll say I'm hittin' the head. You head to the bar for a refill and sneak out. We'll meet in the parking lot. Already stowed my guitar in your Bel Air's trunk so I'm ready to go, Hoss. Ain't no shame runnin' in the face of overwhelming odds, right?"

Rubbing more chalk on the tip of my cue, I said, "That doesn't sound like a good plan, either, son. This is these boys' neck of country. These fellas know these roads, such as you can even call 'em that. Not at all sure we'd outrun the bastards."

"Better'n trying to duke it out with them," Logan pressed.

I smiled. "*Nah*. We just need to draw more into the fray if it comes to blows. We'll slip out once everyone else is fully engaged." I looked around, smiled. "Hell, this dump screams for a makeover, wouldn't you say?"

Logan smoothed a hand back over his glossy black pompadour. Despite his youth, Logan had gone prematurely gray a time back. When I met him the previous year in L.A., his hair was already fading to snow white. Yesterday he'd sprung for some Kentucky dye job. Boy had his reasons.

"Oh Gawd, but this is a big-ass mistake," Logan said. "Last thing I want to do is show up at Jake Gantry's funeral with a black eye or missing teeth. On account of Genevieve will be there." That was Logan, aces over spades—always the dreamer.

Jake was a country music legend, the self-proclaimed "King of Country Music." But the "King" was presently one-week dead.

Genevieve Gantry was Jake's latest ex. (The minx had baldly confided to the Nashville press she'd kept the famous surname "for business reasons.") Genevieve was also Logan's primary obsession and trigger for his do's new hue.

Slender and busty, nineteen-year-old GG was tanned and radiant. Babe had big green eyes, long blond hair and a devastating smile. Also dimples to die for under chiseled cheekbones.

Her pale hair was piled high and she scandalized Music Row by performing in shoulder-baring sweaters and skin-tight black pedal pushers. She tottered on heels high enough to raise a Music Row vixen halfway to heaven.

GG was walking sex for sure, but despite my wanderin' eye, even I knew enough to give that wild one a wide berth.

Logan picked up his cue, freshened the tip, then said, "I'm gonna pocket that eight ball. We'll scoop up our god-damn winnings, then we're gonna politely call it a night, Hec." He gave me the eye: "Am I right?"

"Oh, give it your best shot for sure, kiddo," I said. As gambits go, I didn't give this one a prayer. I dipped my hand in the right pocket of my sports jacket for the taped roll of nickels I always carry there. See, when it came to Basil, I figured the first punch had to count and would make all the difference.

I drifted over to a table of outlaw bikers, maybe twelve in all, long-gone on piss-poor beer and left-handed coffin nails.

Leaning down close to the biggest one, I jacked a thumb back at Shiv and said, "Scarecrow there has been bad-mouthin' you, brother. He said you suck cock better than *his* mama." As I stated that, I pointed at the second biggest biker at the table. "I thought Scarecrow, *Shiv*, that's to say, was just drunk," I plunged ahead, "but after a couple of games of stick? Well, I don't think so no more. I think that skinny son of a bitch truly means it about you and your buddy's mother."

I stepped back as the first biker bellowed and flipped over their table, rushing Shiv. Logan gave me this big eye-roll, simultaneously scooping up our winnings—those, as well as the cash we *hadn't* yet won. Then he started back-pedaling to get clear of the biker's red-eyed, berserker's charge.

Shiv had one leg up, digging into the cuff of his boot for the gun I figured he had tucked in there as he jumped around on one leg.

My aim truly wasn't to get anyone killed this night. So I snatched up a half-empty bottle of Jim Beam and flung it in Shiv's face, buying the biker time to close the gap and wrap hands around Shiv's pencil-thin neck.

Others in the roadhouse were tossing in about then.

The bartender reached for something under the counter I feared would be sawed-off—something that might put a jiffy and lamentable end to the barroom brawl I'd inaugurated. I jerked my head toward the door and Logan nodded his understanding, ducking a flying bottle that took out the jukebox. The Louvin Brothers' cover of "The Knoxville Girl" ground to a halt.

It was snowing outside, big fluffy flakes that were starting to stick as we stalked toward my Chevy. Logan, counting bills, said, "This snow is some fine luck, Hec. We make tracks fast enough, we won't leave tracks for anyone to follow." His breath trailed frostily from his mouth as he talked and counted, walking fast and closing the distance between us.

I angled off toward my newish turquoise 1957 Bel Air. I dropped the roll of nickels in my pocket and fished out my Zippo and pack of Pall Malls. I shook one loose and got her going. "*Maybe*. You know, Logan, it's actually kind of nice to walk away from one of these frays without testing the bones of my hand against some joker's jaw. A real nice change."

Then this shadow stretched out across the downy snow in front of my Bel Air.

It was Basil. He swung a baseball bat so it slapped over and over against his right palm. The Louisville slugger was stained with what looked like mud or old blood. I figured most likely the latter. Basil was alone, but that didn't give me much heart. Old boy looked more than up to his task. I pocketed my Zippo and retrieved my roll of nickels. My palms were suddenly sweaty, despite the snow and cold.

You can do real damage with a Louisville slugger, as I've seen: Key West, 1925.

With my left hand, I took the cigarette from my mouth. "Whoa there, pard'. We don't want trouble and your friends were losing all on their own. If you're honest with yourself, you know they surely didn't need our help doggin' it."

"Their problem," Basil said, pointing at me with the bat. "But they were playing with *my* money, so that makes it *your* problem."

Goddamn it all.

I lobbed my car keys at Logan, said, "Look, I'm fixing to play *peacemaker* with Basil here. No reason we should both freeze our asses off, right? Get her warmed up, eh, Logan?" I could only hope the kid divined my deeper intention. Had to hope he caught that wordplay and didn't bolt in my Bel Air.

Basil watched Logan, wary, stepping wide away from my Chevy to keep us both in sight. "Just give me all the fuckin' money and we'll call it even," Basil said.

Logan was behind the wheel of my Chevy now. He had the engine going and I could see he was groping for the glove compartment. Figured another three seconds and Logan would have Basil in the sights of my Cavalry model, 1873 Colt Peacemaker.

Six shots and a very long barrel.

Deliverance.

All I had to do was wait.

But I felt like testing myself against Basil, at least a little. I closed distance, emboldened by the extra two inches of height I had on the bastard, as well as the promise my trusty old Colt would soon be backing my play. I flicked my cigarette in his eyes. As he flinched and ducked burning ash, I kicked Basil between the legs. That wasn't cricket, no, but I figured as he had maybe three decades of youth on his side, and that goddamn bat, and so...?

Yet something just wasn't *right* down there 'tween Basil's legs. He gave me this cross look, then knocked me on my ass with a lightning right cross to the jaw. He said, "Land mine. Korea."

Licking blood from my lip and seeing little flashes of light against the snow, I said, "Jesus, I'm *sorry*, pal. No wonder you've got that sour attitude on you."

Logan cocked my old single-action Colt: the legendary click of the chambers rolling gave Basil at least a little pause...and time enough for me to struggle to my feet.

Things sounded crazy inside the roadhouse, a real drunken brawl. Exactly that much was goin' to impulsive plan.

Basil half-turned, gauging where Logan was standing I reckoned. "You ain't gonna shoot me," he said to Logan. "I can see it in your face. You got no stomach for that, boy."

Logan shot me this sick look like he'd been found out.

Well, goddamn it anyway, again.

I thrust out a hand and said, "*Uncock* the son of a bitch *first*."

The songwriter gingerly lowered the hammer then tossed me the old Colt. I caught it on the fly. Basil was turning, raising the bat to take a swing at my hands. He was in plenty of range to put me down.

So I cocked and pulled twice—shot Basil in both feet.

The sorry son of a bitch dropped the bat, screamed and fell. Little geysers of blood from his boots spritzed snow-covered gravel in time with his pulse. I said, "Sorry again, pal. Really, I am sorry about this, old kid. But you surely shouldn't have pushed."

2

We hustled into the Chevy and I skidded her out of the lot, slip-sliding onto the rutted county two-lane, spitting ice-coated gravel and southbound on old 23.

I dialed around and settled on a fresh country station. The Blue Sky Boys crooned that spooky old murder ballad *Banks of the Ohio*. Logan smoothed his hand back over his born-again black hair and said, "I swear to Christ, Hector, no more going in bars with you. Not ever. Just once, I'd like to walk out of one of those joints with you without carnage ensuin'."

"Wasn't me challenged those in-bred types to pool for *dinero*."

"Well, I've learned my danged lesson tonight," Logan said.

"Me too: No more leaving my Colt in the car around you."

Chastened, we settled into silence for a mile or two. A year-end news round up was squeezed between songs.

Murder, mayhem and loss, all around:

Lana Turner's boyfriend, Johnny Stompanato, had allegedly been shanked by Lana's little girl. Roy Campanella had been rendered a paralyzed basket-case by a car accident.

Caril Ann Fugate and Charles Starkweather, cross country thrill killers, had been caught after a frenzy of murders.

The Soviets were having themselves some crazy year. Sputnik 1 fell from the sky, finally. The Russkies had earlier killed this poor pooch putting the hapless bastard into orbit. The Reds had a new boss too, some fella name of Krushchev.

In Cuba, an upstart called Castro was causing mob and D.C. hand-wringing.

And old Pope Pius XII had turned up his toes. That last didn't strike me as such a terrific loss: not long before taking the dirt dive, the crazy son of a bitch had declared Saint Clare "patron saint of television." As a people, did we *really* need that? *Really?*

The Jews and the Arabs were freshly at one another's throats and so things looked bad for Israel again.

And a couple of major boners involving big bombs had folks edgy. In one case, a B-47 had accidentally dropped an A-bomb on the town of Mars Bluff, South Carolina. That errant bomb wrecked a house and hurt a few, but luckily didn't detonate on a nuclear level.

Another aircraft flubbed and dropped nearly eight-thousand pounds of hydrogen bomb somewhere off the coast of Savannah, Georgia or thereabouts. Sucker was still down there in all that salt water or marsh mud, the scribes claimed.

Those last two items got me itchy to get back west. At least when they drop big bombs around New Mexico, they do it with planning and intent.

Some music returned, Woody Guthrie and *Bad Lee Brown*. Not my cup of tea.

Logan said, "Maybe we should drive straight on through to Nashville." Boy had it bad, sure enough.

I dialed the radio around some more and found *Have Gun, Will Travel.* I'd recently agreed to provide a script for the new radio oater for walking-around money. Figured maybe I'd better sample the sucker before sitting down to write for it. I said, "You sleep then, son. I'll get us through Virginia and into Tennessee, then you can take over."

Logan nodded. "I'm real sorry, Hector. "Your mouth okay?"

I tested teeth with my tongue. Firm. "Nothing to sweat, kid."

"I'm real sorry."

"Truly, it's okay."

I got a fresh cigarette. My Zippo was sputtering; probably needed a new flint. "G'wan and rest up, kiddo," I said. "You wanna look pretty for the grieving almost-widow. I'll drive us straight through. It's an easy enough trip ... weather permittin'." I wasn't sure it would.

Logan nodded and settled back in the seat, closing his eyes. I braked as I saw some other eyes glowing in the headlights. It was a family of deer, crossing the road amidst the snow flurries.

As I waited for all the deer to pass, I checked the rearview: no tails, no trouble.

Logan was soon enough out, softly snoring. While *Have Gun* was on commercial, I dialed around and found Genevieve Gantry, singing a cover of Peggy Lee's hit *Fever.* Sounded okay, but not nearly up to Peggy's definitive, sex-soaked version.

Logan's face was limned in the glow from the dashboard lights. No question: the kid was in way over his head with jailbait GG. Well, nothing I could do for him on that front. In the end, we all have to kill our own snakes, after all.

Twelve miles later, Paladin's adventure wrapped up in tidy fashion and I already had a few germs of ideas for a radio script of my own episode of *Have Gun*.

Suddenly, there was some late-breaking Sunday night news out of Tennessee. The death of Genevieve Gantry's elder ex was now being termed a homicide.

I glanced over at Logan again. Sucker was snoring up a storm.

Then there was more: GG was being questioned in connection with the suspected murder.

Good thing Logan was out, blissfully unaware of his unrequited inamorata's plight.

I thought about waking Logan, then figured the news about the dead "king" could keep.

3

I hit the brakes turning into the parking space, surprised to slide into the curbstone. Much slicker out 'n I
thought. I whipped out an arm to stop sleeping Logan from
kissing the dash. I pushed him back in his seat.

He stirred. "Jesus, what's up?" Cotton-mouthed, Logan
dug knuckles in his eye sockets.

"More like what's down," I said. "And that'd be the temperature. Hit a little patch of black ice."

Logan sat up straighter, blinking and looking around.
"Doesn't look like Nashville."

"Because it isn't. Weather turned once we crossed into
Tennessee. Lots of snow, little visibility. Figure it'll cost us
at least an hour. More probably two. And I'm starving. And
I badly need some time away from the wheel. All those flurries dancing in the headlights get to you after a time. Make
your eyes tired and reflexes dull."

"So I'm driving next? You *never* let me drive."

"Tonight you can," I said. "I'm wrung out. But first,
let's grab some grub and get warm."

The diner was near empty: just some stray truckers and
a young couple who looked like they'd just eloped from the
way they pawed at one another at this early hour. The kids

still had that not-too-choosy, horny zeal. I reckoned inside a year, one or both would be twisting wedding bands and casing escape hatches.

Logan paused at the jukebox, an ongoing ritual this trip. But this time, he looked up at me, beaming. "Boy howdy, *at last!* It's here, Hec!" Logan shoved his hands in his pockets, frowned, and said, "Spare me some change?"

I shook my head. "How many of your LPs do we have crowding the trunk of my Chevy?"

We'd been selling his albums in parking lots after each "concert" stop. Figured we'd probably sold a couple of boxes worth the past three weeks. It was the game though—building a fan base, one buy at a time. Same as in the book world, really.

Logan gave me this big kid's sheepish shrug. "Got no home. Got no turntable, and so far, got no radio airplay as I've heard. I haven't heard this recording since I cut her, Hec."

Now I felt bad. I handed over a heap of coins. "Let's hear her a few times, then."

We settled into a booth and ordered up some eggs, toast and blessed coffee.

Logan's voice filled the diner. The other travelers shot us a look when the song ended and then promptly started up again. Logan said to them, "That's *my* song playing. I mean, that's *me*, singin' that song!" The boy with the girl raised his orange juice in a toast then. A trucker followed suit. Logan's voice:

> *You're a stranger in this town*
> *Where the only bar is closin' down...*

I pricked the skin of my eggs-over-easy and dashed on some pepper and salt. Dipping a corner of toast in the oozing yolk, I said, "Jake Gantry, how'd he exactly cash out?"

Chewing and talking, tapping time to his own song with his free hand, Logan said, "Heart problems, I hear. Jake always had a bad ticker, they say. Heart murmur from birth, or the like. Newspapers say they found him on the toilet. Massive heart attack. You know, from the straining, I reckon."

There was some imagery I surely didn't crave, eating or not.

And, Holy Jesus, what a way to close out your life: Pants wadded around ankles and tits up in *that place*, likely not even granted the good grace for a last flush. Holy Christ, how forlorn was all that?

"Who found him, Logan?"

"The maid. Jake has—*had*—a pretty big house," Logan said around more eggs. "Needs a staff to keep up the place."

"Lucky son of a bitch," I said. "Or he was when he still drew air. Don't think much about radio singers livin' so high on the hog like that." Lord knows poor Logan was in no danger of such extravagance. Not yet, anyway. But the kid had world-class pipes and a way with words that moved me, well enough. I was a believer—part of the reason I was playing chauffeur to the near-unknown.

Our gum-popping waitress came over with a fountain pen. "Get an autograph, hon'?"

Logan was taken aback: pretty kid was the first ever to ask him for one of those.

Nervous, the tyro troubadour wiped hands on pants and took her fountain pen. He tried to write something on a napkin that promptly tore. Just as well—not a lot of white space there for a message, or even a signature, really. It was one of those "Cocktail Laffs" napkins, covered with ribald riddles and cartoons of naked ladies. I rose, said, "'Scuse me," and went back outside.

I popped the trunk on the Bel Air and fished out one of Logan's 33 RPMs. I ducked back inside, shivering and stamping slush from my feet. I handed the album to Logan and said, "Sign this to her, kid." I sat there blowing warm breath into my cupped hands.

The waitress was maybe three years Logan's junior, but she had a look about her. I figured I'd layover if it seemed young Logan stood a chance of sparking her. Hell, better this one than that pedal-pusher-clad she-demon he had deluded himself into dreaming awaited him in Nashville. Logan signed the album's sleeve to the waitress. She hugged it to her chest and beamed. She gushed, "I'm gonna frame this and hang it over this very booth. You come back through, this will be your special seat, sugar, for always and for always."

She left and Logan said, "Gawd, that was strange."

I smiled. "But real, *real nice*. Best you get used to it, kiddo. You're just starting. Going to be a hell of a lot more of that kind of thing as you get out there now. Especially with that blue-black Elvis hair you're sporting. You look your age again and dangerous in a way that entices certain kinds of compelling young women. Take that pretty young filly serving us, for instance." I ate some more of my eggs and toast and guzzled coffee. "Now, back to Jake. This heart problem of his—his bum ticker a pretty known thing?"

"S'pose. I mean at least around Music Row." Logan stirred his scrambled eggs around, then doused them in some catsup. *Jesus.* "Jake had a heart attack back in fifty-five, I think. Had another in fifty-seven. He was somewhere touring in Texas that second time. Maybe Lubbock."

"Don't get your back up son, but I have to ask this one, you understand? Was Genevieve ever blamed for any of those attacks?"

"Just please stop there, Hector." Some real gravel in Logan's voice. "How the hell do you give someone a heart attack on purpose?"

I held up a hand. "Whoa, son. Didn't mean it like that. Just meant medication gets forgotten now and again. Or maybe it's given in too-lavish doses and toes things in dire directions. Or maybe bottles just get confused."

"They aren't even together, and haven't been, not since the divorce in fifty-six," Logan said. His brow furrowed. "Where are you heading with this?"

The waitress freshened our coffees, pointedly leaning further over on Logan's side so her breast brushed his forearm. Somehow Logan didn't seem to notice like I did. She left and I said, "While you were sacked out, there was a news bulletin. Police think Jake's heart attack was induced. They're now treating his death as foul play. They're questioning Genevieve about all that. Or so the Nashville newshounds claim."

"Then we need to get to Nashville, *now*," Logan said, wide-eyed. Poor kid looked truly stricken. He said, "Hell, Genevieve was nowhere *near* that bastard when he had his first two attacks. They were only married for maybe six months."

"Whirlwind romance, eh?" Then I hoped that one didn't come across with the sarcasm I thought I heard in my own voice. And, of course, nothing in Logan's assertion precluded Genevieve's complicity in Jake's last big attack. But I didn't point that out to Logan. Instead, I put my foot in a *different* pile:

"Waitress is really making eyes at you, kid. Must like your music well enough. There's a motel across the road. Saw a vacancy sign passing by on the way here. I'm really not up to another several hours' driving. And the roads are getting' wicked perilous. Don't want to risk my Chevy in this heavy snow. This car's looking to be the keeper, already becoming regarded as *the* classic American wheels. And now that I'm sitting here, I realize I'm beat well beyond the wide. So I'm going to go get us a couple of rooms. You ask at the desk for your room number. I'll leave you here a bit to talk to your new fan."

Logan shook his head. "I want to get to Nashville, Hector. I want to leave *right now*."

"No way, Logan. I know where your heart and head are, and you can go to your room and work that telephone for all its business, if that's your notion. But I'm too old for all-nighters on icy back roads, far from any hospitals. According to the news hawks, GG's already been a prime suspect for a *couple of days*. Seems the police are following the money as cops tend to do and the gal stands to inherit that big old house where Jake died. She's been bequeathed all his publishing rights, too. Some tidy nest-egg just in that, they say."

Logan's eyes accused me. "Then you believe these damn stories on the radio, don't you?"

I slumped back in the booth and waved a hand. "Hell, kid, I don't even know the gal or what to make of any of that. But I surely do know how cops think. To cops' minds, piles of money equal *mucho* motive. Hell, we all think that way, right?"

"Hector, we need to get to Nashville. We need to do that *right now*."

I picked up another slice of toast, pushed its corner around in that yummy and syrupy orange yolk. "And what are you going to do for G-Squared when you get there, pal?" I searched his dark eyes. "Really, Logan: What's your first move going to be? You need a *plan*. Never confuse movement for action."

Logan didn't seem to have an answer for that one. I said, "So, us having no good plan in this moment, tomorrow will be soon enough for us to rush to the damsel's rescue. Assuming there's really anything we can do for that little gal."

I'm so seldom the quiet voice of reason, I smiled at my own sensible circumspection.

But Logan wasn't smiling back at me.

Seething was the word that came to my writer's mind.

4

I looked out the window a last time around two in the morning, applauding myself for making the right decision.

At least two inches of snow already mounded the roof and hood of my Chevy. The wind was gusty and setting to squall all that unpacked snow, wrecking what was left of any visibility. Looking out there at the mini-blizzard, I heard wind-driven icy rain starting to click against the glass. I was glad to be warm and safe.

Through the swirling snow, I made out the haze of the diner's neon sign across the parking lot: The lights were still on inside the joint. There was no noise next door so I figured Logan must still be in the diner with that adoring young waitress.

Good for him. *Better for him.*

I closed the drapes, drew my old Colt from its shoulder holster and tucked it under my pillow. I tugged a piece of tissue from the box on the nightstand and folded it into a rectangle. I slipped the Kleenex into my current reading material to mark my place. It was a new, crazy-ass novel called *Lolita* enjoying buzz: A darkly comic tale of an older man burning down his life for this hot young thing.

Hell, but for my being "typed" as a crime novelist, I might have written one like it, though more likely set along the Borderlands and the female lead would have been Latina. Tossing the book on the nightstand, I reached over and clicked off the reading light.

Stretched out there in the dark, hearing the frigid wind play across the roof and windows, I shivered and pulled the covers up tight under my chin. I could hear a train's whistle blowing at each crossing somewhere in the distance, the melancholy drone of its horn making distant dogs bay.

Tired as I was, the wind and the ice and the train whistle and all those sad-sounding dogs wouldn't let me sleep.

I got up, tuned the radio to a quiet classical music station and parked the dial there, the radio's glowing tubes like a half-ass night light.

I awakened to Wagner's "Tristan and Isolde."

No wonder the last dreams I remembered were so out-of-scale and terrifically *whacked*, recalling a long ago February in 1920s Paris, when we were all still struggling unknowns, and maybe unknowingly happier for not being known... The City of Light besieged by a religious cult of suicidal nihilists.

It was a period of my life I seemed to find my mind turning back to more and more as the years and the losses accumulated over me.

In my dream, more of a memory, really, Brinke and I were curled up close and warm with one another in bed in my apartment above the Rue Vavin. Brinke already had several published books behind her and she was counseling me about shaping a "public persona," advising me about constructing the "calculated face" I'd need to put out there to the world as a fiction writer. I needed an image, a kind of actualized character, she counseled, but one coldly calculated to sell books.

"There's Hector Lassiter, the man I adore," Brinke said, lips brushing my cheek and ear, "and then there must be Hector Lassiter, the man whose books people read. They're apt to be two *very* different men. A well-crafted and calculated image sells books, darling. At the same time, you have to be mindful of the game you're playing with people. Don't start believing your own lies, Hec. Becoming what you create can destroy you. Hardly any of us can truly live up, or *down*, to our fiction, not all the way. So you be careful what you dream, my darling Hector, or else you might find your dreams are dreaming you."

Brinke and others of my lost ones as they too often do, ambushing me in my dreams.

Not much new in any of that, sad to say. It had been going on for decades, really.

But it was good and pleasing to spend time with Brinke again, as it always was, even if it was only in a dream. She was the person I dreamed of most often and intensely.

If there was such a thing as Heaven, my first wife was the one I hoped waited for me on the other side.

And my darling Brinke's long-ago advice still struck home, all too squarely.

Hell, it reverberated all too resonantly to a weary writer the reading public had long-ago come to call, "The man who lives what he writes and writes what he lives."

To the man they also labeled, "The last man standing of the Lost Generation." That was surely not something anyone sets out to be.

Struggling up onto elbows, I found my spectacles, then climbed bare-assed out of bed and dialed over to a country station where Johnny Cash's *Ballad of a Teenage Queen* played. I slit the "protective" paper cover from a drinking glass and poured myself tap water to offset the booze-induced dehydration. After getting my first cigarette of the day going, I squinted at my watch. The trusty old Timex read eight in the morning.

I rarely slept past five.

So I hustled myself under the stinging shower spray, turned up just shy of scalding.

Last night's young waitress, the one who was all eyes for Logan, was behind the counter.

She didn't look, *well*, she didn't look *loved.* I mean in that luscious, sultry and ravaged morning-after sense. She sported no swollen lips from hungry kisses. No tired eyes or tousled hair. No slow moving because of sore muscles *down there* born of passionate striving.

Nothing like that.

Conway Twitty on the jukebox: *It's Only Make Believe.*

Taking up a seat at the counter I said, "Lord, the hours you keep, darlin'. They got you working a double shift, hon'? Don't they ever let you go home?"

"Shift starts at midnight," she said with a tired smile. "I wrap up in five minutes."

I decided to risk it after accepting an offer of black coffee: "Listen, my young friend—"

"Seemed like a really nice guy," she said, cutting me off. "He sings real good." She pointed at the booth where Logan I sat together hours before. His autographed album cover was already tacked up on the wall there. "Just like I promised, mister."

"Thanks, darlin'. My friend, Logan, he been in this morning?" I figured I'd put that innocently enough.

She scowled. "No, mister. He left not long after you did. Had me call him a cab. Heard him say he wanted to be taken to a Greyhound station, bound for Nashville. Closest bus station's two towns over. With the weather, I bet he paid some fare gettin' there."

Boy never had pocket change, but he did have that fat roll from the pool debacle, goddamn it. I said rather thickly still partly disbelieving, "He left?"

The waitress, I saw now the tag over her left breast read "Raylene," nodded, frowning. "Sorry. I guess he didn't tell you, mister."

"Call me Hector." I sighed from my boot heels. "He was in a danged hurry to get to Nashville, that's for certain. A *friend* of his is in some trouble," I sipped more coffee, said, "Guess I just didn't know how much of a hurry Logan was in. And so I guess I best get moving along in pursuit."

My stomach growled. My vision was a tad fuzzy, too. Few months back, I'd been diagnosed with a mild form of diabetes. Didn't have to shoot up with insulin so far, but I was flirting with the boundaries of that sorry line. So far, cutting back on hooch and some careful dieting was keeping it in something like check. I said, "I gotta hit the road and pronto, darlin'. Could you maybe have your cook make something I could eat behind the wheel? Say, throw a fried egg, some ham or a sausage patty and cheese on a bun? Maybe a strip or two of bacon? Somethin' I could eat with my hands?"

Raylene wrinkled her nose. She really was very appealing in her own quirky way. Logan freshly struck me as a goddamn fool. She said, "Sounds kinda wrong as breakfast goes. What do you call that?"

I shrugged, tossing some bills on the counter and draining my cup of coffee. "I dunno, sugar, maybe, 'breakfast-to-go'?"

"Doesn't seem anything close to right, mister," she said.

I'm a big believer in a hearty breakfast. I love to linger over same with strong black coffee and good conversation. What the Spanish call *charla profunda*. A book or a notebook and pen if I'm solo lobo. It's probably the day's meal I look forward to most.

"Nope," I agreed, smiling sadly at the pretty young thing behind the counter. "It surely doesn't sound anything within spitting distance of right." I pointed at my coffee and said, "And more of this brew in a travel cup?"

After struggling a minute or so with my car door, the ice cracked, the door creaked open and I put the bag with my biscuits and "breakfast sandwich" on the front seat. I turned over the engine and cranked the heater way up. I set to work with a scraper and got the windows scratched clean enough to see to drive.

I saw no way for him to have gotten at them without my car keys but popped the trunk anyway. Indeed: There were Logan's luggage and his vintage ebony Martin guitar. Kid sure enough was a goner for his Music Row temptress—had to be to leave behind his beloved Martin, like that.

I slipped back behind the wheel and checked my Timex again: ten in the morning. I figured to make Nashville not long past noon if the roads were now reasonably cleared.

Just as I was about to put the Bel Air in gear, I saw the waitress, Raylene, all bundled up in a big padded jacket, risking a fall on her penny loafers as she made her way across the icy lot toward my Bel Air, waving a hand. I turned down the Everly Brothers and rolled down the window; she leaned in, all smiles.

"Couple more goodies for you, for the road," she said. "Slice of apple pie—still hot if you eat it now—and a Danish. They're on the house."

"Thanks, sweetie. You're far too kind, darlin'."

She smiled. "You two ever get back this way, please tell your friend not to be a stranger."

"Promise to do that. And I'll darn sure try and see that Logan makes it back this way." A smile. "I was him, wild horses couldn't have dragged me from this joint last night."

Raylene smiled again, said, "One more thing I forgot to tell you, sir. About six this morning, a big man and a couple of other guys, about his size, stopped in. The one big man, the one who did all the talking, he was on crutches. They were looking for two men. Sounded like they were maybe looking for you and your friend, Logan."

"That's strange." I chewed my lip. "They seem friendly sorts?"

Her soft brown eyes widened. "Oh, golly, not at all. Just the opposite."

"I see..."

"I told them nobody like you two was through."

I patted her shaking hand. It was wrapped in a big knitted mitten and tightly gripping my car door. "Thanks again, darlin'." Her teeth were chattering. I said, "You headed home now?"

"Have to wait for my mother to come and pick me up. She can't do that 'til Daddy's shift at the factory wraps up in an hour." She seemed a little embarrassed. "We only have one car."

"It's too brutal to wait in this weather, and you've spent enough time in that hash house for the night," I said. "Hop in and I'll drop you at home. Save your Ma that nasty drive in on the ice." I held up a hand. "Please don't say it—it's no trouble at all. Get in, darlin'. Likely as not, you're even on my way."

As we drove through light flurries, I checked out her shoes. They looked new, but the pennies tucked into them were tarnished. I dug around in my glove compartment with my right hand and found a couple of shiny centavos from my last border crossing back home. "Here," I said, handing her the Mexican coins.

Raylene looked puzzled. "What are these for?"

"Your snazzy shoes," I said. "Figure nobody around these parts will have coins like those."

"I should say!" She beamed and spent the rest of the trip studying the coins. She said at last, a little wonderingly, "You've been to Mexico, mister?"

Watching the icy road, wary for crossing deer, I smiled and said, "A time or two."

THE KING IS DEAD
(*G*NASHVILLE)

Frank Robbins veered into Tubb's Record Shop. He was trying to escape the chilly wind sweeping in across the river, sure, but his real aim was to isolate his tail, see if he could spot today's Fed.

Because he tended to dress them the same way, and to favor a certain *type*, J. Edgar's stooges were never that hard to pick out in a crowd.

Frank had spent the early morning working on his prison novel, then moved on to operational details. It was all a bit of a hash now that that wacky son of a bitch they'd foisted on him to tend the weapon had gone off and died unexpectedly while perched on the crapper.

Frank had mightily resisted having That Man play *any* role in this operation.

But Frank hadn't gotten far with his resistance, despite the Brotherhood's leaders' acceptance of the logic of Frank's arguments against Jake and the fact That Man's increasingly erratic, drug-addled behavior clearly made him a terrible risk.

Frank stomped snow off his shoes and looked around the interior of the record shop. Swaths of black bunting

hung everywhere. There was also a big display of the bastard's forty-fives and long-playing record albums set up next
to the cash register. Alongside those was a big old painting
of Jake Gantry in a ten-gallon hat, gripping his signature
guitar that was striped red, white and blue. This big, shit-
eatin' grin painted there on his stupid, bloated face. The
portrait's frame was draped in more black cloth.

On the record's store audio system Gantry warbled a
cover version of Willie Nelson's *Hello, Walls.*

A man in a severe blue suit and crisp trench coat had
followed Frank into Tubbs. The man dusted snow off his
hat and wiped fog from his black horn rims. In that suit,
coat and hat, the man certainly stood out on Music Row.

Frank had this much to say for certain about the Feds:
they were *not* subtle. They could never blend in with *the
folks.*

But maybe they didn't *want* to be subtle. Maybe they
wanted to rattle Frank's cage. He'd only been out of stir for
a few months, after all. They probably figured they could
cow him by making it obvious they were watching; that
they suspected him of something. Maybe they thought
they'd get him so rattled he'd screw up, somehow.

The Feds rightly knew something was up, something
big, but Frank sensed they hadn't grasped what exactly was
in the wicked winter winds.

Hell, that must surely be so. If they suspected even a
fraction of what Frank and the others had planned, surely
the whole goddamn government would be jumping through
hoops to slam on the brakes.

Frank and his cohorts just had to be careful, that
was all.

Just a little longer.

Frank pretended to browse, flipping through stacks of Elvis Presley records and occasionally stealing glances up to further study his federal shadow.

Next to Frank, some doughy cow with extra chins and a black beehive was going on to her wasp-waisted, pinched-face girlfriend about Gantry's death.

The big gal said, "I was out to his house, at the gates. But it just got *too* cold standing out there and the reporters had stopped interviewing mourners anyways, so I thought I'd come here to warm up and wait for the restaurants to open."

The skinny friend, a mousy, dirty blonde with flat, lifeless hair, eyed her friend's towering tresses. She said, "I don't know how you get it all up there and *keep* it up there, Veronica."

Half disbelieving, Frank paused in his browsing over records and also studied the heavy-set woman's big, gravity defying bouffant.

The big girl proudly said, "Honey, it's the *style*. It's all faith and cans of Clairol, sweetie. But it's well worth the effort. And you know what they say? The higher the hair, the closer to Jesus!"

Frank smiled bitterly. *Yessiree*: Hell, more than hairspray could get you there—and *faster*—if that was truly your aim.

If that high-haired cow hung around town a couple more days, she'd be facing those pearly gates, surely enough.

5

The roads were a bit worse than I expected, getting more hazardous as I neared Nashville. I finally made town just after two in the afternoon.

Faced with the need to start my search for Logan somewhere, I decided to head over to Broadway and Mom's café, the *de facto* axis of Music Row, in most ways.

Mom's was to Nashville kind of what Café du Dôme or Le Select was to Paris in the 1920s. Mom's back door was famously just thirty-seven steps from the Ryman Auditorium. Well, *thirty-seven* steps by a drunkard's count.

I scoped the streets as I looked for a parking space. Christ, you'd almost have thought Abe Lincoln had died and his funeral train was rollin' into town. Men and women with black arm bands wandered the chilly streets; black bunting dangled over storefronts and framed photos of Jake Gantry grinned back from nearly every business's picture window.

The struggling, begging buskers all sang Gantry covers and old Jake's hit singles poured from the sound systems of the Music Row bars.

There were lots of cars and trucks with stenciled radio station call letters lining the streets. Cameramen pointed their rigs at TV reporters and mourning locals were asked to share Jake Gantry memories.

Call it a goddamn carnival of grief.

Christ, even that crazy dead pope hadn't merited this flavor of frenzied media attention.

I parked about a block down Broadway from Mom's in the first open space I could find, then hoofed it to the warmth of the tavern, brushing snow off my black overcoat's shoulders once through the door.

A couple of musicians in cowboy hats were at a table in the back—Ernest Tubb and Hank Snow. The former was pretty plastered for a Monday morning. Dot was creeping up behind Ernest with a hatpin, her infamous "get-along" for patrons on the verge of drunken disorderliness. I took her by the arm. "Christ, Dot, old Ernest isn't that far gone, is he?"

"He will be, I know the signs," she said crossly, turning on me with her wicked pin. She smiled as she recognized me. "Ah, Hec!"

A warm hug. I said, "I'm lookin' for a wayward crooner."

She gestured around her with the pin. "No shortage of those in here, not ever. Take your pick, sugar."

"This one is an up-and-comer. Name of Logan 'Buddy Loy' Burke."

"Never heard of him, Hec," she said, "so he can't be comin' up too hard yet."

"He's bigger down Texas way and out along the West Coast, presently. Just hasn't done much in Nashville yet."

Dot shot another look at Ernest Tubb: he could barely keep his head up. Scrawny as he was, I never could figure where old Tubb stored his hooch. She said, "Get you anything, Hec? What're you drinkin' these days?"

I bit my lip. "Probably nothing at the moment. I may have to push on to another bar. Really kind of urgent about finding this kid. Callow bastard could get himself in no end of trouble without my steady, sure hand to stay his stupidity. It's a woman thing, you know?"

Dot rolled her eyes. "Then you'd know better than most."

This nasal voice from a back booth called out, "Hector, I've written myself into a corner, I think." It was a smallish, skinny guy with a red pompadour. Willie said, "Hec, can you think of any rhyme for vamoose?"

I gave that some thought and said, "Not much other than chanteuse."

Willie smiled and squinted his eyes. "That works. I'll just change the girl in the song from a waitress to a girl singer. Hell, this one's just for the money, anyhow."

Dot had her sights set again on Ernest. Her hatpin glinted meanly in the low lounge light. "I've got business before me, Hec. A bottom-line to attend to. If you change your mind about a drink, you just holler, hear?"

Another voice, this one behind me: "Jesus, Hector? Is that really you? My God, Hector it *is* you!"

This skinny, jug-eared young guy with brown hair and glasses coming my way, his arms spread wide. It actually somehow took me several seconds to recognize him.

Holy Christ: Eskin "Bud" Fiske.

Bud closed the last few feet between us, limping slightly.

I clapped his back. "Holy Jesus, kid, how on earth are you doin'?"

Hands on his bony shoulders, I pushed Bud back from me for a better look. Fiske was wearing a pair of western boots and a white cowboy hat he'd picked up last year along the road with me in fifty-seven. He had on a black suit and this crazy tie emblazoned with an image of a big-breasted, naked red she-devil strumming a strategically placed mandolin that covered her nether regions.

He hugged me tight to him. Bud said, "Foot hasn't ever quite healed. The diabetes gets in the way, you know?" This sad smile.

I was tempted to say, *Hell, name a single thing that* ever *does, son*, but held my tongue this one time.

The young poet had been tortured by a sadistic Mexican legend last time we'd teamed up, all his misery a result of throwing in with me on a crazy caper I got caught up in down in old *Meh-hico*. An evil old bastard had burned Bud's feet with cigarettes. That, and other forms of even worse abuse.

"And your belly, Bud?"

"Still healing, too." He stepped back on his own and gave me a once-over. I braced for it, but Bud surprised me: "You're lookin' real good, Hec. Actually better than last year. I mean that."

"Somewhat cleaner living, mostly," I said, pleased. "And you were catching me at a kind of ebb-tide last year, son. Arguably my lowest low and that is saying something."

I took Bud's bony arm and steered him to a back booth. I said, perhaps too urgently, "You hear anything from Alicia?"

Alicia Vicente, the only woman since Hallie Dalton to truly touch my heart. Alicia was along for last year's wild, bloody ride, too. Fact was, I was still lugging around a torch for my Mexican beauty. Still nursed visions of a settled, happy life with Alicia and her toddler daughter. It was one of those rare, elusive dreams this writer couldn't seem to make real.

Bud didn't look me in the eye, now. "No, Hector. Hell no. You?"

"*Nada.*" I slapped his arm, heard my own voice still cracking a bit, "Ah, well, hell. So...why are you in Nashville, kid?"

"Sent here on another profile for a magazine," Bud said. We'd met last year when *True Magazine* dispatched young Fiske to New Mexico to write a piece on me.

Dot's shadow fell across the table between us. "Drinks?"

After boasting to Bud about my cleaner living, not a terrible exaggeration, I couldn't bring myself to order booze. I said, "Coffee, tall and black." Bud ordered the same.

Bud said, "*True* sent me down to write a piece on Johnny Cash this past April. I stayed on. Been trying my hand at some songwriting for Acuff-Rose. You know, poetry is my thing, Hector. Journalism just pays the bills, and barely at that. Well, songwriting is a little more lucrative, at least so far, and it's a hell of a lot closer to writing poetry than penning profiles for stag magazines. And then there was that windfall last year, thanks to you. Got myself a nice place here with that. A spanking, cherry red new used car, too. I like this place, a lot, Lass. A lot of good writers starting to come to town. Something's happening here. Or it's about to. I can feel it, silly as that may sound. I think this is becoming one of those places you told me about last year, a writers' place, you know?"

I knew. He meant like Paris was for me in the early 1920s. Like Key West was in the early 1930s: an accidental crossroads for simpatico artists.

Such sacred places come unexpectedly, they come hard and they come fast, and usually in the damnedest spots.

And they are infernally fleeting. Gone soon after—or even before—they're quite recognized for the wonderful and special thing that they are.

But if you are young and you are there? Hell, nothing compares. Not *ever*.

"Good you're here, then," I said. "You stay right here and you reap the benefits for all they're worth, son. You pen any songs I might know, Bud?"

He shrugged and nodded at Dot as she poured our coffees. I suppressed a smile: Bud had this air about him now, some kind of gravitas he'd lacked when I met him in fifty-seven. Back then, Bud had been this callow young sucker not much older than Logan Burke, but acres greener. But Bud was a hellcat in a scrap in a way Logan didn't seem to be. Bud hauled my ass out of several tight spots last year. Dot nodded at Bud and said, "You know this beanpole, Hec?"

I smiled, rasped, "We're acquainted."

Bud said to her, "And you know Hector?"

"Sure," she said. "Hec gets through about once or twice a year, every year since, what, maybe forty-nine?"

"Or fifty," I said. "Like to catch the good ones before the world knows their names," I said to Bud. "I like to sneak up to that little studio upstairs now and again to see what's being recorded out from under the heavy, dark hand of the major record labels."

Quieter, to Bud, I said, "And I'm workin' on a novel set around the country music scene."

"Hec plays piano, you know," Dot said. "He can even sing pretty good, with a few drinks in him."

"I didn't know that," Bud said, giving me this funny look.

"I play at playing piano would be the better way to put it," I said. "Play by ear, and maybe my ears aren't quite right. As to singin'...? Nah."

Dot waved a hand. "Don't believe that," she said to Bud. "Hec plays a little like Jerry Lee, kind of attacks those keys. He sings a little like Jim Reeves. You should hear Hec's version of *Distant Drums*. Gives me chills."

She smiled at me. Then it was Fiske's turn to squirm:

"Bud's okay as these green writer boys go," she said. "He could be a 'comer'. Some of his songs surely aren't terrible." She frowned, then reached into her apron and drifted off, holding up her wicked pin again. Some other poor drunk was about to be given the stinging heave.

Bud sipped coffee, said, "What are you doing in Nashville this winter, Hector? Really just scouting new talent and researching a book?"

"Sure. Goes back to last year, as it happens," I said. "When we were in Los Angeles I found that singer-songwriter, Logan 'Buddy Loy' Burke."

"I remember," Bud said. "You and—" he hesitated, like he shouldn't say "Alicia" again but he was too far along to stop gracefully, "—Alicia spent several nights at the club listening to the guy."

Now there was this funny look on Bud's face that I couldn't quite read. Didn't sense it was something to do with Alicia, and that troubled me still more. He said, "And...?"

"And I've been hanging with the kid the past few weeks," I said. "Logan split with his partner, recorded a solo LP, and decided to try and grow a fan base outside the Southwest and West Coast. But Logan took a quick powder a bit north of here last night. Boy's got himself an infatuation for Genevieve Gantry. We heard she was being investigated in connection with her ex's death. Logan promptly got a wild hair to get here, pronto."

"A jones for Genny." Bud shook his head. "Logan and every human with a Y chromosome craves a piece of that one."

Wow, Bud really had grown up some on me. Or at least he'd gotten cruder. The Bud I knew last year would never have made an assertion as raw as that last. Was Bud's coarseness simply a symptom of too much time with me, maybe? I leaned that way, and privately cursed myself for being such an enduring bad influence.

"There is that," I said. "Anyway, I'm here lookin' for Logan before he does some damn fool thing."

Bud looked at the steam curling from his coffee mug. "May be too late for that, Lass. I'm sorry."

I narrowed my eyes. "*Christ.* What's happened?"

"Your boy was arrested according to the radio this morning," Bud said.

I scowled. "Arrested? What in God's name for?"

Bud looked at his coffee mug again. "Logan's being held on suspicion of complicity to murder."

6

The tails of Bud's black duster whipped in the frigid wind. He clutched the brim of his cowboy hat against the Alberta Clipper. I buttoned up my own overcoat and turned the collar up around my cheeks.

"Sorry, just a block more," I said as we passed the turn to the Ryman Auditorium. "Closest parking I could find with all these reporters and mourners clogging the streets."

Bud said, "At the best of times, weekdays, your surest bet is to park either side of the Opry and cut through the alley." He paused, said, "I mean, if Mom's is your destination."

I smiled. "Is there another worthy Nashville bar?"

"I've actually managed to find a couple," Bud said. He smiled and pointed at my Bel Air. "God, I was afraid you might have moved on to the fifty-eight model."

I shook my head. "No way, they got it just right with the 1957 design," I said, fishing around my pocket for the keys. I squeezed the Bel Air's left tailfin with my other hand. "Chevrolet shouldn't have tinkered with this piece of perfection. Should have just built these babies from here to forever." I held up my keys, jingling them. "Remember how to drive her?"

Bud grinned and held out his hand and I tossed him the keys. "Hell, I'd have paid for the privilege, Lass," he said.

Because of my fuzzy vision from my own then-undiagnosed and far milder diabetes, Bud did most of the driving when my Bel Air was new, kind of broke her in for me the previous year. I said, "Actually, I figure you know the way to whatever jail where they're holding Logan. Be quicker than you directing me there."

"Likely so," Bud said. "We go there now?"

"Right now."

❧

A tired-eyed man in a rumpled, off-the-rack suit shook our hands and said, "You two lawyers?" He eyed Bud's tie, then looked at me and said, "At least you, I mean?"

"We're writers," I said. "Name's Hector Lassiter. I—"

"I've read you," the cop cut in. "I loved *The Big Siesta*. Great stuff."

Recognized, again. It was getting fiercely tiresome.

The captain, a man named Rick Corin, said, "Give you this much, Mr. Lassiter. Unlike some others of your ilk, the cops in your books aren't stupid. You're okay."

I thanked him and said, "What did the kid, Logan that is to say, do to justify you holding him?"

"Lied to us, mostly," Corin said. "That much I know for certain, anyhow. Burke claimed he was with the former Mrs. Gantry to give her some cover. But his story doesn't jibe with what the young woman in question already gave us. I thought the Gantry girl's alibi was lame until the crooner foisted his cock-and-bullshit tale on us. We're trying to sweat Burke now. See if he'll give us something useful on the former Mrs. Gantry."

"Logan really can't do that." I shook out a Pall Mall, offered one to the cop and lit him up after a couple of false strikes on my Zippo. "Way I hear it, old Jake burst his pump on the can."

"More or less," the cop said. "That's where he died. But that's not *how* Jake Gantry died." He gestured to a table with a few chairs arrayed around it. I spun one of the chairs around backward and planted my ass, resting my crossed arms across the back of the chair.

"Kid's only guilty of south-of-the-belt-buckle noodling," I said. "Logan's been with me touring a good deal north of here the past couple of weeks. You don't have to take just my word for that. You can talk to two-dozen tavern owners between here and Flint, Michigan. We were in Akron, Ohio, when word reached us that the *King* died."

The cop looked skeptical. "Why didn't Burke tell me this when he saw his lies about the other wouldn't work?"

"Like I said, pal, Logan's thinking with the wrong head." I took a hit of my cigarette and grimaced through a blue-gray haze of smoke. "Logan's far from the first to foul his life up chasing a tight skirt. Hell, I've written the book on that topic. Penned an entire bookcase full of 'em, in fact. In this case, boy's put his foot in it for the sake of a woman's he's never even touched. Not like he aspires to touch her anyhow. Makes it somehow sadder. Almost poignant, don't you think?"

The cop just shook his head, all disgust. "Jesus H. Christ. Well, I'll need some phone numbers of those taverns to check against, Mr. Lassiter."

"Call me Hector." I pulled out a Moleskine notebook and my fountain pen and started scrawling down information taken from various scraps of paper and business cards I'd been collecting along the road. As I wrote, the cop ground out his Pall Mall with a frown and got out one of his own Lucky Strikes. He struck a match on the edge of the wooden table. "You saying this kid has some kind of crazy lust thing going for this girl singer and that's all? This boneheaded alibi bid was the result of some damned crush?" He shook his head. Hell, I couldn't fault his reaction.

Bud arched his eyebrows and said, "Have you seen her, sir?"

"Under the lights in back," Corin said. "I don't think there's a soul behind those eyes of hers. I've seen my share of hollow people. Ones capable of anything. I count Gen Gantry among those, but emptier than most. Vacant. Lacks any *there*."

I dimly heard the echo of Gertrude Stein in my mind, speaking of some wide-spot in the road: "There's no there, there, my handsome young star."

"Logan doesn't seem to know her well enough to know that," I said. "He's seen pictures. Seen Gen Gantry on the TV. Met her in passing in a bar or two. Those were brushes that meant the world to Logan, but I doubt Gen even recalls 'em. In short, Logan's seeing GG's chassis and getting all the expected lusty notions, like most of her male fans likely do. Why should Logan be any different than those horny humps buying her LPs? Hell, it sure ain't her voice that's enticing him, or the others. As singers go, I don't much credit the buxom thrush."

Bud always did have a tendency to provoke the wrong sorts. And it seemed he still had a yen to put too fine a point on things. Bud took my lead but went furlongs further:

"In other words, it's not her voice Logan wants to screw," Bud said. "It's that sweet young body of hers he craves."

The cop shook his head and said, "Soulless as Miss Gantry strikes me, I've got a daughter just a year older than that young gal. So best watch your mouth, son."

I stubbed out my smoke and passed the cop the slip of paper covered with names and numbers and remembered show dates. "Call on 'em as you will," I said. "Then, maybe after, you can kick the kid loose. Now that I'm in town, I'll keep him on the short leash, best believe that."

"Even if these check out, the fact remains the boy lied to me and mine," Corin said. "He mucked up an official investigation. And perjured himself. Consequences for that alone are pretty steep, you know. I've got enough on my plate without having some yahoo sending me down a blind alley."

Bud said, "Could we see him now?"

Corin grunted, said, "I'll have one of mine pat you both down and take you out back. Give you ten minutes with him while I work the phone on some of these numbers."

A cadaverous flunky who was too infatuated with his badge and uniform led us back to the holding cells. The young cop was going for swagger, but scrawny as he was and with his exaggerated posture, it looked more like he'd recently sat on his nightstick.

The jail was hosting just two prisoners. The one closest to the door was a snoring old wino who smelled like he'd pissed himself in his sleep. A transistor radio by his head played *My Special Angel.*

Our boy was quartered two cells down, sitting on the end of the cot with his head in his hands, staring at the floor. I said, "Some jam you got yourself in, eh, kiddo?"

Logan looked up sharply. He was torn between grinning to see me and trying to act like some case-hardened, surly sort in order to cover up his obvious relief. Logan ended up standing and wiping his hands down on his pants nervously. Boy gripped the bars so hard his knuckles were white. "Hector, thank God you found me!"

"Thank this hombre," I said, jacking a thumb at the poet by my side. I introduced Logan to Bud. I said, "Bud alerted me to your predicament. Otherwise, I'd probably be bending my elbow in Mom's about now, at a loss to know where to start looking for you. Maybe I'd be caring less with each sip. You ran out on me, son."

Logan wet his lips and said to Bud, "Thanks. But how'd you know?"

Bud split a look between us and said, "Heard it on the radio. WSM."

Hanging his head again, Logan said, "Not the kind of airplay I was angling for."

"Don't expect so," I said. "What'd you tell those cops, you knucklehead?"

"Sort of tried to say she was with me," Logan said. "Tried to give Gen some cover."

Shaking my head, I passed him a cigarette between the bars. I broke out my old Zippo. Took three strikes to get a viable flame. I really needed to get her a new flint.

"I set 'em straight on all that," I said. "Top cop's calling some of your concert venues right now. Confirming what I told 'em. Sorry, kid, but this was never a way to help that gal. You're just not nimble enough a liar, God help you. Surely not enough to fool a seasoned lawman like the old boy running things around these parts. He strikes me as the sort that play-acts leagues dumber than he is."

Logan ran his fingers back through his hair. "So they'll let me out once they see we've been on the road, far from here?" He searched my eyes. "Right?"

I bit my lip. "Top cop's cross that you lied and loused up his investigation. You cost him important time. And you cost the good Tennessee taxpayers *dinero*. I made a pitch for springing you, but the cop doesn't seem too awful warm to that notion. Not so far, anyhow."

"You're teasing me," Logan said. "Kidding me and playing with me as punishment for runnin' off, aren't you? It's not funny, Hec."

"Hector's not kidding," Bud said. "I heard that cop. He's no nonsense."

Now Logan looked a little ill. "This cop, he thinks I know something, but I really don't. You know that, Hector."

"Yes, I do. And I told Corin so. Like I said, he's checking all that right now. Thing is, police detest people who muddy the waters, who make their hard job even harder. Can hardly fault them for that." I squeezed Logan's hand that was gripping the bars. "I'll talk more to him, son. See what can be done."

Logan slammed his palm against one of the iron struts. "Should have listened to you back there. Jesus, I was so stupid."

"Argue that? I can't." I reached through the bars and gripped the back of his neck. "I'm gonna remind you of that admission next time you seem in danger of stepping stupid. Headstrong as you are, there'll be a next time, likely as not. Get this through that skull of yours: simple bravado is not a winning strategy against anyone with a decent brain."

Bud was smiling crookedly, looking sadly amused. Couldn't blame Bud for that. The young poet had stood witness to too many of my own circa-1957 excesses and foolish moves. I shook Logan by the scruff of the neck. "Don't you lose hope on me, son. Not yet."

This tug at my sleeve: Bud. He pointed at the skinny cop waiting at the door back to the squad room. The man was glaring all hell at us. The surly cop said, "Skipper wants a word with you two assholes. Now."

7

B ud and I were left to loiter a while. That maneuver struck me as probably some low-rent show of power on Corin's part. If I was right, he was starting to disappoint.

To pass time, I picked up a discarded newspaper and checked the cover. Something there about some recently released jailbird and this white supremacist movement he'd gotten stirred up here in Music City. The man's name, Jasper Coleman, didn't resonate.

I followed the jump to an interior page and found a photo of the fella standing on the roof of a Cadillac in an all Negro neighborhood, hoisting a noose and fulminating through a bullhorn.

Then I realized I *did* know the son of a bitch.

Hell, for a fleeting time there, I was his goddamn writing mentor.

It was later in 1957. I was finally starting to put it all back together after the crazy winter-into-spring I'd spent tied up with Bud and this fiasco involving the stolen skull of Pancho Villa. I was putting my life back in order while still lugging my torch for Alicia. All the while, I was struggling to tamp down my hard living ways, so I'd maybe have an honest shot at surviving my new blood-sugar affliction.

On a whim, I'd accepted an offer from Johnny Cash to make a circuit of prisons in which he was performing concerts for the long-termers, bringing country and rockabilly to murders, rapists and career criminals of every stripe.

In one of the prisons out west, the warden had this other notion: Some of his inmates had formed a writing circle. He thought it'd be a fine thing if I spent a little time with them before Cash's concert. The warden figured I could maybe give those prison poets and possible Edgar Allen Poes a few prose tips and writing pointers.

"Hell," Warden Davis Ruthers said, pouring me two fingers of rye, "lot of good books have been written in prison, right? Such as that *Don Quixote* book, and the like?" The warden pronounced Quixote with a hard x and a silent e—*Quicks-oat*... like *that*.

"Sure," I said. I might have added, "Or like *Mein Kampf.*"

I was led to a prison library where three guards with riot guns stood at my back as I sat across a battered table from half-a-dozen hard-case prisoners, all of them armed with legal pads and crayons.

The poets mostly unknowingly ran to the primitive school, sans anything in spitting distance of so-called art.

Their poems surely rhymed a lot, though. (One would-be jailbird Wordsworth pressed me for help on his earthy ode to a cocktail waitress. I sourly offered up "runt" and "bunt," when he realized he'd surely enough written himself into a coarse corner with that c-word.)

One of the cons was a child rapist who wrote skin-crawling short stories about children and "loving" neighbors.

It was a real act of will not to drive those dull kids' coloring sticks through either of that son of a bitch's eyes.

As it was, I lavished praise on his prose efforts and encouraged him to share the fruits of his labor in the yard, figuring matters would sort out from there in something close enough to justice to spare my scraps of conscience.

One fella however, a guy who called himself Frank Robbins, showed flickers of not-inconsiderable talent. That fella had a real ear for putting words together in interesting ways and some of his short sketches—stuff that just missed the mark as fully realized short stories—held promise.

So I focused most of my attention on Frank. I worked over some of his stuff with the inmate and gave him pointers for steering some of his better but unfinished works home to port. We kept at it until someone came to fetch us when Johnny's concert was mere minutes from kicking off. The prisoner wanted to keep on with our lesson; I wanted to lose myself in Cash's music. As a civilian, I got my way.

But from fall of 1957, until Easter Sunday of the present year, Frank and I had kept up a kind of rambling correspondence about the craft of writing.

Frank sent me those rewritten pieces, and I actually managed to place a couple of his works in some men's magazines, so the guy would have a little gelt when he was finally sprung; money to give him a better shot at an honest, post-stir life as a free-lancer, I hoped.

Last word I had from Frank, he was three months from release and was starting a novel.

Then all became silence.

I'd fleetingly wondered if something happened to him in prison before he could leave, or if he'd gotten out and fallen through the cracks pronto, same as so many long-timers are wont to do when finally kicked loose in their new cheap suit and given a bus ticket to anywhere but the state in which they've done their hard time.

I stared at the newspaper photo a time.

Now I knew: Frank had come to Tennessee and reinvented himself. I didn't know Frank, or Jasper, had racist leanings. Those surely hadn't come across in any of the writings he'd shared with me.

But he did have these strange and lurid tattoos, one of them a bluebird on his arm.

Bud was watching me. He gestured at the newspaper and said, "Why so interested in that son of a bitch?"

"Think I know—knew—him," I said. I checked my watch, looked around the squad room. I said, "Wonder how long *this* SOB's going to punish us making us wait?"

"You're all done waiting," a gruff voice behind me said.

8

The three of us were arrayed around that table again, sipping coffee that tasted slightly burned. It's the same thing in every precinct house where I've sampled jailhouse java: Maybe it's a by-product of intentionally burning coffee grounds at so many crime scenes to mask the stench of decomposition.

Corin said, "Now your young friend seems even more the fool to me. I mean, to peddle some story that can be so easily knocked down? What kind of reasoning is that?"

"Sure, it's easy to knock Logan's story down when Hector hands you a phone list of witnesses to the contrary," Bud said. The poet shrugged as I glared at him for that one.

"Take it as proof of how turned around this kid is on this gal, Cap'n," I said, softly. I checked my watch. "What do you say I stand you a drink or two for a late lunch? Maybe a couple of deep doubles? See if I can't talk you into releasing the boy singer to me. I'll keep him in line, I swear."

The cop half-smiled. "Another time on the drink maybe." He rubbed the back of his neck and rolled his head. "Okay. Take the sorry-ass boy singer and keep him well out of my sight, Lassiter. He crosses my path again, no empty threat this, I'll bury him and you."

I believed the cop. "Got it," I said. "He won't."

"Your head if he does."

"Got it," I said again. We stood and shook hands. I said, "Gen Gantry, what've you got on her? She in some other cell around here?"

The cop frowned. "Not in custody, not that it's any of your business. Expect she's with some interior designers or the sort. She's already moved into Jake Gantry's big old house. Nice enough Nashville mansion, but the way Jake fixed it up, it looks a little like what might result if a house-trailer dweller came into the big money."

Bud smiled. "That swanky, huh?"

Corin said, "Yep. What my wife would call *gauche*. And dark. Heavy drapes on all the windows. Guy lived like a vampire."

"But in other words," I said, "you've not got much of a case on Gen Gantry yet."

"I've said as much as I'm prepared to confide to a couple of writers," Corin said, colder now. "It's an active case." A real edge creeping in there. I held up a preemptive hand to stay Bud's tart tongue.

"Deeply appreciate you letting the kid go," I said. "He's really quite harmless. You won't hear of us again. Swear. Good luck making your case against the vixen, Corin."

I hesitated, then opened the newspaper to that picture of the jailbird writer. I said, "Before we go, what can you tell me about this fella?"

Corin grunted, said, "He's big trouble, I think. I wish I knew more for sure. Guy's an enigma. I think the name is a fake."

"Probably," I said. "He like, oh, Klan, or something?"

"Maybe even worse than that," Corin said.

I told him then what I knew of "Jasper" under that other name; where he'd been serving time in the stir this time last year. Then I passed the cop a slip of paper with my answering service number. "Get something, or need something, you call me there, won't you?"

"He a friend of yours, Lassiter?"

"No, more like an accidental acquaintance," I said. "He's surely no damn friend."

Bud and I were left loitering on the chilly steps out front while Logan was pushed through the usual hoops toward release.

The country crooner finally came out buttoning up his coat and shaking his head. "Thanks guys. Really thought I might be moved to the county jail."

"You've used up all your favors in this town," I said, "and all mine, too, I fear. So hear this Logan—you're released to *me*. So your ass is mine. Step stupid and I pay the price. Bear that in mind in the time we're here in Music City and don't you forget it if I start riding you on something. You can hurt me in this town, big time, so no more thinking with your pecker."

Logan's face got red. I'd shamed him in front of Bud. Well, so be it. Hell, I wasn't going to land my fifty-eight-year-old ass in jail for some young buck's ungovernable urges.

We were making our way down the steps between a pair of stone lions when I heard the doors squeak behind us. Captain Corin was standing there, squinting against the snow squalls. He said, "Lassiter, you should know my men chased off a trio of roughs while you were inside. One on crutches. Other two looked like even rougher trade. They

were asking after you and your stupid young friend here."
He gestured at Logan who was freshly red-faced. Thank
God the boy held his tongue. But I could feel Bud staring
at me.

I nodded. "Where'd these boys go?"

"My men ordered them to move along," Corin said.
"Now here's a second favor I don't owe you. They were driving a fifty-four Ford with Kentucky plates. My boys made
a call. Plates are registered to some guy named Basil Sloan.
You know him?"

Callow young Logan shot me a look. I could tell as I
said it that neither Bud nor Captain Corin believed me.

"Nah," I said. "Hell no. Never heard of that son of a
bitch."

9

We trudged through ankle-deep snow to my Bel Air. As we approached the Chevy, I pulled out my key ring from my overcoat's pocket and lobbed the keys to Fiske.

Logan frowned at Bud. "He lets you drive?"

I shrugged. "I trust Bud. Haven't had to finesse him out of any jail cells."

Bud folded the driver's side seat and held it forward so Logan could squeeze into the backseat. The poet started up the Bel Air and said, "Regardless of what you told that cop, Hector, you clearly do know who this Basil Sloan is. Both of you know."

Logan bit his lip and waited to see how I'd play it. I tipped my head back against the seat. "Crooner and I ran into a spot of trouble in a tavern in Kentucky last evening," I said.

Bud just shook his head and sighed. "There's a surprise."

"It's not exactly like you're thinking, Bud," I said. "Logan and I were shooting some stick. There was some money involved, sure. But a brawl broke out and Logan and I hotfooted it out of the joint before we could be drawn into the fray."

So far Logan was holding his tongue, but Bud still looked skeptical.

I said, "Honestly, we never laid a glove on anyone inside that bar."

"Basil met us outside," Logan said. "Hector ended up shooting the bastard in both feet, purely in self defense."

A deep sigh from Bud. "You're wrong, Hector. It's exactly what I thought." He got my Bel Air in gear and edged out into traffic. Bud said, "As I'm with you guys presently, at least tell me what this Basil guy looks like. Be nice to see him coming in time to run or duck." Bud palmed us on to Broadway.

"Just imagine a grain silo on crutches," I said. "And don't waste time kicking him between the legs. Poor bastard lost his plumbing in Korea."

"Only one way you'd know that," the poet said sourly. "Guess that's why you resorted to the Colt." Bud shook his head. "Seems this Basil has good reason to want a piece of you."

"What I can't figure out is how he found us," Logan said.

"Really isn't much to figure," I said. "Not many roads lead away from that Kentucky roadhouse but the one we drove out on. Factor in your name on those concert posters all over that joint, and the radio announcements about your arrest here, and, well, there you have it."

I turned up the heater a click and turned down the volume on Sonny James singing *Young Love*. I sighed and said, "Bad thing is, you've got that gig the night of Jake's wake here in town. Another *advertised* appearance. That makes us sitting ducks unless we cancel the show and beat out of town, which if we're sensible, we'll do right now."

"I don't want to leave," Logan said. "And I don't want to cancel the show."

"That gig's a few days away," Bud said. "Days of ducking and dodging and looking over our shoulders." Bud gave me this funny smile. "Seems like good old bad times all over again."

I decided to ignore that crack. "Have to smoke-out Basil beforehand, that's all," I said. "Draw him out in a time and place of our choosing." I gestured at the road ahead. "We just rambling, or do you have some destination in mind, Bud?"

The poet shrugged. "My place has a second bedroom, and a long couch. Unless you prefer a hotel."

I turned around in my seat. "You're on the couch if we go to Bud's, Logan. What say you?"

"Safer than a hotel," Logan said. He twisted around and looked out the back window, as if maybe he thought Basil Sloan might be back there, tailing us.

"Your place it is," I said to Bud.

"Genevieve," Logan said, "are those police holding her?"

"No," Bud said, checking Logan's face in the rearview mirror. "But that cop who had you locked up pretty clearly thinks she's guilty."

The young songwriter's brow furrowed. "How do you know that, Fiske?"

I flicked Bud in the thigh and wagged a scolding finger at him below seat level where Logan couldn't see. "Heard it on the radio," Bud said lamely.

Logan said, "I just got out of jail. Before we start hiding out, think we could hit a tavern? I could really use a drink."

Bud gave me a sidelong glance: "Mom's?"

"Huh-uh, one of those other watering holes you talked about," I said. "Some place fresh and *new*, please."

10

Bud's tavern of choice was a cozy joint on Fifth. Naugahyde wraparound booths, low lights and a sunken center bar. The Platters on the jukebox crooning *Twilight Time*. My kind of seedy joint, and I guess Bud's kind, too. Logan, on the other hand, looked leery. He checked the jukebox and shook his head. "Closest thing to country on the box is Cash."

I said, "Johnny Cash isn't true country to you?"

A waitress hugged Bud. She wasn't bad looking. She had a blond beehive and rhinestone spectacles. She wore a bullet bra under her white waitress uniform, and I could see the twin vertical trail of black garters under her semi-sheer server's togs. Promising, in a tawdry way.

And she had a nice enough smile.

She steered us to a corner booth I figured was Bud's usual place as it was a writer's table—gave one the view of the room and was far enough from the jukebox to maybe pick up a conversation here or there. Perhaps snag a line of dialogue or snatches of some compelling patois.

The waitress said, "Usual, Bud?"

"Sure, but make it a pitcher," he said, short-circuiting my own drink order. "Brought friends this once."

Logan fished his still empty pockets. Frowning, he said, "Spare some change?"

I just assumed he meant for the jukebox and passed him some coins, bracing for some Cash.

Bud must have been sharing my line of thinking, because he scratched his now longish sideburn with his index finger and said, "Logan just passed the jukebox, headed back toward the restrooms."

"Probably where the damn pay phones are." I shook out a Pall Mall and made a face at my trusty Zippo when it failed to light. I scooped up a complimentary box of matches from the ashtray between us. I got my smoke going and said, "You quit the coffin nails, Bud?"

Bud had really only ever started smoking because of me, I suspected.

"Yeah, took too much of a toll with the diabetes," he said. "Thought you were quitting, too."

"I'm gradually cutting back," I said. "Now limit myself to eight a day."

Bud smiled. "That's down from what?"

"You mean individuals cigs, or packs?"

He smiled again and fished his own coat pocket. "At least you didn't offer up cartons as an option." He tossed a Zippo on the table between us. I recognized it. Last year, Bud had had the lighter engraved with the opening lines of one of my early novels. It read: "Whores Die Hard."

Bud said, "If you need another lighter…"

I held up his Zippo and turned it so the engraved letters caught the light. "No thanks, Bud. You keep it. If I carried around a Zippo quoting myself I'd just remove all doubt about me for the two or three still maybe on the fence." Through a haze of smoke I said, "You and the beauty who seated us, something goin' on there?"

"No," Bud said firmly. "I've got my eye on a girl. Works for *Cashbox*. Becky Thorpe."

I repeated the name aloud. "Sounds promising. Bet she's a brunette."

Bud narrowed his eyes. "How'd you know that?"

"The name 'Becky' exudes brunette. And in the time I've known you, I've got a reasonable sense of your tastes, I think."

"Always the writer," Bud said.

I let that one fly by. "What am I going to be drinking, Bud?"

"Texas Margaritas," Bud said. "Best I've ever found, and I'm counting 1957's tour of Mexico with you in that assessment."

"Can hardly wait." I checked my watch.

"Logan's taking some time," Bud said, again reading my mind.

"Yeah," I said. "I'm getting swarmed by visions of a momentary visit by Gen Gantry," I said.

"Me too." Bud loosened the knot in his swanky, satanic tie. "We can't both be wrong."

"Figure not," I said. "So, more trouble's brewing in Music City, USA. How can a fella like Logan, who can write such smart, true songs, be such a chucklehead in living his life?"

Bud shrugged. "A lot of folks still ask the same thing about Hank Williams, the so-called Hillbilly Shakespeare, you know? I mean a lot of younger artists around town now doubt Hank actually wrote all those songs." A face. Bud said, "Hell, they say he wrote none of those songs."

I smiled. "I met Hank a few times. He knew of what he wrote, sure enough. Not much distance between Old Hank and his songs in that sense. But Logan? It ain't a gulf, it's a goddamn canyon."

Thirty minutes later, we'd made a healthy dent in Bud's pitcher of margaritas. Logan finally slid into the booth next to me. He gestured at the jukebox. "See, no country music to be had. The damn Everly Brothers, now."

Me? I like *All I Have to Do Is Dream* well enough. And some I know consider the Everlys a country enough act. I needled Logan a bit then. "Drink up, son, but be jiffy about it. Bud and I are thinkin' of pushin' along in a few minutes. Time to move on, yeah?"

Frowning as he poured himself a drink from the pitcher, Logan said, "We can't leave. Not yet."

I sighed. "Expecting company, aren't we?" I shook my head. "To what likely good end, kid?"

Logan stared at his drink. Bud gave me a look like I should ease up on Logan. Looking at the two of them together, it was hard for me to fathom Bud and Logan were about the same age. Despite that once prematurely white hair, Logan just seemed much more the kid.

Relenting a bit, I said, "Whatever you have in mind, Logan, whatever happens, we are staying wide of the police, right?"

"Oh, for sure." Logan sounded reasonably convincing.

We sat in silence for a time, drinking tequila. Bud and Logan drifted into songwriting talk, started swapping lyric problems. Soon enough, they were scrawling lyrics and song hooks on napkins. I just sat back and took it in, savoring the belly-warming tequila and low light and Jim Reeves' *Four Walls* on the jukebox.

I closed my eyes, listening to those young writers going at it with verve and passion. I was again carried back to my own days as a tyro, Left Bank writer, finding my author's voice and arguing theories and philosophies of writing— a Montparnasse *comer* and not yet "Hector Lassiter," that increasingly tedious, increasingly public commodity.

Out of the blue, Logan said, "Gawd, I hope this jail beef doesn't dog me."

My eyes still closed, still partly back there in the City of Light, I mumbled, "Friend of mine used to insist that any publicity is good publicity."

Harsh light struck my eyelids then. I blinked and squinted at the source.

Framed in the light through the front door was this tiny, shapely little thing.

Funny: contrary to other recently voiced opinions, it didn't look like Satan's silhouette.

11

Logan and Bud were still mired in music talk.

I watched sleek and curvy Genevieve Gantry tarry at the door, not yet really looking for us, or so it seemed at first. Seemed more like she was waiting on someone else to arrive. Gen was looking back over her shoulder when she wasn't tearing at her nails with her teeth.

Eventually, she drifted to the jukebox. She dipped a hand in her purse and fed coins to the momentarily quiet jukebox. No country for the Music Row vixen: *Summertime Blues*.

Genevieve saw me watching her and smiled, impulsively flirting. Figured right then if I was thirty years younger, hell, maybe twenty years younger, I could easily enough play the fool for her. She was momentarily startled when an older, taller woman took her arm. Genevieve Gantry then pointed at our booth.

"Enough of the shoptalk boys," I said. "Logan's guests have arrived." I scooted around in the wraparound booth so Genevieve would be more likely to sit closer to Logan. "Gonna be tough to talk above old Eddie Cochran's singing," I said. I pointed at Logan. "Little Gen selected that tune, country boy." That made Logan frown; his frown made me smile.

Then Logan's inamorata was standing right there.

Genevieve was surely dishy enough for bein' hardly more than a kid.

And looking at her, it was hard to fathom she'd ever been married, particularly to pasty-faced and wig-wearing, doughy old Jake Gantry.

Jesus, is a fat wallet *that* potent an aphrodisiac?

I looked at Logan and Bud looking at Genny. Yep— goners, both of 'em.

For my part? I'd been to Milan, Madrid and Paris. Been to Monterey, California, and to Tarpon Springs and all points in-between.

But I'd never seen green eyes like Genevieve's. That is, until I looked at her companion's face. The mother's face was that of Genevieve Gantry at maybe forty. Still fetching, still sculpted and damn well keeping her looks and curves. But wise and wearing a perpetual and knowing half-smile that surely challenged a mature man.

The woman introduced herself as Donna Perkins. I checked the woman's left hand: Five slender, naked fingers. Knowing better, but characteristically not caring, I said, "And Mister Perkins?"

Gen's mother gave me a long, appraising look, then said, "Deceased. And not so recently that you need feel obligated to say you're sorry." Mother and daughter were quite the pair, for sure—rather like Aryan wet dreams.

"All the same," I said. "Very sorry for your loss."

Genevieve was looking between Bud and Logan, probably trying to decide which of the young bucks was the one who'd gone to jail lying for her. She was still tearing at her nails. They were chewed down to the quick.

And Logan, the sorry son of a bitch, was positively mooning over her.

I gestured at the young songwriter and said, "Logan here has been telling me all about you, Miss Gantry." I winked at Gen and said, "Love what you did with *Fever*."

Gen draped herself on Logan then. She gave him this lingering hug. Logan's face flushed and he awkwardly patted the small of her back. Kid was in so far over his head I almost hurt for him.

Gen Gantry said, "Thank you so much for what you did to try and help me, Logan."

It was *almost* sweet.

Gen was wearing an almost demure dress and her pale blond hair was down and careless.

She almost looked like the girl next door.

That was until you remembered it was a young thing with a faulty alibi thanking a horny twerp who'd gone to jail lying to cops to spare her an arrest in her ex-husband's murder.

When you recalled all that, *almost* went away faster and farther than I could follow.

As planned, Gen sat down alongside Logan, pressed up tight against him. I scooted around closer to Bud. Donna, slender, tallish, busty and attractive Donna, stubbornly squeezed in alongside me. Donna said, "What are you handsome fellas drinking?" She pulled out a leather cigarette case and I struck a bar match with my thumbnail. The humidity of the place was on my side: the match flared *like that*.

"You like Margaritas?" I held the match up for her then shook the flame out.

Donna leaned back and blew smoke from the side of her mouth, away from me. "Never heard of one. I'm mostly a fiend for gin and tonics."

Damn it all. Now I had this longstanding distrust of gin drinkers to overcome, somehow: a prejudice to fight that went all the way back to Paris and Scott Fitzgerald in his gin soaked cups.

And now another of Genevieve's musical picks was blasting out of the jukebox: Carl Perkin's *Blue Suede Shoes* shook the walls.

I lit my own Pall Mall and pointed at the jukebox. "Old Carl family of yours?"

Donna smiled, blowing more smoke. "Not so far as we know."

"Would have been helpful career-wise for sure if he was," Gen said. She scooted Logan's drink closer between them and took a sip. Gen's scarlet lipstick stained the paper straw. "That's kind of yummy," she said to Logan. "What kind of liquor is that?"

"Tequila," Bud said, watching her. Jesus, the poet was nearly as smitten as Logan.

Gen's green-eyed gaze swung my way then. "I want to thank you for offering to help me, Mr. Lassiter. For coming to my rescue."

Couldn't help it: I shot Logan a cross look. Donna squeezed my arm then. I could almost feel the heat of her hand through the sleeve of my sports jacket and shirt. She said, "It's a relief I can't describe, Hector, to have a man of your famous talents looking out for our interests."

Our.

Famous talents.

Jesus bawled and bled.

And once again, my goddamn outsized reputation preceded me. I glanced at Bud. Fiske sat there with his chin on his palm, eyebrows raised. I nodded. Bud's bemused eyes said it all:

Well, goddamn. Here we go again, eh, Hector?

That jukebox had moved on, again, now cranking out *Stop the World and Let Me Off.*

I drained my drink and said to Genevieve, "Well, I don't know enough to help you at this point. You're going to have to fill me in. You have to do that on everything. No secrets. And don't worry, we're nothing if we're not discrete."

"Of course," Donna said. "We'll tell you all you need to know. But not here. Between the trade magazines and the local papers, well, you never know who's listening in. No telling who might be in the next booth, taking notes."

I shifted around in order to face Donna more directly, draping an arm across the booth at her back. "Where then?"

"At our—I mean at Genevieve's home," her mother said.

"Fair enough." I threw down some bills to cover a tip. Donna stood and I slipped out behind her and helped her on with her coat, prompting flustered Logan to do the same for Genevieve. Young Gen looked over her shoulder from under long lashes as Logan closed her coat around her. "You're *so* sweet," she said to him.

Bud was still seated in the corner of the wraparound booth. "I'll settle up for the pitcher," he said. "Catch you all outside."

As we stepped out into the cold, an elderly black man put the arm on me. He smiled and squeezed my bicep. He said, "I'm the Right Reverend Augustus Grafton Robinson, allied to the Reverend Kelly Miller Smith of the First Colored Baptist Church. How are you, my brother?"

"Aces over queens, Padre," I said. "What's precisely shakin', Reverend?"

"Well, we're tryin' to desegregate downtown Nashville," he said. The cleric watched for my reaction.

Donna rolled her green eyes, looking something more than impatient. She fished her purse for an ink pen, then took my hand in hers and scrawled an address on my palm.

Phone numbers and addresses scrawled in the palm of a hand? Seemed teenager, puppy love stuff. Should've told me something, right there.

"Look us up there," Donna said. "We'll expect you to be close behind." She took her daughter by the arm and they made their way on spike heels across the slick pavement toward a glossy black, new-model Cadillac with steer horns mounted on the hood. Holy God, but that was one tacky sled.

I turned back to the preacher. He had a badge pinned to his lapel. The badge was emblazoned with an acronym— "NCLC." I shucked off a five from my roll, said, "Stick it to those sheet-wearing cocksuckers, Reverend Robinson, you hear now?"

The preacher beamed. "We *will*. And bless you, brother."

I took Logan by the arm. "Too damned cold to loiter long out here, kid. We'll wait for Bud in the car." We fast-walked the distance to my Bel Air. A black Ford was parked behind my Bel Air.

The Kentucky plates on the Ford clicked for me precisely one second too late.

Two apes jumped out of the Ford. They shoved guns under our chins.

A third man struggled out of the front seat of the black car. Swaying, he reached back into the Ford and slid out a pair of crutches.

Basil Sloan smiled and winked. He said, "Thus does your last day on earth turn to so much blood and dust, Lassiter."

12

Basil jerked his head at one of the men with him, a hulking giant with a blond flattop and a missing front tooth. He said, "Dusty, you're with me in the Bel Air. You get in back with Lassiter, there. Chip'll follow in the Ford." The man called Dusty patted us down.

My Colt was still in the Bel Air's glove compartment. Would Logan have the courage to use it if he could get at it? Past experience indicated that was pretty unlikely. But now that we were really up against it, just maybe the kid would find the backbone to—

But then Basil robbed me of even that slim hope. He pointed his forty-five at Logan and said, "You drive, boy. Pony up the keys, Lassiter. I'll ride up front, on account of my goddamn ruined feet."

I tarried, groping around my pockets for my keys, trying to buy Bud time to maybe make it outside, to tumble to our plight.

But Dusty shoved his gun's muzzle up against the small of my back. "Step it up, you son of a bitch," he said. "Freezin' our balls off out here." He made a face and nodded at Basil. "Sorry, boss. I fuckin' forgot."

Cursing softly, I tossed the keys to Logan. "You finally get to drive her kid," I said. "Try and savor it."

Dusty shoved me into the back of my Chevy and made me sit up tight against the door so it would be that much harder for me to make a quick reach for his gun.

He also ordered me to sit on my hands. As Logan started up the car, I said, "Look, you can have your damned money back, Basil. Hell, take it with interest. And I'm goddamn truly sorry about your feet, old pal."

"We're well past apologies or even reparations, dumbass," Basil said. "I didn't come all this way just to break even. See, I've got certain enterprises back in Kentucky. These are things I have that run on reputation."

Basil shoved his gun into Logan's side. "Get her movin', crooner. Start her up pronto and get her rollin'."

Sick inside, I said, "How'd you find us?"

Basil said, "Chip's brother is an auxiliary cop back home. Stew has an extra radio he loaned me. Seems, you're under surveillance by the Tennessee cops. We just happened to catch the chatter on the radio. Listened to the cops following you, givin' spots you were stoppin'. And here we are."

If we were being watched by the local cops, then perhaps—

An evil smile from Basil. "I know what you're thinkin' now, and, *nah*: Your watchers decided to grab some grub while you were in the bar. Must've figured you for being in there longer than you were. So you can forget any happy thoughts about the police pulling your asses outta *this* fire." Basil, gratingly, pronounced it "*poe-leece.*"

As we pulled away from the curb, I looked back over my shoulder, hoping I might see Bud with a gun pressed to Chip's head back in that damned Ford.

But no.

"We're gonna take you all out to Old Hickory Lake," Basil said. "Shoot you and weight your bodies. Then I'm gonna enjoy the ride back home to Kentucky in my new fuckin' powder blue Bel Air. Hell, I even like the color scheme, inside and out. So behave—don't want to bloody up her upholstery."

༃

I tried talking us out of the hit on the drive out to the lake. I said, "You realize I've got a pretty prodigious public profile, don't you? Killing me is not quite like shootin' up just any old citizen, Basil. Logan's pretty known, too. Cops aren't just going to let something like this rest. Particularly not my good friend in the Nashville PD, Captain Rich Corin."

"Police have to find your bodies first in order to know you're dead," Basil said, almost nonchalant. "You boys ain't comin' back up once we put you under. Comes to disposal, we're what you'd call well-practiced."

Yeah. And stone mad, too.

"There's the other thing, too," Basil said. "You're not from around these parts, neither of you, so who would report ya'all missin'?"

It was cold inside my car, but in the rearview mirror I could see the beads of sweat leaking out of Logan's black pompadour. I saw some of the dye had stained the collar of Logan's shirt gray. His knuckles on the wheel were damp and trembling.

But then, hell, so were my palms, still jammed under my thighs.

Some gesture of bravado or bluster was needed to buck up Logan, regardless how hollow it might be at base. I cogitated erratically, groping for something and coming up empty. Sour and cynical, I finally said, "Basil, if you don't turn this car around and get your sorry ass out of my way, you're going to wish I'd shot you elsewhere than your feet."

Basil tipped his head back against the seat and sighed. "What do you think the temperature is out there, Lassiter? Would you guess it's twenty-five, maybe thirty degrees? I suspect it's in that range. Here's the thing: the difference won't much matter when you're under those icy waves of Old Hickory. You'll be even colder then. And a home for bluegill."

Logan's eyes searched mine in the rearview mirror.

I smiled back at the songwriter and tried for a last bit of swagger. "Basil, if you don't turn this car around, *right now,* I refuse to be held responsible for every dark thing I do to you in the terrible time stretched ahead of us."

That drew a scornful snort from Basil. "You got no more time, Lassiter, but I promise you plenty of terrible."

We parked on a high, snow-blanketed embankment.

Basil and Dusty ordered us out. Logan's legs were already shaking.

Snaky Old Hickory Lake was starting to freeze around the edges in its shaded places but mostly churning and chopping down there at its center, endlessly driven restless by the chilly wind.

Some ducks paddled around on the lake's center, but they were the only signs of life.

Always wary of heights, I cautiously looked over the edge of the cliff's side, saw an old derelict rowboat way down there beached at the lake's edge. Such a long way down, the fall alone could kill.

Seemed the boys had scouted ahead, well enough. They evidently aimed to kill us, throw us off the cliff, then climb down there and weight whatever was left of us. They'd row our battered corpses out to the center of the manmade lake and sink us for same as eternity.

The snow was falling harder, already making little piles on our shoulders.

Basil grimaced as the crutches dug into his underarms. "Don't look so sad, Lassiter. If the weather wasn't so shitty, and if my armpits didn't ache so much, I'd take some real time killing you two. All thing's being relative, you both are gettin' off light in my eyes." Basil jerked his head at his flunky. "Go help Chip with the chains and the cinder blocks. I've got these sons of bitches under control."

Basil was leaning on a single crutch now. He pointed a .45 at the space between Logan and I. "On your knees, boys. Put your hands in your pockets and make fists."

Poor Logan looked positively nauseous. As we settled onto our knees in the cold snow the troubadour said softly to me, "This plan of yours, when does it kick in, Hec? I mean, you really do have a plan, right, Hector?"

"Sure," I lied. "Sure I do, kiddo. There's *always* a plan, son. Just follow my lead."

Seemed no use in dropping the pretense of bravado now: no point in making Logan spend his last moments in abject terror.

For my part? I felt like I had instant ulcers. My knees quaked.

Maybe any who noticed would think it was from the frigid wind from off the lake, I told myself. That wind whipped up the fast-falling snow and we were in the midst of a mini-blizzard.

Blinking against the stinging flurries, Basil hollered, "Dusty, Chip! Move your lazy asses, hear now!"

I could hear snow crunching underfoot behind me.

"About goddamn time," Basil said. He pointed his gun between my legs and took a shot into the snow 'tween my knees. My stomach flip-flopped, but at least my kidneys held.

Logan sobbed, then he began to *beg*.

"See no reason to make this *too* quick for you, Lassiter," Basil said.

"We don't deserve anything remotely like this, you son of a bitch," I said. "It was a stupid game of pool against two humps you should have known better than to back."

"If it stopped there, you might even be right," Basil said. "But you shot me in both feet, Lassiter. I'm told I'm gonna walk with a double limp, probably goddamn always. So you best shut up now. At this point, it's all about saving face back home, and that's going to cost you two, all the way up."

Basil closed one eye, taking aim at my crotch.

Logan, voice quavering, said, "Hector, please, this plan—?"

The second shot was deafening.

Its sound was held close to us and the ground by the growing density and humidity of the air and the harder-falling snow. I flinched and waited for the pain to go shoot-ing up my spine; waited to see my blood pumping from between my legs onto that virgin snow.

Instead, a pink spray came from *in front* of us. Some of the blood splashed my cheek.

Basil's forty-five tumbled from his grasp and disap-peared with a plop into the ankle-deep snow, leaving only its outline, like some snow angel lost its roscoe.

Old Basil began screaming, staring at the new hole suddenly there from still another shot—that hole going clear through his ruined palm. He snarled at something behind me. Basil said, "Goddamn! I'll be a sorry son of a bitch! Undone by a goddamn nigger!"

I looked over my shoulder. The Right Reverend Augustus Grafton Robinson and Bud Fiske stalked through the deepening snow. Smoke trailed from the barrels of both men's guns.

I jerked my hands free from my pants' pockets and rooted at the hole in the snow for Basil's dropped automatic. I got a hand around it and felt a dent in the grip where Bud's bullet had struck. I came up with the gun, aiming between Basil's wide eyes.

But before I could pull the trigger, he was gone: Basil took one step too far back and toppled from the embankment, screaming.

I crept up to the side and hung my head over, expecting to see Basil sprawled and broken way down there next to the boat.

Fingers tangled in the hair at the back of my head.

The wounded man was dangling from a tree root with his one good hand. Then his grip failed and he began falling again.

Somehow, he found some slope: Clutching frantically at bracken and smallish, shallow-rooted trees, Basil somehow managed to pretty much control his fall, ending up sprawled on the frozen lakeshore perhaps sixty feet below me, shaking his head and cursing.

I was just taking aim when he rolled into a hollow under the cliff's side.

Logan was behind me now, peering over. "He dead?"

"Didn't look it," I said.

I took Bud's offered hand and he hauled me to my feet. "Honest to God? That was far closer than I can well stomach them," I said. "Thank you, Bud. You too, Preacher. But how in hell did you two come to be here?"

"I ran into the reverend here," Bud said. "He saw what happened back there in Music City, but was too far away to do much to help you when he saw these guys pull their guns."

"Just as that was happening, Bud here came out, looking like he was searchin' for someone," the preacher said. "Well, I pointed ya'll out, pulling away in your Bel Air. We followed in my car. We tailed the gentleman in the Ford."

I pumped the preacher's hand. "Thanks for taking the trouble to get involved, Padre. Most wouldn't have run that risk."

The old cleric grinned. "Hell, these ones were racist crackers. I plum relished it."

I flicked on the safety and shoved Basil's automatic down Logan's waistband. Then I leaned into my Chevy. I popped the glove compartment door and hauled out my Colt. The preacher's eyes widened at the sight of the long-barreled Peacemaker. I said, "What about the other two?"

Bud looked a little sick. The preacher however, smiled. He held up a bloody stiletto. "Stakes were precious high and they had guns, brother."

All-righty, then.

"You're some kind of Old Testament-style sort of cleric, aren't you, Reverend?" I shucked off a twenty from my roll. "That's for your trouble, Padre. You best get moving along. We'll see to the scrubbing up the aftermath."

The preacher smiled and held up the Jackson. He said, "This, with the other, buys you a plaque on a pew at the church if you'll let me. Your name, right there, for same as forever!"

I shook his hand again; now saw the blood on his shirt cuff. "By all means. Name's John Edgar Hoover."

The padre grinned. "So much bullshit. But I love it, so that's exactly what I'll put there."

We watched as the Right Reverend Robinson trudged back through the snow, still laughing and shaking his head. Bud said softly, "That time in the car with him, well, he's not like any preacher I've come across."

"Good thing in this instance," I said, setting off for the other Ford.

I stooped to pick up Basil's discarded crutch, then took the other one leaning against my car and closed the door against the heavy, wet falling snow. The tire tracks from our cars were already vanishing under a fresh layer of the white stuff.

Logan, still looking sick, said, "There never was a plan, was there, Hector? Us being here now, still alive, it's all just dumb luck, ain't it? Don't you lie to me, goddamn it."

I shrugged. "Bud was *always* the plan. Bud has never *not* come through for me." I called back over my shoulder, "That was some Lone Ranger-flavor of shooting, my poet. I mean knocking the gun out of Basil's hand. Clayton Moore couldn't have topped that on his best day. Though I'll confess, I'd be happier if you'd shot for his goddamn ugly face."

"Actually, I was shooting for his heart," Bud called back. "With my eyes and the snow?" A shrug. "Hell, I was lucky to hit anything."

Catching up and squeezing my shoulder, Bud said, "Best brace yourself, Hec. Preacher slit their throats. He did it before I could stop him. He pitched them forward into the trunk of the Ford. I'm thinking now we would have been ahead to leave them on the ground. You know, because of the mess as they bled out."

Hellish strategy to come from a career poet. Yet it was sound, all the same.

"Surely would have saved us the trouble of what do with the Ford now," I said.

We reached the Ford. It was indeed a sorry, bloody sight.

Chip and Dusty had emptied nearly all of their blood into the trunk. The result was a shallow dark red pool, flecked with a welter of melting snowflakes. The coppery scent of blood co-mingled with the pines: it made for a disturbing but heady aroma.

I grabbed the bodies by the unspoiled hair and dropped them on their backs behind the Ford. The neck wounds were surely grisly enough—textbook overkill. The exposed spinal cords were cut halfway through.

He was some kind of preacher, to be sure—he'd damn near decapitated the men.

I reached in and pulled out four cinderblocks and the bloody chains from the trunk.

The previous year, Bud had helped me with a little necessary grave robbing, so I knew he had the stomach for what was to come; I was relatively sure Bud wouldn't puke his way through it the way Logan was apt to.

I slung the crutches into the blood soaked trunk—call 'em kindling for the fire to come.

"Bud, you help me with these sorry sons of bitches," I said. "Logan, see if you can't figure out how to get that police band radio out of this heap and into mine. Could prove useful down the road. Take its antennae, too. After, fill up the trunk and compartment with all the dry leaves and twigs as you can find them. Any old, fallen and rotting wood. We're gonna torch this bitch to hell and gone."

I figured Logan would have no luck with any of that, but the tasks would keep Logan's hands and fevered brain busy while Bud and I did the real work and sank Chip and Dusty at the center of Old Hickory Lake where me and Logan were supposed to spend all the unknown years to come.

I stooped down at the lake's edge and scooped freezing water up in my crossed palms and washed off my hands. The icy water soon made my fingers numb.

"Jesus Christ, but this water's cold," Bud said, also washing up. He looked around some more.

We'd found no trace of Basil. Hurt as he was—cold and far from the city as this place was—I figured he'd die of exposure or bleed out soon enough, wherever he'd crawled off too.

The young poet nodded at the boat. "And now the inside of that thing's blood-soaked."

"Easily enough fixed," I said. Rising, I put a boot against the bow and kicked the boat back out into the water. I waited until it was twenty-five or thirty yards from shore, then shot it three times at the waterline. There was some gurgling, then the boat began listing to one side and soon sank.

Shaking his head with this humorless smile, Bud said, "Is there anything that can't be solved with a Peacemaker?"

"If there is, I've yet to run up against it." I slapped his arm. "C'mon, Bud. We gotta climb back up there topside. Then we've got us a Ford to torch."

Bud said, "Think they burn anything like a forty-nine Mercury?"

We'd torched one of those babies, a spell back, south of the border.

I impulsively hugged him to me. "God but it's good to see you again, kid."

13

J ake Gantry's place was a white, three-story monstrosity with big old Doric columns propping up its upper porches. There were plenty of old trees and vast expanse of lawn.

All that Southern charm was surrounded by a high, black wrought-iron fence.

The gates out front flaunted sculpted iron silhouettes of battling sporting cocks.

Bud pointed to the hint of a roofline and a smokestack sticking up out of the ground, about a foot off the turf and at least fifty feet from the main house. He said, "What's that, do you think?"

"That, I think, is The King's bid at a fallout shelter," I rubbed my jaw. "Seems Jake feared they might drop the big one on Music City, of all unlikely places."

Tracing the sprouting gray stubble on my cheek, I said, "So let's declare the son of a bitch crazy paranoid, too. Sincerely doubt this town's high on Russia's list of targets."

Donna Perkins answered the door herself, all anger: "What happened to you men? You should have been here an hour ago."

Not sure why, but I felt compelled to put it right out there, nice and naked: "Bloody trouble honey. Blood and thunder. The kind you usually don't come back from. Three men tried to kill Logan and I. Bud and that street preacher you sneered at turned the tables on 'em. That padre saved us."

Now Donna looked scared. "Was it something to do with my daughter?"

I took her hand in mine and patted its back with my other mitt. "Who can *truly* say?"

Bud and Logan just looked at me, probably wondering if this was some sideways strategy on my part, and wondering to what end I was angling.

Bud would of course have notions about all that, all of it based on sound past experience.

What was going through Logan's mind at any given point increasingly struck me as any poor bastard's guess.

Donna squeezed my hand once, firmly, then released it. "We stopped at a liquor store and bought some more of that tequila for you fellows. She mispronounced it in a way that made the Mexican booze sound *très* exotic. "Is that good? Might calm your nerves after your close call."

"It might at that." I smiled and took Donna's arm. "But tequila, all alone, isn't really something for *deep* drinks. That heady elixir screams for some kind of smoothing mixer. Have you got any orange juice around this manse? Maybe some Grand Marnier? Amoretto? Orange cognac?"

"Freshly squeezed orange juice," Donna said. "But as to the other?" A shrug.

"Why don't you show me, darlin'?"

Gen Gantry met us in the foyer of Jake Gantry's big, "gauche" house. She was now wearing her trademark peddle-pushers and a loose-fitting cotton sweater that clung to her saucy curves.

A longhorn's head was mounted on the wall above the front door.

A killed and stuffed black bear reared up on hind legs stood opposite the mounted stag's head.

Donna saw me eyeing and frowning at the dead bear, said, "We're getting rid of it. You want it for your home, cowboy? You can have that thing's head, too. Consider them gifts for services rendered. Or yet to come."

Was there a hint of innuendo in her tone? Either way, unlike at least one other writer of my acquaintance, I was never one for festooning my hacienda with the cadavers of glass-eyed critters.

"Holy Christ, but emphatically *no*, darlin'" I said. "I eat stuff like that when it's fresh, not display it to gather dust."

I followed Donna to the kitchen to make our drinks. Gen led the boys off to some other portion of Jake Gantry's kitschy hacienda.

The kitchen was no smaller than the average tennis court.

A servant's table in the middle of the room looked like it could seat twenty and still have plenty of elbowroom.

Donna slipped a bottle of tequila from a paper sack. From a cabinet over the sink, she pulled out a bottle of gin drained by perhaps half. I found the refrigerator on my own and poured myself a couple of fingers of tequila over ice and topped it off with orange juice, some apple cider and a dash of cinnamon.

I sampled my improvised concoction and decided it hit the spot well enough. And hell, it was ripe with citrus vitamins. Call it a jacked up juice drink.

Donna handed me a tray for the other drinks I was evidently expected to make. "It works, Mr. Lassiter?"

"Call me Hector. And yes, it works just fine."

Donna mixed herself one of her gin and tonics. We tapped glasses. "Down to cases," I said. "What do the police say killed your son-in-law?"

That got a bit of a rise out of Gen Gantry's mother. "Please. Jake was nearly twice my age. I mean, he was *at least* that."

"Yet you couldn't talk your little girl out of marrying the old coot?"

Donna scowled. "I've done some accidental research on you, Hector. The gossip magazines...Seems to me upon even cursory reading there's quite the string of younger women in your past, mister. *Significantly* younger women."

It indeed wouldn't have taken much browsing over copies of *Confidential* or *Hush-Hush* to suss out that sorry fact about me.

Between Bud's recent piece on me for *True*, as well as a couple of other not-so-long-ago profiles in *Argosy* and *Screen Gems*, my private life was, pretty sadly, very much public property this season.

"Sure," I said. I sipped my drink, carefully choosing words. "But there's younger and then there's far too young. By that, I mean jailbait stuff. Quite a spread there, between the King of Country Music and your little girl, Ma'am. Hell, by my math, your baby girl was probably even a bit less than legal when old Jake first came a-courting."

Donna scoffed at that. "Welcome to the true South, Tex. Look at Jerry Lee Lewis and his recent nuptials. At least Genevieve and Jake weren't blood."

"True so far as it goes," I said, smoothing an eternally stubborn comma of hair back from my forehead. "When it comes to doubtful life choices, I reckon we reap solace from relativism as we can. Good thing for you all Jerry Lee Lewis is even more flexible in his moral standards."

"You know, I've never found sarcasm an appealing quality," Donna said.

"I don't much care for it in others, must confess," I said.

I mixed a couple more drinks for Bud and Logan. More than a tad reluctantly, I said, "What's your little girl drinking, this hour?"

"Water," Donna said, licking liquor from her full lower lip. "She's put on a little pudge of late. We can't have her looking like that cow Patsy Cline, not with a tour about to start in a couple of weeks, can we? Not the way she's expected to dress, with those painted-on pants."

Nice bit of patter, particularly coming from one's mother.

"Perish the thought," I said. "You never have confided to me what the police said killed Jake Gantry, Donna. As I said, I need candid information if I'm going to stand a chance of helping with anything."

"Don't know exactly what the medication was, but the police said the medical examiner who performed Jake's autopsy found traces of a drug used to treat depression," Donna said.

She held up the half-empty bottle of Gordon's gin, looking at the label. "They said the medication has lately been blamed for heart problems in other patients."

I freshened my drink with a fresh splash of tequila. "So, Jake was the moody sort, was he? Probably prone to black studies? Maybe old Jake was still down in the dumps over your little girl leaving him? You know, badly fazed by her loss. Turned to the pill bottle?"

Donna shrugged. "I suppose he was sad enough to lose her. He still loved Gen, clearly. I mean, he left her everything, right? So he was still carrying a torch it would seem, wouldn't it? But, according to police, Jake wasn't under any official psychiatric care of any kind."

"And so the cops presume foul play," I said. "Tell me this, is your daughter some kind of secret pharmacologist?"

"Of course not," Donna said archly. She picked up a bell and rang it. A heavyset, elderly black woman bustled in from an adjoining room off the back of the kitchen.

"We're out of gin," Donna coldly told her servant.

The old woman nodded and fetched a careworn cloth coat from a hook on the back of a pantry door. "More Gordons, ma'am?"

"Two—no, *three* bottles," Donna said. "And be quick about it."

The old woman shrugged on her coat and adjusted its collar. On the lapel of her coat was pinned a metal badge. The piece of tin read "NCLC." I watched the woman leave through a back door. Indulging a hunch, I said, "That lady and some others I've seen around here, they holdovers from old Jake's employ?"

"I'm in the process of re-evaluating staff for our—I mean, for Genevieve's—needs." Donna hesitated. "You were asking about the drug that killed Jake and about Genevieve. I tell you this next in strictest confidence: Genny has been under a doctor's care for the past several months. For her own nervous condition. The drug prescribed for Gen is the same as the one that killed Jake. You can see now how that might be made to look. What thoughts it might put in a certain kind of a dark and suspicious mind."

My kind of mind, for instance. But I didn't react to that.

I just nodded slowly and said, "What's the problem? I mean, Gen surely strikes me as edgy in some ways, fidgety. Her fingernails chewed down to the quick and all. But she's young. All those crowds—is it stage fright has her in its grip?"

Donna waved a hand. "That's just another part of the recording business. No. She's being told it's important now for her to find some original material. Even better, it's been said that she write that material herself. Her new album is all covers of songs already recorded by other singers. I'm afraid sales are looking to be weak. The label's fretting."

"And Gen is just no songwriter, is that it?"

"Not at all. Not even a musician."

So the fetching young country star was just a pretty face and body and electronically enhanced voice. It was like some of these pretty-boy up-and-coming authors…these *Beats*.

I looked around us. "All this inherited money should buy her some time to look for options. Maybe recruit some honest songwriters to pen some original tunes for her."

Gen's mother shook her head. "Maybe, if she isn't arrested for something she didn't do."

Donna had drained her drink. I took the glass from her hand and mixed her one like mine.

"Best we get back out there," I said, gesturing with my own drink. I looked at the big servant's table in the center of the kitchen. "Lead on, honey. Sprawling as this spread is, I'll confess I'm afraid of gettin' lost between place settings."

Donna smiled and led me through a formal dining room dominated by a table even bigger than the one in the kitchen. Two suits of armor stood sentry at one end of that table behind a hard-carved chair that looked like a redneck's notion of a throne.

Of a sudden, I could hear singing. Logan had found a guitar somewhere and Genny was crooning the tune Bud and Logan had been polishing in the bar before our kidnapping. They had tentatively titled the ditty *She Didn't Have Far to Go to Be Gone*.

"I think it could work real well for you," Logan said. "And it's no big deal, is it, Bud?" Logan was sliding the pick between the strings up above the fingerboard as we moved into a sitting room. Logan leaned the guitar against the sofa arm where he sat.

The damn young fool: Nashville was positively lousy with war stories of shortsighted and scuffling songwriters trading just-written hit tunes for a mere drink or a couple of sawbucks to make rent.

Yet presumably wiser Bud was just smiling and nodding his head at the vixen. Damn fools, both of 'em.

Logan picked up the guitar again. He started strumming as Genevieve began singing Logan and Bud's song, changing all the "she's" to "he's."

He's living in a pretty house now on the pretty side of town
See his kids playing out there on their pretty lawn
Ain't no great distance between here and over there
He didn't have far to go to be gone

Young Gen's voice was thin, even thinner than it already sounded to me captured on vinyl with all the benefits of echo and reverb.

Memories of our time together
They go on and on and on
Of times when nights were better
But it took him only one night to be gone

Jesus *Elvis* Christ:

Donna jumped right on Bud and Logan's hormone-stoked largesse. Smiling, she said, "Of course the record company will require you to sign a waiver to that effect. I mean that you're signing the song writing credits over to Gen."

There was real excitement in Donna's voice.

I passed their drinks to Bud and Logan. "That won't be necessary," I said to Donna. "My boys have forgotten I'm serving in the capacity of their manager presently. Hell, manager, chauffeur and sometimes spiritual advisor. Actually, I expect I'm their Dutch Uncle too, in a tight. Like goddamn *now*."

I took a deep drink from my glass. Sucker burned and almost briefly shut down my windpipe. I said, "With her recent jaw-dropping windfall from old Jake, I expect Gen can *well* afford to pay the thousand that song will cost you, Donna. And we will not cede *all* writing credits. Though, for another five hundred dollars, we'll cheerfully extend Gen a *co*-writing credit. Future royalties will be divided three ways, less my up-front ten-percent agent's fee for my lads."

Donna sat down and crossed her long, lissome legs. She noticed me noticing and smiled. "That's agreeable, Hector. But this deal shouldn't be construed as a template for any future deals between us regarding other potential songs. Agreed?"

That little fiduciary two-step left me with no lingering doubts about who was managing Gen Gantry's career to this point.

"Case by case, and tune by tune it is, my darlin'," I said. Raising my glass, I smiled. "I'll confess here and now that I do *so* enjoy the *dance*."

I tapped my tumbler against Donna's and looked around the living room. I spied more taxidermed dead things, including a full-grown horse and yes, even a damn dog. That last made my blood boil.

There was also a painting of Robert E. Lee hung above the chair where Bud sat.

Remington sculptures and still more paintings of Indian war parties and Civil War battlefields gathered dust here and there.

At the center of the room there dangled a chandelier fashioned of elk horns. I sipped, said, "This place is *all* like this?"

"This is actually one of the more subdued settings," Donna said, savoring my sour reaction. "We'll start with the bedrooms and work our way through each room redecorating. We plan to make this look like a place where right-minded people live rather than some cowboy museum."

Gen was greedily eyeing Logan's drink. She said, "The billiard room actually has leather walls."

"And so a pungent room, I'll bet." I stood and offered Gen a hand. "Why don't you show me that crazy pool room now? I enjoy shooting a game of stick, as Logan can well attest. And we need to talk a bit, anyway. Just the *two* of us," I added that last as Logan started to rise.

Gen looked to her mother: Donna chewed her lip, then nodded her assent.

"Hector is a *worldly* man," she said to her daughter. "One of the last of the men's men left in this sorry, pale world, or so some who should know say. That's all a windy way of saying you can trust in Hector."

14

The billiard table was as over-the-top as everything else in the house: ponderous and supported by claw feet carved from mahogany. Sucker sported tousled leather ball catchers and pristine crimson cloth.

One end of the room was dominated by a fireplace that looked like something out of my presently ex-buddy Orson Welles' *Citizen Kane*—a near *walk-in* affair.

At the other end of the room was a four-by-eight-foot, full size oil portrait of Jake. The dead songwriter looked thinner and tanner than I remembered from album covers. The painting depicted him commanding the stage of the Ryman Auditorium.

As Gen had said, the walls of the billiard room were covered with some kind of leather wallpaper.

The room smelled like saddles and the ghosts of too many cigars.

Rebel flags dangled from the ceiling like bunting around the room. There were a few Nazi flags, too. With all those Rebel and Kraut banners, the place looked a little like it was snatched from a Klansman's wet dream.

Nodding at the German emblems, I said, "You know me and a lot of good others took real risks never to see that sorry image again, honey. You should have those swastikas pulled down, *pronto*."

Gen just smiled and nodded.

Sighing, I racked the balls and selected a cue stick from a stand. "You play, sweetie?"

"Too short to reach much," Gen said. "You go ahead, though. Maybe I'll pick up a trick or two."

She was eyeing my drink. I held it out and let her take a sip. "God, those are yummy," she said, savoring that mostly Mexican firewater.

Already second-guessing myself, I handed her my drink and bent low over the table, stroking for the break.

The balls scattered with a pleasing crash. A couple of solids dropped and I started playing a game of eight ball against myself. "When did you last see your ex-husband, honey?"

"Like I told the police, I really, really don't know. Not for anything like sure. When you're in the country music business, and you're living here in Nashville, you're constantly bumping into other singers. It's really a pretty small town in the end. Only two real streets in the whole town."

The vixen parked a shapely hip on the rail of the pool table, distracting me and fouling my shot on the one ball. Or maybe it was my aging eyes at fault—there was a lot of red "green" to cover and I was shooting sans spectacles. That was frankly goddamn needless vanity in this case. I had no designs on the kid, not like *that*. Yet, as a man, I had some measure of pride left: one still hoped to catch the eyes of the girls of summer, now and again.

I said, "When approximately did you last see your former husband?"

"You sound like that cop, Corvin or Corben … whatever."

Genevieve sipped more tequila. Her cheeks were already glowing from the booze. There were spreading red blotches on her sleek ivory neck, disappearing down into her neckline.

I was starting to feel unsavory for having handed the filly that poured-for-a-long-lived-veteran drink.

"The cop's name is Rick Corin," I said. "And, yeah, we've met. Now tell me, honey, and I realize it's a best guess on your part, when the last time you think you saw Jake?"

Gen wrinkled her brow. "At the Opry. It was the weekend before he died. I *think*. Backstage."

"And all was cordial?"

"Jake was *always* friendly to me," she said, firm-voiced. No particular surprise, that: She'd so far offered nothing I'd seen to dislike. Jailbait didn't come much more fetching than this too-young delicious thing.

I glanced at the fireplace again. A couple of concrete lawn jockeys squatted on the big mantel, clutching matching brass rings, held out in ebony right hands. Their faces were also painted jet-black and the size of their lips had been exaggerated with copious coats of red paint.

Fact was, nearly all I'd seen so far of Jake's place's décor flaunted a decidedly racist vibe, in addition to all the cowboy stuff and the dead stuffed animals.

I stepped a little more carefully for the next of my parlay with the young singer: "Your mother told me about your...well, about your *nervous condition*, Gen." I said softly, "She said you've been on the same medication the cops blame for causing Jake's heart attack. Did you two ever swap or share medication, hon', or maybe just—?"

Pure acid: "Now you *really* sound like that cop. Honestly, Mr. Lassiter, I don't even know what exactly I'm taking. I can't pronounce that fifty-cent name on the label, it's so long."

"Then who sees to your medication, sweetie?"

"Mom." This look of total incomprehension: "Who else?"

I sighed and slung the cue stick across the table, sending billiard balls rolling helter-skelter.

A lip bite, then I took a different angle: "Tell me about your father, honey."

"I was only five when he passed."

"So you don't remember much about your old man, then?"

Confession time here: *My* only daughter died at age three.

Little Dolores never had time to forget those three years the two of us shared ... for all the comfort *that* afforded me.

"Don't remember much at all," she said. "Sad, yeah?"

She shrugged in a way that made it clear it wasn't anything in hollering distance of what I regarded as *sad*.

But then I'd lost my parents when I was still in single digits.

"Or maybe that's a blessing," I said. "I mean, it's hard to miss what you don't remember, yeah?"

"Maybe," Gen said.

I wondered then if Donna had subjected her daughter to a succession of "uncles" following Gen's father's death.

But I didn't wonder enough to put that question to Genevieve.

Instead I parked my ass on the pool table rail next to Gen's. The black pedal pushers that indeed seemed painted onto the Nashville thrush's fetching thighs gleamed in the light of the Tiffany chandelier dangling above the pool table.

"How'd your Daddy die, sweetie?"

"Heart attack."

That got my attention. I let my voice go softer: "Older gent, was he?"

"No, I don't think so," Gen said. "Pretty young for that. It was a real surprise, I think."

"Heart problems run on either side of your family?"

I sure hoped not if Gen was taking the same depression medication the medical examiner had ruled tripped the trigger on Old Jake's bum ticker.

Gen shrugged. "None that I know of." She searched my face: "The private investigator Mom hired to research you brought over some of your books. I was looking at the photos of you on the older books. You look a bit like some pictures of my Dad, back in the day."

Huh. How about that?

"What about your mother, Gen? What'd she have going in her life before hooking up with your father?"

"A career. Or the starts of one."

I smiled. "That be in music?" It might explain Donna Perkins' Mama Rose Lee airs.

Gen looked at my left hand and its bare fingers. "Oh, no," Gen said. "Mom can't carry a tune to save her life."

Some critics said the same of the daughter. Hell, more than a few wags had been brutal in their critiques of this pretty young thing's singing voice, arguing it was a studio creation. I was with what Billy Blake would have called the devil's party in that sense.

I said, "What was your mother's intended line of work, then?"

"She was a nurse," Gen said. "She wanted to be a doctor, but you know women *never* get to do that."

"Right."

I watched Gen tear again at her nails with her teeth; watched her green eyes watching me watching her.

I thought about what the cop, Corin, had said about the vixen being soulless, even hollow.

That was a very bad reading of Gen's character, in my opinion.

Truth was, she was simply young and shallow. And not particularly educated.

Child was a bit vapid and callow like a dozen or more pretty kid actors or teen idols I'd crossed paths with over the years as a result of screenwriting. Good looks precluded cultivation, even education.

There was "no there *there*," as my old acquaintance Gertrude Stein would again have put it.

And Gen was doped up, to boot, so to speak.

The minx was drifting through a drug-fortified life of fog and fumbling with fouled-up motor-coordination. Mix in a little or a lot of booze...?

I took my glass away from her then; drank from the side *not* stained with her lipstick and the taste of her too-young, Cupid's-bow mouth.

I stood and wrapped my hands around Gen's trim waist, lifting her off the table and setting her down before me. She smiled, surprised; flirty and a little drunk. "Let's get back out there," I said, now very much regretting letting her almost polish off my drink.

I could only hope dubious Donna wouldn't notice the booze on her daughter's breath and start thinking even worse of me.

Those sloe green eyes of Gen's searched my pale blue. "You're going to help me, Mr. Lassiter. I just *know* you're going to get me out from under this crazy mess." She hugged me, hard. I chastely patted her back.

"Call me Hector."

Maybe I really would. Help her, I mean.

"I mean to lend a hand," I said, untangling myself from her embrace.

Hell, I'd already just about convinced myself that the cop, Corin, had picked the wrong blond-haired, green-eyed woman to pursue in mounting his murder case.

15

"We reached a decision in your absence," Donna said. She foisted over a fresh tequila and orange juice. I sipped. It was about twice as strong as I would have made for myself. Figured I'd just have to cope.

I said, "Have *we?* And what decision have we made, Donna?"

"As you can see, this place is very, very large. We'll put you and your young friends up for a few days. There's a guest cabin out back where Bud and Logan can bunk. If it doesn't bother you, we'll get Mr. Gantry's room prepared for you. You'll understand when you see the décor. Until we can redecorate, no woman would want to sleep in that place."

I shrugged. "As I hear it, Jake died elsewhere than the bedroom, so at least there's that. But really, we have our lodging seen to and—"

Donna was having none of that. "I *insist*, Hector. *Please.* After this attack on you today, it makes sense that you stay here. If it was related in some way to my daughter, the attack, I mean, we'll feel better having you three men right here with us. To protect us. If it *wasn't*, well, who would think to look for you here?"

She smiled, awaiting my verdict. Some flirtation there that didn't hurt my ego.

"It is a thought, viewed in that light," I said. I looked to Bud and Logan, not that I had much doubt as to which side of the proposal they'd favor. "You lads simpatico?"

Vigorous nods from both boys.

"There's something else," Donna said. "Tomorrow is Jake's funeral."

I took Donna by the arm. "And so you're looking for escorts to that sad affair?"

Donna bit her lip. "Not so sure that *escort* is exactly the word for it. But essentially, yes."

"Can do," I said. "I do need to pick up a couple of things, however. Bud does too, I expect."

Logan gave me a look. "You stay here, son," I told him. "Protect the fort. Gen here has a hell of a pool table down one of these great halls. But she has no training. Maybe you can work on improving her game while Bud and I step out."

The poet struggled up to his feet. "We best get cracking," I said to Bud. I smiled at Donna. "We should be back before ten."

Donna, with her mocking half-smile, said, "Maybe just in time for a nightcap."

"Maybe. Just."

Bud and I pulled on our coats and stepped out into the dusk. It was a bit after five, but the December sky was already black. The snow spiraled in the lights arrayed around the outside of the house and in the distant streetlights.

Bud said, "Who's driving?"

"How's about you do that again?" I tossed him the Bel Air's keys. I slid in, fastened my lap strap and searched radio stations while Bud cleared the windows of ice. We slowly pulled up toward the closed wrought-iron gate until some electric eye hidden somewhere was tripped and the fancy gates parted with a rusty groan.

We rolled out onto the street, straight into three matching black sedans that slid sideways across the slick pavement, blocking our path.

Bud gestured at the glove compartment. "Your Colt?"

Urgency there in my poet's voice.

I brushed his hand away from the glove compartment. "Huh-uh, Bud. These guys scream government muscle. If you're packing anything yourself, best get it under the seat, pronto."

16

Bud jammed an automatic under the seat and sat up straighter, just as a man, perhaps in his mid forties, climbed out of the lead black car blocking our path. He sported a gray crew cut and wore a dark suit under a long black overcoat. He slipped a black fedora on as he slid from the sedan.

The poet wetted his lips, said, "A Fed, you're thinking?" Clearly my lamentably left-leaning young friend was thinking that.

"Not FBI, Bud, if that's what you mean. Not with the cutting-edge lapels that overcoat's sporting. And not with its length. Not with the wider brim on that hat, either. Threads are way too stylish for J. Edgar's tastes."

"But he *is* government," Bud said. "You think that much, right?"

"He surely has that sorry air," I said. Or the stranger aimed for that look, at any rate.

Bud adjusted his glasses, watching the stranger making his way toward us across the slick pavement. "Anything you want to tell me, Hector?"

"Honest Injun, kid," I said, "Basil Sloan was my only known potential agent of strife, presently. I mean, apart from a few of last year's lingering friends from Yale who still turn up now and again, looking for Pancho's noggin. Goddamn Skull and Bones Society..."

The man in dapper black rapped his knuckles against the window on my side. He called through the frosty glass, "Mr. Lassiter?"

The stranger held up some kind of government I.D. I couldn't quite make out through the fogged glass and the snow flurries whipping between us. I rolled my window down a crack.

"I didn't quite see your affiliation on that card," I said.

The man nodded. "That's by design, Mr. Lassiter. My organization isn't, well, it's not one you, or most any civilian, is apt to have heard of, let alone to have run across. Most in the federal government don't even know of us, presently. Could I climb in back there? Candidly, I'm freezing my nuts off out here."

I stepped out and lifted the seat so the man could slide into the Bel Air's backseat. I twisted around and shook the man's hand. "Didn't quite make out a name on that badge, either."

"Sorry again," the man smiled. "*That* much wasn't by intent. By that I mean the illegibility of the name is a result of poor graphic design. Name's Charles Easton. Call me Chuck."

"Hokey-doke, *Chuck*. You maybe CIA of sorts?"

Chuck smiled. "No. Really, it wouldn't ring any bells if I told you. Not one of the better-known acronyms as federal agencies go. We're pretty new." Another smile. "Very fresh alphabet soup as the name runs."

I shrugged. "Well, I'm pretty sure I haven't done anything this year to merit government attention." I hesitated and frowned a little. "Christ, this isn't some Skull and Bones fallout from fifty-seven, is it? Not something to do with that damned silly-ass religious spear from even further back when?"

"Your escapade with Villa's skull last year freshly raised your profile in certain official sectors, to be sure," Chuck said. "As to whatever spear you're talking about, I'm not sure I'm up to date on that one. But no, this is something quite apart from anything you're likely thinking of. Although your handling of the various competing parties last year, the way you finessed them, did not go unnoticed, and, by some, unappreciated. Here's how it is: I'd like to buy you gentlemen dinner. Treat you to the very best steak in town."

Bud looked a bit uneasy. "Am I in some trouble?"

"Not at all," Chuck said. "You're simply known to us through your affiliation with Mr. Lassiter last year, Mr. Fiske."

Didn't see much choice for the moment but for Bud and I to go along with the invitation.

I said, "So where are we eating, Chuck? And can we lose your entourage, or at least *most* of it? As it stands now, it looks like President Eisenhower's in town. I mean, this is only Nashville, Tennessee, and you sorts do stick out in a loud kind of way traveling in caravans as you are now."

"Sound reasoning," Chuck said. He rolled down the back window, waved a minion over. He gave some instructions. Two of the other cars backed out and drove off. The third moved enough to make room for us to get by, then followed at a discreet distance. Chuck reached over the seat and squeezed Bud's shoulder. "You know Jimmy Kelly's on Louis Avenue?"

"Been by it a time or two," Bud said.

"Go there now, then," he said. He winked at me. "Best steakhouse in town, Mr. Lassiter."

"Sounds dandy," I said. "But a steakhouse seems like a strange setting for the kind of talk I feel in the air. Some frank talk about government-type business is in the offing, am I not right?"

"Let me worry about our privacy and security, Mr. Lassiter," Chuck said. "But there is something else to address first. That is regarding you, Mr. Fiske. I read and enjoyed your recent profile of Mr. Lassiter in *True Magazine*. From that I deduce you're aware, or at least suspect, some of the, *er*, well, let's term them 'colorful dealings' with U.S. and foreign intelligence services that your friend Mr. Lassiter here has had down through the years. I mean, affairs going well beyond that crazy caper you were a party to with Mr. Lassiter last year."

Bud glanced over at me and then said, "I've heard some things." I figured Bud was afraid of hurting me in some way if he got drawn into telling tales out of school to a mystery Fed.

"Go ahead, Bud," I said. "Hell, this fella probably knows it all, anyway."

Bud nodded. He said, "I performed a few more interviews for that article than found their way into print in *True*. I've heard many things about Hector tied to the Spanish Civil War. Learned about some things during World War II and his running a guerilla unit that got Hec in some real trouble with the brass and Patton because he was supposed to be only a war correspondent. I heard about some crazy stuff in the early 1950s when the Cold War was just heating up."

"Right," Chuck said. "What I'm getting at, Mr. Fiske, is this: I can sit down with myriad dossiers running back to the 1930s and I can talk to some older agents of various government agencies. Doing all that, I can arrive at what I sense to be a pretty trustworthy assessment of Mr. Lassiter's loyalties and the sorts of causes he'll reliably ally himself to. I'll confess I can't quite get a fully firm handle on his politics, yet I know without doubt that Mr. Lassiter is archly patriotic. You, on the other hand, Mr. Fiske? You're something of an enigma to me." A tic at the corner o the Fed's mouth. "You're frankly at least a mild *worry* to me."

I could see the tension building in Bud, could see it in the muscles of his jaw and tendons in his skinny neck that were starting to stand out. Could see it in this *throb* at his temple. Bud was about to get his back up in a dangerous way. He was about to run his sometimes reckless mouth again.

"Look, Easton," I said, "I'll confess to some curiosity regarding this little talk we're toeing up to. But if you know anything about events last year, then you should clearly know Bud and I were in it together, fly or fall, all along the crazy way. Bud saved my ass time and again, and he's battle-tested and found worthy by me. He's sound under the gun and has come through for me under some pretty horrific circumstances. What I'm saying is, I vouch for Bud, without reservation or exclusion. If you want me to hear something, Bud hears it, too. If you aren't on board with that, then we're through, right now."

"Very well, Mr. Lassiter. Apologies if I offended you, Mr. Fiske."

"Might help Bud, and me, too," I said, "if I had some inkling as to what we're going to chat about. What the hell's driving this mystery confab?"

Chuck gave me a sober sizing up. It was a practiced look, I was pretty sure.

He at last said, "Rest assured it's a national security issue, Mr. Lassiter. This is a crisis whose scope and implications will exceed your wildest imaginings, my friend. Yes, even the imaginings of a wildly creative mind such as *yours*. What I'm going to share with you two could, and this is no exaggeration, it could *easily* cause mass and deadly panic if it was to become public domain."

Now Chuck had my full attention. Christ, what the hell could it be? And how could I be of any use in something of such crazy magnitude?

Bud pulled curbside in front of an older, big red brick house converted into a restaurant. The place looked empty to me: there were just a couple of cars at the back of the parking lot where the staff might be expected to park. Bud said, "What's this crisis, Chuck?"

He hedged. "You *sure* you're up for this, Mr. Fiske?"

I reached across the seat and smacked Bud's knee. "Long pants time again, Bud. In or out?"

Bud didn't hesitate. "I'm in, Lass."

"Then so be it," Chuck said.

He put it out there, cold and scary: "Gentleman, this is all about a missing hydrogen bomb."

17

Shaken, silent, we made our way up the snow-covered path to the near-empty restaurant. "Joint looks closed," I said.

Chuck just smiled, then opened and held the restaurant's door for us. "We have the place to ourselves this evening," he said. "My men will mostly monitor our needs in terms of drink refills and so forth. I'll just ask you gentlemen to avoid substantive discussion in front of the wait staff and servers as they are required to see to our needs directly."

One of those waiters stood at attention by a table set for four; he waved us over, then pulled out our chairs.

"Sense I'm going to need a real drink for this one," I said, scooting in my chair. I ordered a vodka martini on the rocks with three olives. Bud ordered a single malt and Chuck asked for a Ballantine ale.

When our official waiter was out of earshot, I said. "A missing H-bomb? That's some showstopper, to be sure."

"Actually, what's missing is a radioactive component that can conceivably be used as a weapon in its own right," Chuck said.

The presumed G-man knocked loose a Lucky Strike from a pack and patted his pockets for a match. Bud broke out his Zippo and held it out for Chuck. Blowing smoke, he said, "If the component falls into the wrong hands, it's no exaggeration to say it could threaten the lives of several thousands. It could be responsible for the destruction of an entire city, or even a portion of a small state."

"Okay, I'm squarely on the hook," I said. "Now, a fella like me would tend to think such a bomb, or one of its *key components*, would be a very closely held commodity. How'd Uncle Sam lose one of these damned things?"

"*Lose* is almost an appropriate word choice on your part in this case," Chuck said. "Because that's nearly what happened." Chuck glanced over his shoulder. "Drinks will be here soon. To minimize further interruptions, would be good if we could order our food when those libations come."

Bud and I picked up our menus. Frowning, I pulled out my spectacles and put them on, drawing a curious look from Easton. "That's right," I said to him. "It has come to *this*. Getting old is a pain in the ass."

Chuck said, "There is a darker alternative, Hec."

Our drinks came and we ordered our food. Alone again, I turned to Chuck and said, "So, was this some military base incursion? A waylaid convoy?" I bit into an olive. "Internal espionage, maybe?"

Chuck scratched at the label of his ale bottle with a manicured fingernail. "The component's loss was the unintended consequence of an accident. Or, at least the discovery it was missing was a result of that accident. Perhaps you gentlemen heard of this: Earlier this year, one of our own bombs was dropped near a heavily populated area of North America."

Bud evidently hadn't heard that bit of news: his brown eyes were wide.

I plucked another olive from its skewer and popped it in my mouth. "We talking that bomb that got dropped on Mars Bluff, or is it the H-bomb you all lost near Savannah?"

"The former was an atomic weapon whose constituents were recovered without incident," Chuck said. "I mean, other than the damage caused by several thousands of pounds of metal falling from considerable height. No, I'm referring here to the latter incident. To the H-bomb, as you call it."

Bud was still reeling. "You crazy bastards lost *two* bombs? You actually accidentally dropped two atomic bombs here at home?" Bud blurted it out.

Chuck lashed out at him: "Keep it down, goddamn it, Fiske, or I'll order you to leave!"

"Whoa there; steady on now, boys," I said. "Bud is a poet and so not too concerned with the front pages—more focused on the eternal. You cut Bud some slack, Chuck."

For Bud's sake, I said, "I'm pretty sketchy on that H-bomb accident. Not that a lot of hard detail was forthcoming at the time, as I remember. So this really was a hydrogen bomb you boys went and lost?"

"What's called a Mark 15 Mod O," Chuck said softly. "Nearly eight thousand pounds and a hundred times more powerful than the bomb we dropped on Hiroshima."

Bud was aghast. He said, "Where in God's name did his happen?"

"Wassaw Sound, off Tybee Beach," Chuck said. "It was February 5 of this year, at about 3:30 a.m. The bomb was in a B47 that accidently collided with an F86 fighter in midair. The jet's pilot bailed out and the F86 crashed at sea. The B47 was still airworthy, but it was badly damaged and couldn't reduce airspeed sufficiently to ensure a safe landing."

"So to avoid the bomb going off in a possible crash landing, the crew dumped it, yes?" I sipped my vodka. "Seems to me that was the story at the time."

"And essentially an honest one," Easton said. "The bomb was dumped, as you put it, in order to avoid accidental detonation of the TNT portion of the weapon. The bomb, put in the simplest terms, consists of two key explosive components. There are four-hundred pounds of what we'll call conventional explosives—the TNT. There is also a canister that can be taken out in order to prevent nuclear detonation. The canister, or nuclear component, for wont of a better term, contains the uranium. The plutonic ingredient, in other words."

Bud stared into his whisky. He looked like he'd just learned the world is flat. "And that's the part that's now missing?"

Chuck was sour-faced. "This is where it all gets into the realm of confusion and conjecture."

"Do please try and un-confuse it for us, Chuck," I said.

He nodded and signaled for three more drinks. Once the bartender hustled off again and our steaks were delivered, Chuck said, "When a decision was made to risk a crash landing of the bomber, a crew member was sent back to extract the plutonium component. The idea at the time was for that crewman to parachute out with the uranium capsule on his person in the event the crash landing resulted in complete destruction of the plane and the bomb. Even if the bomb didn't detonate with the uranium inside, we could hardly afford to risk having a radioactive debris field on our hands, could we?"

"Of course not," I said. "Then what happened?"

"The canister was already missing," Chuck said. "The theft had to have happened prior to the bomb being loaded."

"Obviously," Bud said with an edge.

But Chuck pressed on: "There was little time to try and investigate how that happened in the moment, of course. The bomb, or what remained, was jettisoned somewhere in the vicinity of Tybee Island, not so far from the mouth of the Savannah River, as reported in the media. Fortunately, the conventional explosives didn't detonate on impact. Even that explosion could have been potentially devastating. The crew of the B47 made it out alive, by the way. Hell, the pilot, Major Richardson, was given the Distinguished Flying Cross for getting her down with her crew alive. That was some feat, believe me."

I said, "But then came the headlines and the hand-wringing. Those I well remember."

"That's right," Chuck said. "We spent two months looking for the Mark 15 and never found her. She may be sunk deep in marsh mud or quicksand. Hell, a search is *still* quietly going on. We've assured everyone, quite honestly, there is no danger of a nuclear detonation there."

"Though you really had intended to fly an armed hydrogen bomb out of Florida," I said.

"And of course many still don't believe us," Chuck continued, ignoring my interruption. "Hard to blame them, in a sense. Imagine, thinking a hydrogen bomb could be sitting off the shores of Georgia with one-hundred times the killing force of the bombs we dropped on the Japs. If it *did* go off, it's not just the horror of the actual nuclear event, but the ensuing tsunami that would be generated in all directions by the underwater explosion. Hell, even if we *do* find the Mark 15, the risk of a TNT detonation is still unthinkable."

"Quite a tale," I said, working at my steak with knife and fork. Sucker was very tasty. "Reminds me of something from my limey buddy Ian Fleming's James Bond thrillers. But what the hell has this got to do with Bud and I? What's with all this scary secret sharing?"

Chuck paused, going for effect, I reckon.

"We're ninety-percent certain the missing uranium component is right here in Tennessee. Right here in Nashville, we believe."

Another dramatic pause. "We think you, Mr. Lassiter, are in a unique position to help us recover it."

18

With our shared sugar problems, Bud and I passed on dessert. But old Chuck was working on a slice of pecan pie *à la mode*, talking while he ate. Not a pretty sight. The poet and I steeled ourselves against it with more vodka and single malt.

Around his pie, the man from the mystery agency said, "You're obviously acquainted with the former wife of hillbilly singer-songwriter Jake Gantry."

"You *did* waylay us leaving his crib, after all," I pointed out. "But we're only just acquainted."

"Yet you've already been invited into the home for lodging," Chuck said.

Well, well. Letting my voice drift to gravel, I said, "Only one way on earth you could know that already, mister."

"As you clearly deduce, Gantry's house is bugged, of course," Chuck said matter-of-factly. "Well, the living room is bugged, that is. The dining room, of course. His bedroom, ditto. That was all we had time for in the guise of installing a second water heater last month. Oh, and his phones are tapped. Of course, that last goes without saying."

"Of course," Bud said, all venom. "Mr. Hoover being Mr. Hoover."

I leaned back in my chair. "And why would Uncle Sam be snooping up on crazy old, bad-tickered Jake Gantry?"

"Nashville is a racial powder keg," Chuck said. "I'm not sure how familiar you are with the current racial tensions here, but believe me when I say they are running quite high. As a New Mexico resident, this might be quite alien to you, but—"

"As a southern New Mexico resident," I cut in, "as a Rio Grand-banks dweller, I'm well-acquainted with racial tensions peculiar to a border."

"Of course," Chuck said. "But those are just *Mexicans*. The colored population here is *organized* and *active*. What some of the white locals might even call *uppity*. That activism, it will not surprise you, has led to the formation of opposition groups among some whites."

I waved a hand, trailing cigarette smoke and took another slug of my martini. "What, you mean the Klan? Those fools are nothing new, nor particularly effective in terms of broad-base effects. And the other side? The Civil Rights types? That's a tidal wave, old pal, and one that likely won't be resisted in the long run, not by J. Edgar or anyone else. Hell, they've got the closest thing to any moral high ground."

"I'm *really* not making any judgments here," Chuck said. "I'm just describing the milieu. And I'm not talking about the KKK. The FBI is already focused on that organization."

Bud said, "What then? What did Gantry do to merit illegal bugging of his home and phone if he wasn't KKK?"

That got Chuck's goat. "We're the federal government, Mr. Fiske, so regards your allegations of illegality—"

I cut Chuck off. "Legality aside, Bud's central question stands, Mr. Easton: What precisely was Gantry into?"

Hell, I'd voted against FDR *four* times, so God knew I had no patience to hear left-leaning Bud and some fascist, crypto-spook like Easton tear at one another over the issue of privacy rights.

At base, I had no meaningful partisan politics.

Chuck focused on me as he spoke: "Mr. Gantry was a member and key contributor to an underground organization of particularly well-organized, and shrewdly directed white separatists. Some of those came out of the California prison system. They came from a gang called the Bluebirds and centered around San Quentin. They're a very powerful organization populated by some very powerful men on the outside. These are men with very deep pockets and a very dark agenda."

I tsk'd.

"Please, a *dark* agenda?" I said. "What is that, some attempt at poor-taste humor or a pun?"

"No, Mr. Lassiter."

Chuck pushed his empty pie plate away and daubed at his mouth with a linen napkin that he then slung across the pie plate. He fished a wooden toothpick from his pocket and began gnawing at that. "This organization Gantry was tied to and its objective is to entirely annihilate or eradicate the colored race in North America. There is no question of that being anything less than the endgame. And they will not stop short of that goal, according to the tenets of their own organization. They propose to achieve that end through murder, terror and a focused effort on forced Negro immigration to Europe, Mexico, Canada... back to Africa. Anywhere but *here*."

"That's goddamn crazy," I said. "That's a sick pipedream."

"Of course it is. Yet these are smart and powerful men, Mr. Lassiter. Prominent southern university professors, captains of industry, politicians, former military men, even a West Virginia representative of some note, whose avian surname echoes that of the organization in question. Hell Robert Byrd was an Exalted Cyclops and recruiter in the Klan. Even a few radicalized novelists and historians are part of the Bluebirds. And one of them is a man you know, Mr. Lassiter. Your arrival here is really propitious for *our side*—for the *righteous* side—you see."

Our side: some real presumption in there.

Still, I was listening.

He continued, "Call it double lucky. You're already in the Gantry house. But you also know a group leader. A man you knew as Frank Robbins."

So there it was.

"A bastard who is now also known as Jasper Coleman," I said. "I saw something in the newspaper about him a few hours ago. He's leading some kind of white supremacist gang here, according to the Nashville newsboys. I guess, based on what you're sayin', this gang is worse than the journalists know."

"Far worse than even the local police know," Chuck said. "Imagine what this racist cabal might achieve through blackmail or terror if they could threaten the destruction of a city or region with that has a significant racial population. Somewhere in Alabama, Louisiana or Georgia, say. New York City, even…Or right here in Tennessee. Maybe in Memphis."

"You saying this group has got that canister that you boys lost?"

"As I said, their membership includes many military men, some of them high ranking, as well as lesser officers, some of whom are still in service," Chuck said. "These are men in a position to engineer the theft of the radioactive component prior to that B47's ill-fated flight this past February. These are men with the knowledge to put that device to use in myriad destructive ways. Just attaching the device to a few sticks of dynamite and setting it off in a populated area would create a panic and a long-term health hazard. And a real problem for local authorities to try and cope with. The demolition site would be small, but still a toxic spot for decades."

I stretched out my legs under the table, crossing them at the ankles. I laced my fingers behind my head. "Maybe so," I said. "But Jake Gantry was a hillbilly singer of middling intelligence, near as I can tell. I'll confess that having walked around his joint now, I'll whole-heartedly buy into the proposition the old boy was a racist cracker, and of the first water. No doubt about any of that. But on his best day, he was just a redneck rhymster in a Nudie suit and ten-dollar toupee. He was hardly some kind of evil genius or super-criminal."

Easton shook his head. "He didn't have to be any of those. There were plenty of others in Gantry's organization capable of doing the brainwork. Robbins/Coleman, for instance. But Gantry was also a 10th-level Mason. His possible connections stemming from that fraternal secret society are unknowable, even to us. He had lavish amounts of money, a private estate and a terrible hatred for the Negro race. Hell, he left the bulk of his fortune to a Knoxville-based arm of this racist brotherhood."

Bud was still incredulous. "Jake Gantry left his big tacky house to his much-younger ex-wife, Gen," he said. "He left his publishing and recording rights to Gen. It's why the cops are looking at her for a murder rap. I mean because of that big damn inheritance she's facing."

"Yes, Mr. Fiske, all true, but the crooner did that just for the songs he penned and recorded under his own name," Chuck said. "Mr. Gantry actually wrote an amazing array of hit songs for other performers under a variety of pennames. All of those royalties have been willed to his racist fraternal organization. Our accountants have been all over this, Mr. Fiske. Trust me when I say what was left to Genevieve Gantry, the house and the music rights under the name 'Gantry'—substantial though they might be in and of themselves—comprise merely a fraction of the late Mr. Gantry's net worth."

Chuck smiled and moved his toothpick from one side of his mouth to the other with his tongue. "And hell, he didn't intend to die when he did. Who's to say if Jake Gantry had lived a bit longer he might not have written his ex-child-bride out of his will entirely?"

I shook my head. "No way, Chuck. I think old Jake nursed tumescent dreams of some kind of reconciliation with his jailbait ex. But back to this Brotherhood as you call it. The missing trigger—if they even have it—what is their objective? What's the goal here?"

Chuck toyed with his toothpick. "As I already said, terror. Extortion of some sort, I expect. We think they mean to ransom a city or even a region. Hell, they may even have intended to detonate some kind of homemade bomb using this stolen component and then claim they had many others just like it to deploy. When it comes to this flavor of terrorism, they only have to succeed once. Those of us on the other side have to win every fucking time, which isn't doable, by the by."

Munching on a last olive, I said, "What would that gambit you theorize about have entailed? Would they really try to order the Negro population out of here? 'Back to Africa,' to coin a phrase, at the risk of wiping out a city if they stayed?"

I almost laughed at that. "That's a bit much to swallow, Chuck. And if it was that easy to build a bomb? Hell, more than these would be troubling you folks, and for all kinds of wrong-headed causes, I figure."

Mr. Chuck Easton shook his head. "It's not so much to swallow when you know the Brotherhood is salted with former members of the Soviet and Nazi atom bomb projects."

"Jesus Christ," I said, truly reeling now. "This just gets better and better."

I ran my fingers back through my hair. "Is it remotely possible they could have taken this trigger and made such a bomb?"

"More than remotely possible," Chuck said. "Look what Hitler's refugees have done for our own missile and space programs. Look at what they've done for the Russians. So, yes, we think it's an entirely plausible scenario."

"So what is Hector's—our—part in all this?" Bud drummed his fingers on the table, looking more than a little crazed by a night of outrageous, even nightmarish revelations.

Easton leaned forward, punctuating points with his dulled toothpick clutched between thumb and forefinger. "We think Gantry's house was the nexus for the transfer of the stolen trigger," he said. "It might not still be there, but if it was, even shielded, it could leave trace elements that can be detected. It would certainly leave something to show us we're on the right track. And, hell, given Gantry's untimely death, it's possible the transfer wasn't effected and the trigger is still somewhere in that crazy mansion."

I said, "But this secret society trusted Jake Gantry to be the facilitator for the swap of a nuclear weapon." I knitted my brows. "I thought you said these Brothers were brainy, Chuck. If that's so, why pick this guitar plucking cracker with a headline-grabbing May-December romance to be their key man?"

"They *are* smart," Chuck said, "make no mistake on that front. But among all the professors and military men populating its ranks, Gantry was a rare property owner with sufficient acreage to thwart our detection devices if we employed them from public property. Gantry's place is also *in situ*—his mansion is close to Georgia and the beating heart of the Old South. It's close to major roadways leading to a host of potential target cities."

"Jake's untimely death, followed by Gen's swift move into the joint and all the resulting police presence tied to the suspicion around her regarding his death could have kept the Brothers at bay in terms of retrieving the capsule, Hec," Bud said. He looked at the agent. "Is that what you're thinking, Easton?"

"It's one of our theories," Chuck said. "And probably the best possible scenario for our side."

"That mansion is just damn large," I said. "Conducting a blind search as house guests may sound easy, but it plays different when you have to sneak around the place with the ladies of the house and all the hired help."

Chuck snapped his fingers. An older balding man appeared toting a black leather case. It was larger than a briefcase, but smaller than a suitcase. Baldy bustled over and pushed aside some dishes and glasses and then opened the case.

The man said to me, "You're a noted author, Mr. Lassiter. We have therefore secreted the Geiger counter inside this reel-to-reel tape recorder. You'll use the cover story that you use the recorder for dictation, of course. To that end, you flip this switch here to actuate the actual recording device. In this original position, the unit works as a radiation detector."

"I didn't catch your name, Ace," I said.

"I didn't—and I won't—share that with you," the bald man said. "My sincere hope is that you'll never see me again when I leave here, Mr. Lassiter."

He paused, said, "I loved *The Land of Dread and Fear*, by the way." That one was my 1957 novel about Tex-Mex border tensions. At least the anonymous little bastard was a fan.

"Right." I pulled the recorder from the case and hefted it with both hands. It weighed about fifteen pounds, I guessed. "Aren't Geiger counters kind of noisy? Sort of clickity-clackity, loud, I mean?"

"Indeed," the stranger said. "That's why you'll use these headphones when you search the premises. This is the *on* switch. Any reading on this meter here, that is to say any reading that moves the indicator into the orange zone, indicates you're in proximity to the radioactive canister or a place where it has been stored. If the needle slides into the red, then the component's protective capsule has been compromised or perhaps even removed. Then you'll need to get it into the protective lead box we'll be giving you, as well. You must do that with all haste. No hesitating. Do you understand?"

I scoffed at that. "First things first. I haven't agreed to do *anything* for you people. Second, I know enough not to pick up some goddamn radioactive gizmo of any stripe. Not if I don't want strange burns, hideous cancers, internal bleeding and projectile shedding." A shrug. "Hell, I may yet want to spawn, a last time or two."

"We'll give you special gloves," the man said with a somber face.

"That's almost funny," I said. "That's more than a little like having grade-school students hide under desks or trying to con wage-slaves in the suburbs into accepting the lie that life will go on plenty dandy after the niggling bump of a Big One being dropped in their environs by the Soviets. Or maybe after the destruction wrought by one of our own bombs. I mean if you boys have another damned so-called *accident*. I wasn't born yesterday, or even the decade before that. You want me to play ball? Don't insult my intelligence."

"Be all that as it may," the gadget man said, "this other, smaller unit here is a radio that can only be received by a radio in Mr. Easton's hands. A secure radio, in other words. You will—you *would* if you agree to help us—use it to contact Mr. Easton upon immediate confirmation of a positive reading on the Geiger counter." A frosty smile. "*If* you choose to cooperate, of course."

I could see Bud's head was swimming. The young poet said, "Given the stakes, why don't all of you just raid that big house of Gantry's and conduct your own search? You're government. You can do anything you want, isn't that so?"

Chuck nodded at his anonymous colleague. "That will do. Thank you. Please give the radiation-proof lead container to my driver to hold for us." Chuck turned back to

Bud and I. "We can't just barge in, Mr. Fiske, because at the moment the Brotherhood's members don't know we know what they are up to. You see, we think they don't know that we know they even *exist*. We're also obviously trying to avoid creating a public panic if word were to leak regarding the quarry of our search. Trust me on this, please. The announcement that even a partial hydrogen bomb was dropped off the coast of Georgia has been nightmare enough." He paused. "And there's the other thing—it could tip foreign interests to the fact that some of our nuclear materials are in play."

That, too, was an unsettling prospect, even to me.

"What a mess," I said. "What a bloody awful, unthinkable goddamn mess."

"Yes," Chuck said. "All of that and more. Truly a waking nightmare. So, Mr. Lassiter, you will please help us fix this mess?"

I looked to Bud. "You know me, and you know I can't say no to this kind of thing. But you, kid? You can surely still walk."

The poet shook his head. "If you're in, I'm in, Hector. Someone has to back you up, Lass. Besides, if I'm ever going to have another decent night's sleep in this city, I really need to know how this comes out—that everything is okay."

I squeezed the poet's arm, then said to Easton the Fed, "Where is Coleman now?"

"No clue about that, I'm sorry to say," Chuck said. He shrugged, looking small. "Frankly, we're really hoping you'll draw him out in some way. You are a kind of hero of his, after all."

19

The snow had stopped for the moment, but enough of it had already fallen to persuade most to stay at home, maybe cozied up by a crackling fire.

Bud and I meandered through the empty, un-shoveled streets of downtown Nashville in a near silence. I was at the wheel, and Bud in a rare instance, rode shotgun, staring out at the city lights glowing on the fallen snow. We rolled by the closed and darkened Ryman; pushed on down Broadway past Mom's and Tubb's record shop toward the icy Cumberland River.

I u-turned at the end of Broadway and headed back west.

We'd stopped at Bud's place just long enough for him to throw some things in a suitcase and pick up more of the precious insulin that kept him vertical.

As Bud packed, I'd sat in the Bel Air with the radio on, but mostly unheard, running it all through my mind again.

"God, I just can't get it out of my head," Bud said as we once more rolled by Tubb's, flurries whipping around the neon guitar out front. "This notion of white light, then a mushroom cloud rising over the Nashville skyline. I just can't forget the idea."

"If you're close enough to see that flash of white light, chances are you won't be seein' the cloud that follows, Bud. If there is comfort to be found in the fact, everything here will be ashes in the bat of an eye."

"And that's supposed to be some sort of consolation?" Bud sighed and held his hand up to the heater vent on his side. "Tell me more about this Coleman guy."

I did that. After, Bud said, "How do they expect you to draw out this insane writing student of yours?"

"Search me, kiddo. And, Christ, he hardly qualifies as a student."

"So what do we do next, Hec?"

"For starters, I beg out on Jake's funeral tomorrow. I'll use that time with the emptier house to conduct my search with that gizmo Easton gave us."

"Just which branch of the government or the military do you think this guy Easton is tied to?"

"I really have no notions about that," I said. "And that gives me some serious pause in terms of handing over this doomsday component to the smooth-talking son of a bitch. I don't like his caginess about his affiliations. All that is its own flavor of unsettling."

Bud said, "We going to tell Logan about any of this?"

I came on emphatic: "God, no. No way. Bad enough you have to risk the ulcers from knowing all this stuff, buddy."

He hesitated, then Bud said, "You know, Hector, after last year, and some time apart from you, I came to think that stuff with Villa's head and Skull and Bones and all the rest was really maybe some kind of fluke. But Alicia actually called it all right, didn't she? This kind of intrigue is just an ongoing scene with you, isn't it?"

This was a *moment*, in all kinds of senses. Maybe *the* moment.

If Bud had some kind of open line with Alicia still going, what I said next could cost me what—perhaps from being a tad delusional—I still hoped for.

I took a breath, thought about what I wanted to say next, then forged ahead:

"As you see, Bud, I didn't exactly come looking for this one. At some point, you get a rep like mine, and it just becomes a chicken-and-egg proposition. Intrigue begets intrigue—that's gospel truth. More truth to tell: I'm more than goddamn *tired* of it all. Exhausted and left feeling burned by it all. I increasingly envy the ones who lead anonymous lives in safe and comforting ruts."

Bud shook his head. "I don't believe that, not for a minute, Hector. Sorry, but I just don't."

Goddamn my poet for not recognizing a real moment.

But, hell, he was still growin' up.

I sighed, down deep. "Well, you're just flat wrong, kid," I said. "I'm bein' utterly honest, Bud. Lord knows I've collected twice my share of enemies over the years. Plenty have reason to hate my guts, that's for sure. Plenty of those are maybe yet laying in wait for me somewhere down life's crazy road. But nobody is more tired and finished with so-called *Hector Lassiter* than I am, anymore. You know Bud, I sometimes think of getting myself a big old roll of money and a false driver's license and just goin' out on the open road under some other hombre's virgin handle. Kind of curious to see how life might roll for me without that Lassiter moniker that sells copies for *True* and *Argosy* and parks asses in the cinema seats and the like. Increasingly, I flirt with the yen to let the world think Hector Lassiter has shuffled off to Valhalla. To Heaven or Hell, assuming there's really some difference between the two if either or both exists."

I was quiet a while, then added, "And it's the *other*, you know. I stood on a porch outside that restaurant in the rain last year with wicked old Emil Holmdahl and we were talking about outliving the world. A lot of *my* good old world is *gone* now, Bud, and the rest is standin' in line to board a train that's leavin', fast and soon. That eats away at you, too, kid, as you'll one day know.

"You should also know extreme longevity runs in my family. My great grandpap saw 105. My grandpap Beau is still very much in the game. Despite all my vices and bad choices, I just might be around for a long while, yet. That might sound like a gift, but, as the saying goes, at some point, you're just the last man standing, which is same as sayin' the *loneliest* man standing. So I stand to maybe lose a lot more than most, goin' forward."

Bud smiled. "But did your long-lived grandpap have all your vices?"

Leave it to Bud to dodge the point. I snorted and smiled back. "Nah. Not at all."

Bud was again quiet for a time.

Raw-voiced he finally said, "You really should do that, Hec. Just take a year off from being yourself. Do that and see what comes of it."

The name Alicia somehow hung in the ensuing silence between us, at least for me.

"Maybe I really will, after this mess is cleaned up," I said.

We were crossing the bridge over the rail yard. "Got me some business to close out down in Cuba next month," I said. "A friendship to try and repair. But after that's behind me, maybe I will just get out of the way of history for a year or two. Maybe try and write the kind of book I was trying to pen back in January of 1924, in Paris."

I'd toyed with this sort of reinvention thing from time to time, over the years.

But this one night it didn't seem like hollow talk, somehow.

The notion was actually taking root in me, at the core.

I gave Bud a look and said, "We writers, we have to front a persona, as we've discussed a time or two. I can see you've got one under construction, kid. Just be choosy and careful and make sure you can live with the beast you build. Trust me on this next: A writer's reputation and identity can become some kind of heavy and even destructive burden, son. A real fucking albatross."

Bud nodded, looking at me. He got it, in terms of what I was saying about myself.

As to what he grasped about his own budding persona's risk?

Hell, only time, that wicked old whore, would tell.

"You're late." Donna was dressed, if that was the right word for it, in slinky, clingy silk pajamas and a matching robe. Very fetching, even if she maybe was a black widow.

Donna smiled and said, "I bought wine for tonight, for our nightcap. Having browsed a book or two of yours, I've deduced you prefer red wines, Hector. Something robust, with real depth, and a long finish. Am I right?"

"You're quite the booze sleuth," I said as she handed me the bottle and a corkscrew. It was a Spanish wine. She *really* had sussed out my tastes in vino. "This is good stuff, the right poison for me," I said, working at the cork. "But I have to go light on it."

Donna nodded. "Yes, your diabetes. Logan told Genevieve, who told me. I'm also told it's very mild in your case. At least for now."

"So long as I go easy on stuff like this, maybe it will stay that way," I said, hefting the bottle of wine.

"So no other side effects from your condition?" Donna hesitated, letting a little innuendo slide in there, putting a little husk into her voice. "I mean, I've heard about various, well, side effects that it can cause. In men, particularly."

Ouch.

I said, "I have to use spectacles to read anything smaller than a billboard. But that's strictly all." A beat. "At least so far."

"I'm *so* relieved," Donna said, smiling. She gestured to the sofa. A couple of wine glasses waited on the table there. I sat down and poured us both vino. "We should probably let it breathe first," I said. "But as it's rather late..."

We tapped glasses. I sipped. It was oaky, smoky. The wine had hints of chocolate and cherries. A little would go a long way, and I'd already exceeded my liquor allotment for the day, and then some.

Donna arched an eyebrow. "It'll do?"

"For this night. It's perfect," I said. "Do you know where's Logan gotten off to?"

"Out back I believe, in the guest house. He's giving my daughter guitar lessons. Or so the story goes. Now that your young friend Bud Fiske is back there with them, maybe that's really what's going on."

I nodded and sipped more wine. I really should be going easier on the stuff, but I was feeling reckless in all sorts of directions, suddenly.

Maybe it was some kind of *carpe diem* impulse born of visions of Nashville and everything in it—not the least of which being me and mine—going up in some massive fireball at any instant.

"Logan's several shades less worldly than his voice or songs would likely lead you to believe," I said. "He writes like a devil, but lives like an angel. Usually, it runs the *other* way with songwriters. So, in other words, Logan probably really was giving Gen music lessons when they were alone back there."

Donna looked up at me through black lashes with sloe eyes. "Again, I'm relieved. I watch you with those two young men, Hector. I see how you treat them like adopted sons, or something. You don't have any children of your own, do you?"

I savored some more of the Spanish wine. "No, I don't." I changed the subject: "The décor in this pad of Jake's, it's decidedly bigoted."

She wrinkled her nose. "That bothers you?"

"Sure," I said, sipping my wine. "Doesn't it bother you, too?"

Donna shrugged. I watched her chest move under the silk robe as her shoulders rose and fell. There was no brassiere there under all that silk, I figured. Still, for their size, her breasts were pert enough.

"Jake Guthrie was born in the old, never dead Confederacy," Donna said. "His forbearers on both sides, to hear him tell it, fought with Lee. There was also real money on his daddy's side. That is until the family's Atlanta estate was burned to the ground by Sherman. Jake was still nursing a family grudge. He *hated* Ohio for giving birth to Sherman and Grant. You know Jake rarely toured up north, and *never* in the Buckeye State, despite the demand for his records up there."

I considered that. "But all these employees here are holdovers of Jake's," I said. "Have to observe, I haven't seen a single white face around here but yours and your daughter's."

"I think that was deliberate on Jake's part," Donna said. "Think about it."

She sipped the wine and combed her hair behind an ear. "*I* think that Jake secretly liked to pretend it was old days, say, 1850s days, and he really liked to kid himself he wasn't *paying* these Negroes to wait on him."

Okey dokey.

"What a prince the King was," I said. I rolled my neck and winced at some crack just below the base of my skull. Probably muscle strain from hauling around corpses, earlier, I told myself.

Donna clucked her tongue, sat down her glass and moved behind the sofa. She began kneading my shoulders with strong, passionate hands. "You wear your stress, you know. Doesn't this feel nice?"

"Very." It really did.

She had surprisingly strong hands. Something about that gave me a sudden chill, some sense of déjà vu I couldn't put a name to in the moment. A name of another woman who'd massaged me some time ago was just at the edge of consciousness, but once again, I couldn't pluck that name from the ether.

"Your muscles are *so* tight," she said, really digging in now with her fingertips. "You're carrying *so* much stress in your shoulders and neck, it's amazing. You need to relax, to unwind. There's a screening room in this place. I was looking over the film selection while you were gone. I found a crime film, there. It's called *Kiss Me Deadly*. Would you like me to have the staff set up the projector for us?"

Gawd. Fucking Mickey Spillane. That *hack.*

"No thanks," I said firmly, rolling my head as her hands worked the muscles of my neck and shoulders. "Thank you, but *not* that film, and particularly not tonight of all nights."

She moved back around the chair and took my hand; drew me up to her. "Then I have another way to relax you. It's sure to take away some of the pain in your muscles."

The sauna was located off a small weight room. "Towels and robes are to be found in those cabinets," she said.

"This is perfect," I said. "Should really do the trick." I realized I still had my glass of wine along for the ride. That was not a good sign for my lately cleaner way of living. I sipped some more wine before Donna took the glass from me and finished it off.

"Sorry," she said, "I shouldn't have tempted you with that stuff. Not with your condition."

She pointed at a cedar post. There was a white console there with a couple of buttons. "Press the blue button if you need anything more, or a cold drink," she said. "Water would be best, of course. You can dehydrate yourself pretty quickly in there."

Donna excused herself then.

I undressed and hitched a towel around my waist and draped a second towel around my shoulders. I closed the sauna door behind myself, doused the hot stones with some water, then settled down on the wooden bench and tipped my head back against the cedar wall, listening to the sizzle and soaking in all that rising steam.

My notion was to clear my head of all thought, but instead I started planning and plotting.

Tonight, I'd ask to use the billiard room as a temporary writing space. I'd take the "tape recorder" with me and get a radiation reading there. Maybe sweep the kitchen and dining room under the guise of needing a late night snack. The trip from the billiard room to the kitchen would take me through that big old living room. And feigning being lost—a plausible enough gambit in this palace, with its warren of rooms and hallways—would get me into a few other places, maybe.

When I turned in at last, I'd search Jake's bedroom and private bath.

During the funeral, I'd wander the rest of the house. See if I couldn't get access to the garage and maybe even Jake's fallout shelter. The existence of that latter now certainly took on a sinister patina.

I mopped my forehead with the end of the towel draped around my neck. I thought some more about Chuck Easton. Those sleek cars and the gizmos Chuck had given me were nice stagecraft, but they didn't make him a lock as a U.S. government man. Huh-uh.

As Chuck had correctly told Bud, I'd had my share of brushes with various intelligence agencies through the years. Hell, I'd jousted with CIA, FBI and sundry other secret services, foreign and domestic. In theory, I could work the phones. I could maybe get some dope on this Easton character and whatever spooky spy agency he was tied to.

But it would be a fishing expedition that carried all kinds of risks of its own. Christ only knew what it might stir up in official circles if I started making such inquiries.

What I really needed was some kind of contact above J. Edgar or Allan Dulles. Someone who floated well above a single law enforcement or intelligence agency.

Unfortunately, I didn't have the direct number to Ike and Mamie's pad at Camp David.

But there was this *other* politician of recent acquaintance I suddenly remembered.

There was a hiss of escaping humid air and some of the steam started rolling out the now-open door. I could see a silhouette through the steam. It was unquestionably female and nearly nude.

Donna wore a terrycloth towel wrapped around her torso. Given how little it covered, the thing looked better suited for use as a washcloth. "I never promised I wouldn't join you," she said, smiling.

There was no further preamble. Donna doffed her too-small towel, then tugged at the knot in the one tied around my waist.

She kissed me on the mouth, the neck and the chest. She kept heading south.

"We need to close our pores," Donna said, leading me naked through the weight room to a shower. I noticed now she had a bluebird tattooed on her ankle. She kissed me while lathering us up with a bar of soap. She said, "Separate bedrooms tonight, lover—for Gen's sake, I mean."

I could have said, "But Gen's already got a marriage behind her. She's hardly a child anymore." Instead I said, "I get up ungodly early anyway. Usually am up by five writing. And I'm racing a deadline."

Then I took the bar of soap from Donna and began smoothing it over her breasts. I slid it down her belly and between her legs as I gripped the back of her neck with my other hand, searching her eyes. "Afraid I won't be able to squire you to the funeral, but I will be there for you in terms of enduring the *wake*." I said that last between hungry kisses.

"You *better*." Donna kissed me back, using her tongue. She said, "Any more ideas about how to clear this mess up regarding my daughter and the police?"

I turned her around and began burnishing her back, then her hips. "I do have a thought or two along those lines."

Donna twisted in my arms and put her back to the shower stall's wall, stroking me as she wrapped one leg around my waist and guided me there. She panted, "These thoughts... do share, *please*."

I cupped her chin in my hand, tipping her mouth to just the angle I wanted it. "That might be premature," I said.

Breathing harder, breasts heaving, she said, "It's kind of exciting all on its own, you know."

"What's that?"

Thrusting against me, Donna said, "Being taken by a man who's allegedly had Paulette Goddard and Rita Hayworth. Having a man who's also had Ava Gardner and Joi Lansing. Heady company for a nobody like me."

That admission almost cost me an erection.

20

Five in the morning: I was up and at Jake Gantry's hand-carved desk, filling up notebook pages at a feverish pace. But all of it was maybe drivel. Just couldn't concentrate, my mind too full of mushroom clouds, passionate and perhaps murderous mothers and squirrelly master spies.

The Geiger counter showed no readings in Jake's bedroom, the billiard room or in the hallway connecting them. So I showered, dressed and wandered downstairs around six. The black maid I'd met in the kitchen the previous afternoon was squeezing oranges. She smiled when she saw me—not friendly, not false … not anything, seemingly. She said, "Hungry, sir?"

"I could surely eat." I smiled. "I could even help make the meal."

"I'm paid to do that," she said, smiling for real now. "Don't need you upsetting the apple cart or starting any dangerous trends, mister."

"Call me Hector."

"Fine then. I'm Esther." I stuck out a hand and she wiped hers on her apron. After, we shook.

"Good Biblical name you got there, darlin'," I said.

"Sure enough."

She said, "What'll it be, Hector?"

"Eggs over easy, toast? Maybe some bacon if it isn't too much trouble."

"That's no trouble at all. Mr. Gantry, now there was some breakfast to prepare. No wonder his heart was so bad, the crazy things that man ate. And in the quantities he demanded?" She shook her head side to side.

I started working oranges. "At least let me do this," I said. "God knows, me and the boys and all the tequila drinks have upped the demand for orange juice in this place."

She nodded and made room at the counter for me. Not that space was at a premium on the kitchen countertop— I'd seen shorter driveways.

"How about some grits, too, Hector?"

"God, you know, they may be the one thing I've never gotten around to sampling," I said.

"Well, then you're going to have mine, and it'll ruin you for all the rest, mister."

"Sold." I tossed aside a spent orange and set to work on another. "How long have you been here, Esther?"

"Twelve years, *if* I make it to 1959." The eggs sizzled as they hit the frying pan.

"Fifty-nine is damn near upon us," I said. "You really have some doubts about going that distance?"

Esther shrugged. "I see the way that woman looks at me. At all of *us*. I expect a lot more than just the furnishings are going to be changing around here, and soon. Not that redecorating wouldn't help this place. Good Lord, the crazy things that man spent his money on."

"It's all pretty hideous," I said. "Looking around this place, it's clear your former employer wasn't what we'll call an open-minded man. In fact, his mind seemed pretty meanly set in some bad directions. I mean, if you could keep a job with him for twelve years with his obvious prejudices, well, it shouldn't be too hard to stay in these ladies' good graces. Hell, Gen used to live here, right?"

"And her mother was a near fixture, too," Esther said carefully. "No, you're right enough. Mr. Gantry was prejudiced to the bone. He made sure we all knew our place."

"Yet you gave him more than a decade of your service," I said softly.

"His money spent," Esther said, cracking a few more eggs and pushing some slices of bread down in the toaster. "And he paid better for my services than some others around this town would."

"Why? I mean, given his feelings toward non-whites, why would he pay better?"

"Because all of us here were tested and found discrete." Esther made a face. "And I'm talking too much. More 'n I ever do. You're the exact kind that draws such things out of a person, I 'spect. You seem trustworthy, but I don't know why that should be. Anyhow, it's this simple: I needed money to pay for my children's education. To keep them in a clean safe house well away from the harder parts of town. Keep them in a Catholic church's school, where they can truly learn something. So I stayed on the job here. Bit my lip and kept my mouth shut tight. I didn't judge." This look: "I *don't* judge, Mister."

Well, I didn't believe that last.

"Why did Mr. Gantry need so much discretion from the hired help, Esther? I mean, word is out he was involved in some pretty vile organizations where it comes to race."

"There is that. That, and some other things. But I'm talking out of school again, and I just don't know you."

"But you can trust me," I said. I remembered that NCLC badge I saw pinned to her coat the previous day and mentioned it.

She shook her head. "Only started wearing it when that man Jake Gantry was safely in the ground. Usually, I remember to take it off when I'm here. Getting forgetful, now that some pressure's off. That's more dangerous for my job here."

"Either way, you're a member of the NCLC and a follower of the Reverend Kelly Miller Smith, right? Well, we have a mutual ally, I guess you'd call him. I know the Reverend August Grafton Robinson. Even gave him some money. Hear there's a plaque going to be put on a pew in a church here in Nashville with my money."

Esther's eyes narrowed. "You know the Rev. Robinson?"

"Pretty well."

"Well, that man's about half-crazy. He claims he's tied to the Reverend Smith, but that's not so. Reverend Robinson split off and formed his own church about six months ago. He thought the Reverend Smith was too quiet, 'too passive to be effective,' he said. So he started his own church, and it's anything but passive. Word is they're collecting guns, even bombs. That they're fixing for a riot of their own."

I shrugged and tried for sheepish. "Well, clearly I don't know him too well after all. Just met the padre yesterday. Briefly, but intensely."

"Well, watch your back around that man, Hector. Like I said, he's mad, bad and dangerous to know."

"I will, now." I poured the orange juice into a waiting pitcher. "Were you the one who found Jake Gantry dead?"

Esther set to scraping my eggs off the pan and sliding them onto a dish. "That's right."

"He was toes up when you found him?"

"Very. You want jelly and butter on your toast, or do you want to see to that yourself?"

"Just butter, and I'll do it." I poured myself a glass of orange juice and pulled out a chair at that long table. "I should tell you now that Donna Perkins has asked me to poke around the circumstances of Jake's death. On account of the police have this crazy idea that Genevieve—"

Esther was firm: "Genny didn't do *that* to him. She hasn't been back here since she left him back a time. Didn't come back until Jake was dead." The old woman shook her head. "Say what you might about that little girl, but she did not do anything to hurt that man. She couldn't. Not the type. She's just a child."

"Do you like her?"

"I don't dislike her," Esther said. "And she's always nice to me. About the only one around here giving orders who still is."

"I see." She put my plate down before me and I urged her to take a seat next to me. "Do you know why the police suspect her?"

"No. How would I?" She hesitated. "And I probably shouldn't know."

"This is just-between-us talk, Esther. You can trust me like I trust you."

"You don't know me, and all the same," Esther said, "this isn't something I should be hearing, I think. Maybe just in case I do stay on here and have to be around that gal."

"It's nothing that bad. May not even come as news to you." I sipped some orange juice, frowned. It's never quite as sweet when you do it yourself, just like food you make is never quite as tasty to your own palate.

I said, "Your former employer—Lucifer bless his poison soul—died from a reaction to medication. He was killed by some kind of pills he used to treat depression. Stuff doesn't sit well with a bad heart. The stuff killed old Jake, just like that." I snapped my pulpy, sticky fingers—the traction making 'em snap louder; she flinched at their crack.

Esther's hand went to her mouth. Apparently she must have had more affection for the old bastard than might be expected under the circumstances. Shaken, she said, "But what does this have to do with little Genevieve?"

"The girl's under a lot of pressure," I said. "She's a bit young to be in this crazy, often wicked business. So it seems she's gone and gotten herself a nervous condition. The medication she takes is the same stuff that triggered Old Jake's fatal heart attack. That being so, and the cops being cops...?"

"So the police have up and decided that little girl killed her ex-husband for his money," Esther finished for me. She wet her lips. "Is it possible that girl could have left some of those pills here from before, from before they split up?"

"A question I might have asked you," I said. "But the girl's only been under professional care for about a month. From the looks of her fingernails, things aren't moving along so well on the treatment side. No signs to me that medication is really working for her much beyond some water retention in mother's eyes."

"That girl *is* a wreck, on the inside," Esther said, looking genuinely anguished. "Worse than I've ever seen her, the poor child." She started to say something else, but I pressed ahead, hearing noises upstairs somewhere and not sure how much longer we'd have left to talk candidly. I said, "I just can't figure it, that pretty young thing tying the knot with that evil old buzzard."

Esther hesitated, then said it: "That man wasn't a man like you. Mr. Gantry was not like most men." She hesitated, then said softly, urgently, "That girl's marriage to Mr. Gantry was like the one *Confidential Magazine* wrote about. You know—Rock Hudson's wedding. Do you understand what I mean?"

A sham. "A show marriage," I said, incredulous. "A mask for the tabloids and newsboys? Is that what you're saying?" Now that Esther had put it out there, I realized I couldn't remember Old Jake being married prior to tying the knot with Genevieve. Hell, I couldn't even conjure up a memory of Jake being linked in the scandal mags with any women.

More creaking of the floorboards overhead. We both looked up at the ceiling, then locked gazes again. "Esther, did Jake bring men into the house here?"

"Sometimes," she said. "Through the back, after dark. Or so I've heard from the night staff."

Footsteps were drawing near. Esther stood up and scooted in her chair. She said softly, "It's the mother. I know her stride."

It was indeed Donna. She nodded at me and said, "You're up early, Hector."

Esther's gaze roamed between us. I guessed something in Donna's demeanor was enough to tip the old woman to something having shifted between the elder lady of the house and me. Esther silently shook her head and set about slicing mushrooms. From that I guessed that Donna liked omelets in the morning. And I got the sense I'd maybe just slipped a few rungs in Esther's estimation.

Donna said to me, "Thought you had a writing frenzy ahead of you."

I pushed away my empty plate. "Been up and at it since five. The frenzy is past. Took just enough time out to eat to keep the blood sugar under control. I'm headed back up, now."

Scooting in my chair, I excused myself and hustled out of there. I grabbed my overcoat from the foyer's closet and headed to the Bel Air to go find myself an untapped pay phone—far from the prying ears of Chuck Easton.

Three blocks from the Gantry mansion, I found a bar with an enclosed wooden phone booth in a rear corner, a good distance from the jukebox. I settled in with a coffee in hand and began flipping through the bulging pages of my address book. I browsed through the Bs until I found the name I wanted.

I dialed and asked for Senator Bush.

21

Prescott Bush said, "I'm frankly peeved at you, Mr. Lassiter. That business with Villa's head last year—we're *still* not convinced the skull Mr. Holmdahl delivered to us is authentic. Parenthetically, Mr. Holmdahl was also peeved to learn you'd already collected the bounty for said skull. He seemed to think he was to be paid for the delivery."

"Aw, seems old Emil's about half-wrapped in the best of times," I said. "I should have sent a better man. I'm kickin' myself, even now, if it's of any consolation, Pres. As to the *provenance* of the skull, well, that old bastard Holmdahl is vigorously treacherous. I only know that now, sadly for us all. But that's all the stuff of yesterday, sir. I have a situation on my hands now, Senator. Much bigger stakes this time. It's a nasty dilemma you can perhaps help me out with. A man came to me last evening claiming to be some kind of government agent. He came around trying to recruit me to help in the recovery of what he called a kind of radioactive component lost earlier this year—a loss discovered after a midair collision of—"

A whiplash response: "You stop right there, Mr. Lassiter! Please!" I heard some papers rustling; unintelligible whispers through a hand over the phone's mouthpiece. Then: "You're in Nashville, I believe."

Oh, I believed the senator well enough. From past entanglements, I knew Senator Bush had ties to all manners of intelligence agencies. Hell, it was the reason I was reaching out to him. Wouldn't have surprised me terribly if the politician next told me the color of the sports jacket I wore.

"I've made quite a study of you since our encounter last year," Bush said. "Based on my research, I presume you to have a favored bar there in Nashville."

"Sure, I do. Place called Mom's on Broadway, right next to—"

"My people will find it," Bush said. "That man who approached you—"

"Tried to recruit me would be more accurate," I said. "He gave me some devices to aid in this search he wants me to conduct for this gizmo."

The senator's voice softened a hair. "Why are you contacting me now, Mr. Lassiter?"

"Because I'm suspicious of this son of a bitch and you're connected to people and organizations I don't dare imagine. This man talks a convincing game in some ways, but in other ways, he strikes me as somehow suspect. I trust my gut and my gut doesn't like this fella much."

"And you suddenly do trust me?"

"Wouldn't put it exactly that way," I said. "Put it this way: the devil you know ..."

"I see. Did this man give you a name, Mr. Lassiter?"

"Charles Easton." I waited a beat, "He lets me call him Chuck."

"How affable. Did he indicate any official affiliation?"

"No, he dodged on that count. Flashed an I.D. that was impossible to make out. He's got a nice fleet of black cars backing him up. Lots of stooges in black suits, but too stylish to be FBI. Edgy lapels...sideburns. Kind of things to set J. Edgar's teeth on edge."

"Yes, I see. Again, I find myself thinking it's a mistake to ever underestimate you. You certainly still surprise. Go to your favored Nashville bar tonight at seven," Prescott Bush said. "I'll meet you there, Mr. Lassiter."

"I don't know about that," I said. "I really just wanted the true gen on this Easton character. Wasn't really angling for a dinner date, Senator."

"The item you're supposed to be looking for is indeed missing," Prescott said. "And there is in fact a person named Charles Easton. But that's absolutely all I'll say now, over an unsecured line. Now, please don't hang up, Mr. Lassiter. I'm going to put a man on the line. I want you describe to him this fellow who identified himself as Easton. And I need you to recount to my man all that was said between you and Easton, of course being less than specific about your quarry."

"Whoa there, pard'. This isn't quite what I envisioned. And dealing with some flunky? That's never been my style, Pres."

"You stop there, Mr. Lassiter. You're in Tennessee. I'm in Connecticut. I have many miles to cover in a short time. I must start now. You'll fill in my man and he'll fill me in prior to our rendezvous tonight."

"Well, okay then, I guess." Hell, I was in this far. Might as well take the plunge.

The Senator said, "One more thing, Mr. Lassiter. Have you told anyone else about Easton? Some other government contact you might have, for instance?"

"No. But Easton recruited me and young friend of mine named Eskin—"

"Fiske," the Senator cut in. "Yes, I remember this Bud Fiske from last year, too. Well, don't make any more contacts, please. Our government isn't the only one interested in the whereabouts of this, *er*, missing *component*. Frankly, I'd term your current situation appallingly precarious, even by your rarified standards."

"How precarious, Prescott?"

"If I were you, I'd be hiding somewhere, and I'd be well armed. Hector."

Prescient Prescott...

I filled in the Senator's flunky on all the details I could remember about Chuck Easton, then racked the phone. Some commotion up front—men yelling, some woman pleading.

I saw four men; one of them teetered on crutches.

Son of a whore if it wasn't goddamn Basil Sloan! He was now gripping one of his crutches with a bandaged hand—the one Bud had shot through.

Basil saw me and bellowed, pointing with the end of one of his crutches. I tore out of the phone cabinet, ducking low just as a sawed-off reduced a quarter of the wooden cabinet to kindling.

I ran down a darkened hallway past restrooms and a storage area, hoping to Christ I'd find a working back door out of the dive.

22

I twisted the lock on a battered metal door and slid through, slamming the door behind me and tipping over trashcans to clutter my wake. I dashed down the narrow corridor formed by two deeper neighboring buildings, then rounded a corner onto another commercial street. Blessedly, the shopkeepers had taken the trouble to clear the sidewalks so I'd leave no footprints in snow.

Veering left around another corner, I ran to the street which fronted the bar I'd just fled. I glanced at the stenciled canopy of the bar I'd run from and decided to roll the dice—try an old trick that had worked for me before in better old days. Trying to muster some swagger, I *re-entered* the bar through the front door and drew my Colt.

Basil Sloan was stumping down the back hallway toward the rear exit, in no shape to keep pace with his posse. I nodded at the barkeep as his eyes widened at the sight of my Peacemaker. I said, "I'm a cop, brother. If that gimp's pals come back, you be sure to tell them I came back through the front door and left out that back door *again*, but with their boss in irons. Got it?"

Looking confused, the bartender wet his lips and jerked his head vigorously in assent.

Overtaking Basil was easy enough. I was on him before he heard me coming. I clubbed him in the head with the butt of the Colt and checked over my shoulder to be certain the bartender couldn't see us from his post.

Safely out of sight, I hurled Basil into the men's room, then opened the metal door onto the alley again and tossed Basil's crutches into the snow. I slid back into the men's room and grabbed the still-groggy Basil by his shirt and coat collars. I hauled him into a stall and propped him up on the toilet bowl.

The toilet lid was up so I pressed him into the bowl with the toe of my boot, jamming his ass down there into the water. His butt hitting the toilet water brought Basil back around. As he came to, I patted his coat pockets and took a .38 off him, then his wallet. I shoved both in my overcoat pockets.

Basil winced and rubbed the back of his neck with his left hand. He looked down and around and said, "What the hell is this?"

"No, the question is how the hell are you still alive?"

"Thank the fire from my buddy's car you torched, cock-sucker," Basil said. "I climbed back up and stayed warm by the car fire until some couple with a nearby cabin came to check on all that smoke. They were afraid it might spread to their property, they said. They got me back to town after I told them me and my hunting buddies were robbed. They looked around but didn't find my friends. What happened to them, Lassiter?"

I shrugged. "Your pals ran into the strong right arm of the Lord. Street preacher cut their throats. Your buddies are blue gill habitat by now. Same as you'll be if you don't let this thing between us end, here and now. Jesus, on top of your prior wounds, you've gone and gotten both feet and a hand fucked up tangling with me. How much more of yourself do you want to risk losing?"

I could hear fresh commotion outside. Before Basil could call out to his new minions, I took him out with a right cross; saw one of Sloan's front teeth ricochet off the stall wall.

The old boy's physical attrition rate pursuing this vendetta of his really was quite appalling. I closed the door on Sloan and then slipped into the adjacent stall, put down the lid with the toe of my boot and climbed up onto the toilet, stooping and closing my stall's door. I heard the restroom door open, then a voice say, "Nah, looks clear. Let's check out back again!"

When I heard the metal rear door clang shut, I climbed down, slid over to the restroom door and cracked it enough to check the hall both directions—empty. I eased out and headed back toward the front of the bar, fast-walking and waving to the wide-eyed barkeep as I passed him.

Once outside, I dashed across the street and swung into my Bel Air. As I pulled into traffic I sat back and let out a deep breath, feeling very slick, very proud of myself.

That prideful moment was terribly short-lived—as such instances often are, perhaps rightly.

Cold metal at the base of my neck and click of a gun's cock.

This voice—*foreign*. Maybe Middle Eastern.

"Do not panic, Mr. Lassiter," the stranger said. "Just keep driving straight ahead until I tell you otherwise. Do anything else, and I shall shoot you in the spine."

23

We drove three blocks, me chewing my lip all the way and trying to get a glimpse at the stowaway in the rearview mirror but seeing little more than a patch of slicked-back black hair and a dark eyebrow.

The man ordered me to slow as we approached the parking lot of a bowling alley.

Three bearded, swarthy-skinned men, maybe more Middle Easterners, stood stamping their feet in the snow, leaning against a black sedan. One of the men pointed at my approaching Chevy, just like he'd been expecting it. The other two men reached under their coats.

"Turn here," the man with the gun to my neck said.

I decided to risk it. "No, I won't do that," I said.

Then I put my foot to the firewall.

The gun was momentarily withdrawn from the back of my head as my captor was thrown back against the backseat as the Bel Air surged forward.

I twisted around in my seat and grabbed at the man's gun. I got my fingers around the back of the trigger, then I slammed on the brake with my left boot heel, wrapping my other arm around the driver's side seat to keep from being thrown backwards through the windshield as the Chevy skidded to its rubber burning stop.

My captor, a smallish man with Peter Lorre eyes and a Cesar Romero moustache, was now being propelled toward me.

I saw to it his gun got in the way.

The stranger's nose crunched as it collided with the barrel. My kidnapper fell sideways across the backseat, screaming and clutching at his face, so I turned back around and steered my Chevy curbside.

Just as I did that, the man's buddies whipped by in their black sedan, so intent on overtaking me they didn't realized they'd just passed me by. I glanced back over my shoulder at the man back there curled up on my seat, whimpering. His hands were still clutched to his face. His fingers were slick with blood.

I slid across the seat and slipped out the passenger's side door; pushed back the front passenger's seat and grabbed the bastard by his collars, dragging him from my Bel Air before he could muss her upholstery.

Little bastard was still squealing and now he was saying over and over, "My nose! You broke my nose!"

"Gonna be teeth next, pal—I'm on roll today in that area. Who are you? Who do you represent? What was this sorry-ass attempt at snatching me?"

"You know what I am here for."

"Humor me," I said. "Pretend I don't know, because maybe that's the fact."

"Absurd." He moaned again as he probed at his face. "My nose! It *is* broken."

"Pretty clearly that's so. Could be just the start of your problems. Now what is this?"

"We have your car *bugged*, as they say. We did it while you had dinner with that man, Easton. We have heard everything you have said in that car. I know you know what I want." His lip curled and I got a glimpse of bloodstained teeth. "We have heard it all despite that awful music you have playing all the time." He mewled again, said, "My poor nose!"

I ignored his bellyaching. "Fine. Then let's drop all pretenses. I don't have what you want."

"But you *will*, soon quite likely, and we must have it. We'll pay you handsomely for it. And you will want to help us, surely. The Jews are trying to get the bomb first you know! Can you imagine what the world would be like if Israel—if the *infidels*—got it first?"

I just shook my head. "Oh, Christ, stop right there or I'll shoot you now." I motioned with the man's gun. "Get your sorry ass up. I'm going to call Easton and just turn you over to him. Let him and his boys go to work on you to figure out what interested party or desert hell hole you represent."

After his anti-Semitic rant, it wasn't like I didn't have some notion about his likely origins already. "Christ knows what my government will do with you. I really don't care."

The little man struggled up onto unsteady legs, one bloody hand still gripping his nose. "Oh, you'll *care*. And you'll do as I say. Your friend, Fiske—" (he pronounced it *Fee*-ske) "—is now in a bar, sitting in a booth, writing. One of my other associates is behind him, sitting in the adjoining booth. I have only to call the bar and ask the one who answers to shout out to my friend, to say there is a phone call for him. That will signal my associate to stand up, to shoot Mr. Fiske in the head, and depart the bar. I will do that unless you agree right now to turn over the materials to us."

"Jesus, what happened to paying me handsomely?" But thank God this crew was strictly amateur hour. "Listen," I said, "the way you're *supposed* to do this is you tell me that unless you place a call by a certain time your friend will shoot my friend. That's the way you play a scheme like this, Ace. Telling me your phone call is the trigger, no pun intended? Well, that just buys you more damage."

The little man screamed, "Allahu Ackbar!" Then he charged me.

I swung the butt of the man's gun into his Adam's apple and heard something *else* crack. "Samuel Colt begs to differ, cocksucker," I said.

Maybe it was the stranger's voice box I heard give way. If it was his hyoid bone, he was going to be dead before he hit the ground. Either way, he wasn't going to be talking, let alone placing any phone calls.

He crumpled to the pavement and I took a quick look around. No pedestrians to stand as witness. Nobody in any of the passing cars seemed to want to get involved in my sordid and bloody little scene.

I popped open the trunk of my Chevy and rooted around until I found the tire iron. There was a manhole cover about a foot from my kidnapper's feet. I wedged the tire-iron into the inset ring and levered the cover off the sewer hole beneath.

Waves of hot, stinking steam rolled out of the opened sewer. I grabbed the old boy by the feet and got those started down the sewer hole. When his waist finally was swallowed up the rest of him went down fast enough. Sounded like he fell about six feet before he landed in something that made a splash.

Bastard might well suffocate or drown down there, but at least he'd be nice and warm. I rolled the lid back over the hole, slung the tire iron in the trunk and slammed the lid. I was six blocks from Bud's favorite bar. I gambled that was where I would find Fiske and his stalker.

The trigger man was easy enough to spot. He was dressed like his cohorts in a black suit that looked new and off-the-rack.

Bud, thank God, was indeed sitting there in the booth adjacent to his would-be assassin. Bud's head was down and he was focused on his writing. The poet didn't even see me, which was all to the good.

I walked past the man in the black suit like I was headed toward the men's room, then swung back around, grabbed a handful of hair and slammed the man's face down against the table top. I did it again, then once more until I was sure he was completely limp.

Bud slid out of his booth now, head on side as he watched me check for a pulse. He said, "What the hell, Hector?"

The waitress I remembered from before, Bud's friend, was standing behind the bar, mouth agape.

I frisked the unconscious man and pulled out a switch-blade and a .45. I wrapped the man's knit tie around his neck once, then pinned it to the table with his knife. I stripped the man of his belt, got his hands behind his back and tied them with the stretch of leather.

Bud said again, "What the hell, Hector? Really, what is this?"

"Hombre was going to kill you, Bud. I'll explain out-side. Best have your friend call the cops and have this guy hauled out of here, pronto. Tell that gal to just say he came out on the wrong side of a bar fight."

While Bud did that, I went back over and frisked the unconscious man again, looking for a wallet, *any* kind of identification. I found nothing but a money clip filled with crisp ones and a package of condoms, still wrapped in the drugstore receipt.

Bud's would-be assassin had his sorry dreams, I reckoned. Guess he figured to cross the ocean, retrieve a weapon of annihilation to stick it to "the Jews" and just maybe bed a Yankee gal in the bargain.

The waitress said, "Think he'll stay out long enough for the police to get here?"

I grabbed the man by the back of the neck and lifted his face off the table. I let go and he slumped forward again. "He'll keep." I passed her the man's gun. "But just in case ..."

Bud and I hustled out the back door. He said, "This guy really meant to kill me?"

"Yeah, he and some others surely did if I didn't agree to give a cohort the bomb component."

"Who are they?"

"My grasp of Middle East geography is pretty dodgy, I'm afraid, but I suspect if you pick any country bordering Israel you'll be in the neighborhood. Guy who was going to give the killing order on you was sweating the prospect 'the Jews' might get the bomb component first."

"This is crazy," Bud said.

"And it's still early days." As we approached the Bel Air I said, "Your car close by?"

"Around the corner," Bud said.

"I'll drop you. You've got a funeral you're almost late for. I have a bloody mansion to search." Bud was about to slide into the Chevy. I took him by the arm and led him a few paces away from all those bugs. I said, "Oh, and we've got a dinner date tonight, at Mom's."

Bud raised his eyebrows. "Yeah? Who are we meeting?"

"Fella you'll remember from our last little escapade. Senator Prescott Bush."

I relished the poet's double-take as we headed back to my Chevy. Before we climbed in, I said softly, "Choose your words carefully. Bel Air's been bugged."

24

Jake Gantry's garage was a bust. There were some more ostentatious, dubiously decorated sleds and an old motorcycle with a sidecar. It looked like another Nazi souvenir and it surely brought back some bloody memories of WWII, but nothing to set my special Geiger gizmo to clicking.

I moseyed over to the fallout shelter and walked around its perimeter a couple of times, but I got no readings from that sucker, either. On the other hand, if the shelter was really designed to do its job, odds were the walls of the son of a bitch were lined with lead.

I wandered back into the house to continue my search.

Creeping around the basement of Jake's cavernous casa I turned a corner, right into scowling Esther. "What are you doing down here, mister?"

A shrug and a smile. "Thought I had the place to myself," I said.

Esther nodded, searching my eyes. "Mrs. Perkins asked that I stay in case you needed anything."

I smiled. "Wasn't that thoughtful of her? There are others who could see to me. Why aren't you paying tribute? You spent years working for the man."

"I'd have felt like a hypocrite standing over him and saying how tragic it was he'd passed." She gestured at my modified tape recorder. "And my question stands. What are you up to, mister? Creeping around outside and all over out there, and in here, too, with that machine there of yours...What are you up to?"

"Your dead boss they're planting today, he was a worse piece of work than you know, Esther. He was up to serious no good. Really bad stuff."

"You police?" Her mispronunciation of the word didn't grate quite like Basil's did.

"More like a special government agent," I said. "Special recruit, you might say."

She thought about that, then said, "Is this about the school? Are you FBI?"

"Not FBI, but that's close enough," I lied. Hell, as I didn't know what Easton's affiliation was, maybe it didn't even qualify as a lie. "And what school are you talking about, Esther?"

"The elementary school, the integrated one, that got dynamited last September," Esther said. "Here in Nashville, you know? There was rumors around the house here Mr. Gantry might have had a hand in that. Some people from church quit talking to me after that rumor got 'round. 'How could you work for a man who'd do that to a school?' That kind of thing, you know?"

That left me shaking my head: old Jake really was shaping up to be a real first-class son of a bitch on every ugly front.

Figured then and there that, going forward, I'd be swiftly switching the channel every time one of the bastard's tunes got radio airplay.

"No, it's not about a school," I said. "Actually, this stands to be much worse, if you can even imagine that."

I decided to risk it. "This device is a kind of detector," I said. "Feeling is Gantry may have had a role in stealing some government property. Something very dangerous he might use against your people, particularly. This machine can find the stolen device, or traces of it, if it was ever hidden here in the house."

Esther scowled. "I have a hard time believing that. Mister, that sounds crazy."

"Yeah, well, I only wish it was. It's a pretty nasty weapon that's gone missing, darlin'."

"Have you gotten anything from the gizmo there, mister? Anything to show this stolen *de-vice* was ever here?"

"Nothing so far. Not even a flicker. But I've still got a few nooks and crannies to search in this place," I said. "Unless you know of some more hidden spots in this cave. What I'd really like is to get inside that fallout shelter the bastard built out back. His private hidey hole in case the earth went to ash."

Esther smiled. "I *can* help you with that. That door on the outside of that place isn't the only way in. There's a tunnel that connects to the basement in here. I have a special key to get inside because I was supposed to clean in there once-in-a-while. Check the dates on his provisions and restock some of the perishables and potables, now and again."

I squeezed her arm and smiled. "You've really got to let me into that place, Esther. If you have still have that key ... ?"

She rummaged in her pocket and pulled out a big key ring. She held it out to me. "This way."

Trailing her through a maze of hallways in the big basement I said, "Have to say, given Jake's bigotry and apparent paranoia, I'm a little surprised he'd trust you, or anyone really, with a key to his atomic hidey-hole. I mean, if the Big Ones were indeed dropping, what would stop you from using that key to dodge the apocalypse, too?"

Esther shook his head. "Oh, he thought of that, too, mister. Mr. Gantry told me that once he was safely inside he had some special lever on the lock inside that would change the tumblers so my key wouldn't work ever again." Her voice ran to acid: "Man thought of everything, didn't he?"

Spotting every angle? The worst ones, those who are "full of passionate intensity" as Billy Yeats memorably put it, usually do just that very thing. It's a kind of religion with 'em.

Another big nothing: the fallout shelter search proved a bust.

Not so much as a flicker of radiation, according to my nifty gizmo.

So we sat in the bunker after, sampling some of that "potable water" and dipping into some of the old boy's K-rations.

I said to Esther, "You know, if the prospect was sitting down here, eating this stuff for Christ only knows how long, I might just say, *To hell with this*, and pop the hatch on this bunker. Take me a good, deep, radioactive breath and be done with it, fast."

Figured I might get at least a smile from Esther, but it didn't even elicit a smile. Her head was down as she stared at her hands; kneading her fingers. She said softly, her voice raw-sounding, "This job of yours that you're doing for Uncle Sam, does it give you any pull with the local police?"

"I suppose so," I said, thinking of the cop, Rich Corin. "I mean, I could throw some weight on them, if needed, sure." I put down the food and the water and rested a hand on Esther's shoulder. "Something on your mind? Some problem I can help you with?"

She finally looked me in the eye again. "Those pills you say killed Mr. Gantry?"

"Yeah..." I crumpled up the container on some more K-rations and tossed them at a wastepaper basket. "What about them?"

"I gave those pills to him. I gave Mr. Gantry those pills what killed him."

"You did?"

"Night before he died, Mr. Gantry was grousing around at the table while I made him some supper," Esther said. "He talked about how depressed he was. Couldn't get his mind to stop turning things over, he complained. He wasn't hardly sleeping. Tired as he could be, yawning all the time, his eyes burning and tired, yet he said he lay there in the dark and his mind would just race on to nowhere in particular. He told me he thought he was cracking up. Well, mister, my youngest boy, Colson, he's got nervous problems all his own. Wicked insomnia and the like. Had them since he was a tiny thing. I had just picked up his medication. I offered Mr. Gantry a couple of Colson's pills. Told Mr. Gantry it might settle him down. At least give him one night's sleep. Said if it worked, maybe he could get his own doctor to prescribe some more for Mr. Gantry. I, well, I was just tryin' to help the man, God forgive me."

I shook her knee. "*I* forgive you," I said. "And I'm sure God will, too. You couldn't know what would come of it, Esther. You did a real nice favor for the old bastard. Or you meant to."

Some nice irony in there. Almost made me smile, the thought of the compassionate act of this woman of color accidentally killing a mass-murdering racist son of a bitch. Made me want to hug her.

But Esther was starting to lose her grip. "Now that little gal is in trouble because of what I did, and if I go to the police—?"

"You *will* go to the police but with me there to back you up," I said. "Me, and maybe another who'll carry some serious weight if we need still more juice. I've got friends in high places. And hell, if those pills did put Old Jake away, if they *did* put a hitch in his get-along in terms of his other plans, well then, Esther, there's every possibility you may have saved lives. More lives than anyone can rightly say. You're a hero, viewed in that light."

I patted her back and she rested her head on my shoulder. I could feel her shoulders shaking. "We'll get this settled fast," I said. "And no reason your new employers ever need know about it. Hell, they'll just be relieved to see Genevieve out from under suspicion."

Esther looked up, searching my eyes. "You sure they won't arrest me?"

"I swear. We'll end this particular thing right now, before the others get back. Get you in the clear, pronto."

Yep. I figured it was a good afternoon's work, all in all. By the time Donna and her daughter returned, I would have fulfilled my obligation to clear GG of suspicion of murder. I'd also have completed a fruitless search of Jake

Gantry's house and have good excuse to clear out of this hillbilly Hilton. Then I'd go bunk with Bud or find myself my own hotel far from the vexing arms of wicked Donna Perkins.

Esther stood up and said, "So we'll drive to the police now?"

I stood and cracked my back. Somewhere out there between me and the station house was Christ-only-knew how many skulking cretins angling for the missing *component*—a road-trip with Esther just didn't seem the best idea, presently. Too many depended on this sweet old lady staying north of the dirt, and riding shotgun with me about now was in no way a prescription for a long life.

No, safer, I thought, to stay on the grounds of Jake's place. Better to have the cop, Corin come to us.

25

"You believe this maid?"

"I surely do," I said. "Esther's was a compassionate gesture toward a man she had real reason to loathe. Whom she *did* loathe, with a purple passion. And that kind gesture accidentally put the son of a bitch down. Some fine joke, wouldn't you say?"

I heard Corin's sigh across the phone. "If she's sold you, I'm probably prepared to accept it, too."

Huh: I thought of my own assessment of Corin's ability to accurately read Genevieve Gantry's character. Having Rich Corin pronounce my judgment sound didn't make me swoon or swell my head.

I said, "So can you come here, soon, while her new boss is out? Esther's ready to give you a statement. Wants to get this behind her, discreetly, we hope."

"Forget it. You said she gave him a minimal amount of these pills."

"That's right," I said. "Two tablets."

"Wouldn't likely have the done the job. Gantry, according to the docs, was filled to the gills with those pills. About five times a normal dosage."

"Yeah?" I was freshly confounded.

"Yes. That's what the coroner found."

"What else was in old Jake?"

Papers rustled. He said, "Remnants of breakfast, lunch and dinner. Whatever could be pieced together from what was found in the toilet bowl. His blood-alcohol content was pretty high, too. He'd drunk a river's worth of rye."

"So what now?"

Corin said, "So now you tell your friend the maid to quit sweating it out. There's still a killer out there, but she's not on my list of probable suspects."

"So I can tell Esther that? That she's in the clear?"

"Please do," he said. "I don't need any more distractions, Lassiter."

❧

Esther gripped my hands. "You believe this policeman?"

"I do," I said. We were sitting in the front room of Jake's place, surrounded by all that Confederate art and stuffed dead things looking sightlessly down at us. "Here's the troubling thing, Esther. Did Jake maybe raid your purse for more pills?"

"No," she said, emphatic. "Why?"

"Corin said the coroner found about a hell of a lot more of that stuff in Jake's system than you gave him." "He says *a lot* more." I hesitated, then said, "Donna wasn't by here anytime close to Jake's last *adios*, was she?"

Esther narrowed her eyes. "What you're doing with that woman isn't my business, but I hope you understand why what you might be doing with that woman might make me not want to talk about her like that, one way or the other."

"That's fair," I said. "That's understandable. But..." I groped for words. "Esther, I'm a man. I don't turn down certain opportunities as they come my way. Doesn't mean I'm going to go hunting for rings, or even bouquets, though. There's love and there's the other. Call me a tomcat in that respect and it won't hurt my feelings. And all that being said, once doesn't mean twice. Particularly if I clear out of this crazy pad today, which I'm fixin' to do, pronto. Now that I've found I can't find what I was looking for here, I'm seriously leaning toward making tracks from this joint. That lusty widow won't see me again for my dust. Swear."

"Mrs. Perkins wasn't by like you asked," Esther said. "Not her, and not the little girl, either. Least ways, not on my shift."

I believed her. "Hokey doke, then. Two last questions, darlin'. First one: You mentioned these men Jake used to bring through the backdoor. Any of them by in the last week or so before Jake dove south of the sod? And if so, would you know any names?"

"No and *no*. I mean, they might have come through off my shift, but either way, I never knew most names, and I know the night crew didn't, either. Oh, I mean, they might recognize a famous face now and again. An actor or two. Ramon, Billy. That other pretty boy actor was here hiding from the scandal magazines for a time while his face and teeth was being fixed up from that car accident last year. But most all of those sorts coming 'round, that was a times back, when Jake wasn't quite so ..." Her voice trailed off.

I offered up an ending: "Wasn't so fat and bald?"

She smiled despite herself. "That's right. You said you had another question."

"Jake have any other places around you know of? Property he might have owned. Investment stuff and the like? Apartments, or maybe rental units of some kind?"

"I don't know anything about any of that. You really going to clear out?"

"Mean to," I said. "This other thing needs attention I can't give it in this place and around those women. So I figure Bud and I will bug out later this afternoon. Logan, on the other hand? Getting him away from that little gal may take dynamite and a mule team."

Esther smiled. "Like you said—silly tomcat stuff."

I wrapped an arm around her shoulders and hugged her close. "I surely hope your boy gets better." Then I stood and said, "I should go put on something black about now."

"Why?"

"I dodged your employer's funeral, but promised to make the reception. They've got some spread set up over at the Ryman Auditorium. Gotta dress for the wake."

I headed out to the Bel Air first—I wanted to fetch my Colt and holster from the glove compartment so I could pack it under my mourning suit.

There were simply far too many enemies gathering now to walk the streets of Music City unarmed.

26

I was a mile from the Ryman Auditorium, driving in a freezing drizzle.

The ice was just starting to build up on the wiper blades. This strange noise on the passenger seat startled me. Chuck Easton's little radio gizmo was squawking. I scooped it up and clicked a button. "You've had some time alone in the house," Easton said when I picked up. "The fact you haven't contacted me, and the fact you're in transit, leads me to believe you found nothing."

My car was bugged by at least one foreign agency. Maybe others. I decided to press ahead anyway. In coming clean with Chuck, I'd let those others, too, know I'd come up empty. At least maybe enhance my chances of a quiet afternoon seeing Jake safely into the ground. "That's right, *nada*."

I thought of my foreign listeners—particularly the one I'd shoved down a sewer tube. He'd seemed to have a shaky grasp on English. Even basic Spanish lingo was probably beyond that one-percenter's comprehension. I said for universal emphasis, "Bupkiss, zilch, zero, nothing. The Big Empty. I've got *nothing* to show for the search. *Noth-ing*."

Chuck said, "Well, goddamn."

"Yep. I was going to ask you if shaky Jake had any other properties around town, but figured if he did, you'd probably already seen to sifting those yourselves."

"He did and we did," Easton said. "Hell, in an act of true desperation, we even ran a sweep through that crypt they're going to deposit him in. Big old stone thing with naked angels all over it. Clefs and musical notes scrolled into the iron gates on the front door." I could envision the silly bastard. By now I had a pretty good grasp on Jake Gantry's catastrophic, sometimes swishy, racist cowboy aesthetic.

And so far as last resting places?

Me? I wanted to be burned, then left to the wind.

"Where are you off to now, Lassiter?"

"The Grand Ole Opry," I said. "They're having a little party in remembrance of Gantry. I promised the new ladies of the house I'd put in an appearance, particularly since I missed the church service doing your nefarious bidding."

"Well, stay in touch," Chuck said. "I'll try you again tonight. Maybe you'll pick something up at this party."

"We can only hope."

I caught a break and found a parking space in front of Mom's. Dottie, dressed in black, looked up from the register and said, "Hec, I was just about to head over there. You'll hold my arm? Steady me on the ice?"

"My privilege to escort you, sweetheart," I said. "But first, can I get two fingers of Scotch in a wide-bottomed tumbler? Just don't think I can do this thing without a stiff belt in me."

I slung the drink back, took Dot's arm, and climbed the steps to the back room and door down into the alley. Then we walked the legendary thirty-seven steps across the back to the Ryman, Ambrose Bierce's big old handed-down Colt dangling snug and comforting under my left armpit.

I'd also brought along my "recording device," not because I saw the Geiger counter being of any real espionage use in the old converted house of worship—what the faithful had dubbed the "mother church of country music"—but rather because I figured I might play "song-catcher" and record myself some impromptu performances for later, personal enjoyment.

Sure enough, Johnny Cash, skeletal and sweating, squatted alone in a corner, near the rear door, hunched over, strumming and composing as he rocked and fidgeted.

Pep pills, I told myself.

After pulling up a chair, I surreptitiously flipped on the tape machine, and just sat there, listening to Johnny sing an old dark gospel tune. He finished and looked up and then smiled and switched his pick to his other hand. He reached out and shook my hand. Hadn't seen Cash since last year's prison tours. The toll of the intervening days and his addictions had not been kind. I said, "Staying away from the crowds, JR?"

"I've never much fit in around this town, Hec," Johnny said in his basso tremolo. "So I try to limit time here, best I can. You know what they say about this town? They say you never leave it the same person you come to it. There's not a songwriter alive that's passed through here and not been changed by this city. Usually they end up hurt by it. The old-timers call this city 'Gnashville.' You know, with a silent 'G'? Damn hell-hole chews you up, grinds you through its cogs and then spits you out like some nasty damn machine. Town's like a combine accident waiting to happen."

Johnny dragged a sleeve across his damp forehead. His forearm and fingers trembled.

Uppers for sure, I figured—that would also explain his alarming weight loss.

"Been working on a new song," he said. "Started to come to me during the church service, while I was standing at the back. Can't quite bring it together yet, but I'll lick it in the end."

He played a bit of that song for me. Promising, dark…stark and *true*. I hoped it was entirely John R's own.

I said, "I've been staying out at Jake Gantry's place, John. Learning some things about that man. Nothing too flattering. Not at all. You know, I don't think I'm going to be enjoying Jake's music like I once did. He's shaping up to have been some kind of racist monster."

"I've heard stories." Johnny smiled and his skittish dark eyes shifted from me to his guitar. "There's an old saying, Hector, trust the art, not the artist."

That chestnut comes up *a lot* in my daily life.

"That's right," I said, standing and switching off the recorder. "That's an old saying I'll wager was coined by a wig-wearing, Nudie-suit-clad, scum bucket of a crooner. I'll leave you to your songwriting, buddy."

"Just don't leave without saying goodbye," Johnny said, "Hear now?"

"Wouldn't think of it."

I ventured deeper into the Mother Church of Country Music.

A cold cuts table and makeshift bar took up room backstage.

On the floor in front of the stage, mourners mingled, ate sandwiches and swilled drinks. A few more sat in the chairs, listening to various performers tell stories about Jake Gantry between drunkenly slurred tunes.

The old boy himself occupied a mahogany box on stage, too close to the food and booze for my taste, looking like a wax statue in a blue Nudie suit spangled in rhinestones. There was a bolero tie bound around Jake's swollen neck. The tie was adorned with a sterling silver bronco. The body was only visible from the waist up—the lower portion of the coffin lid was closed. Some woman with a red beehive said, "They did a wonderful job on him, yes? He looks so peaceful. So *handsome*."

Yeah?

If she truly believed any of that, then fuck on a bicycle.

Peaceful? Maybe.

Handsome? That's was more than a stretch for the pudgy, racist and bewigged dead dwarf.

A hand took me by my arm. A smallish man, a singer-songwriter named Doc Jenkins, led me off to a corner. "Hector, it's been too damned long."

A trio of other singers sat in a sprawl of folding wooden chairs, passing a guitar back and forth. "Havin' us a guitar pull," Doc said, taking a slug of whisky from a flask. "Just no patience for anymore of Jake Gantry's standards that they're doing up front. So we're singin' our own songs. Jake being in the ground may finally open up some radio time for new voices. Figure some agent shedding crocodile tears for the old son of a bitch might be here, maybe even offer us a contract. Hell, what else to do here? Anyone who knew that son of a bitch surely couldn't love him."

I was introduced to some of those up-and-comers and got permission to run tape on them as they played.

Four songs in, wet and warm lips brushed the back of my neck.

Donna said, "I was beginning to think you were going to stand me up, Tex." I suppressed a chill.

The songwriters stopped to ogle the widow Perkins. Her bond hair was now swept into some French 'do that looked to have cost significant *dinero*. Donna's black dress flaunted beaucoup décolletage.

Donna's ensemble was decidedly not what I would consider funeral-worthy in most places, but in Nashville— or *G*nashville, as I now found myself thinking of it after Johnny's remark—maybe here it was standing garb for a country crooner's sendoff.

Anyway, it was a flavor of threads that potentially made *some* things stand, anyhow.

I wondered if the dishy dark dress was similar to the one Donna had worn when they planted the late Mr. Perkins.

And, looking at her, just like that, I *almost* rethought my plan to depart the Gantry house that night. I thought about what I'd told Esther, then tried to convince myself twice didn't have to mean *three* times.

Tomcat stuff, for sure: Right now I wanted to wreck that fancy hairdo with my fingers; to peel that slinky dress off her fine body and murder the day tangled in her hungry legs and arms, making one another breathless.

Donna said, "I have some people I want to introduce you to."

"Isn't that nice." I stood and began to fiddle with the recording gizmo—to shut it down. Curious, Donna took it from me before I finished and began her own fiddling. She flipped a switch; a strange clicking started. The needles jumped on the Geiger.

Donna gave me the strangest look.

Goddamn if the son of a bitching needle didn't shoot straight into the orange sector.

No doubt about it: A *positive* reading.

There was something radioactive in the Grand Ole Opry.

27

I wrestled the device from Donna's hand and flipped off the power switch. Smiling sheepishly, I said, "Sorry, it's a new model. Boasts all flavor of crazy features, including a radio. Hence the static sans a station, I reckon. Still learning it myself—clearly not effectively."

Donna, looking a bit skeptical, took my arm and led me off toward the bar. "Thirsty?"

"Very, now." My heart raced.

Jesus: the fucking nuclear trigger was apparently under my goddamn nose somewhere.

I said thickly, "You look quite fetching, by the way. I mean for a woman in mourning."

"I'm not mourning much, not for this one—you know that, Hector. What are you drinking, Tex?" She again eyed my gizmo dangling from its shoulder strap at my left flank.

"Scotch and soda will do the trick plenty fine." I fished some coins from my pocket and shoved them into the bartender's tip glass. "Tell me something, darlin'. Did old Jake maybe have some stuff of his stashed around this joint? Say, a footlocker? Something like that maybe?"

Donna narrowed her eyes. "Why do you ask that?"

I bit my lip, groped for a lie: "The boys over there you dragged me away from—the struggling songwriters. Fellas are feelin' sentimental about the old son of a bitch. They live too far from wagging tongues, I reckon to know better. That being so, they're waxing nostalgic about some of Jake's signature guitars. You know—those crazy custom jobs he had made with leatherwork around the rims and sound hole. Like that wild one he had made to look like an American flag. The songwriters have it in their heads they want to pass around one of those classic guitars while they play some of his tunes. Their own final tribute to the sorry old son of a bitch." I patted my gizmo. "I was going to record what follows."

That earned me a funny look from Donna, but she nodded, sipping her gin and tonic. "Jake practically *lived* here. He has a big locker downstairs, full of guitars and mandolins. Those awful spangled suits. More cowboy hats. Probably some more of those awful goddamn jet-black pompadour wigs."

"Can you take me there?"

Donna shook her head. "You'd need a key. That old colored man over there, the one with the broom? His name is Clarence. He's a Ryman custodian. He could get you down there. I mean, if it's really so important."

I patted her shoulder. "Back in a jiffy."

"You'd better be."

Feeling her gaze on me, I put the arm on old Clarence. He said, "Who are you, exactly, Mister?"

"Friend of the great man's wife's mother."

The old man narrowed his cataract-clouded eyes, trying to parse that one. "Guess that makes you ... well ... *sumthin'*... " he said finally.

Smiling like an undertaker, I said, "Boys are planning a little musical tribute, you see. They want to play a medley of Jake's hits, and play those songs on one of his signature guitars. A sentimental gesture, you know?"

"Alrighty, then."

The old man waved a hand for me to follow. He led me to a cabinet marked with a simple tin plaque that read "Jake Gantry."

I checked the headphone set connection to make certain the Geiger counter's clicking would be suppressed this time. The gauge dipped into the faint orange, a weaker reading than I'd gotten on the stage. I waved the gizmo over some mandolin and guitar cases: not a flicker of extra radiation. Not a blip.

Wherever the goddamn trigger was, it was close by the corpse, or maybe close by the cold cuts tables. I decided right there to skip the finger foods.

Annoyed, I put down the Geiger counter and rummaged through rhinestone-studded Nudie suits. I made a sour face and dipped groping digits into fancy leather boots. *Nada.*

For alibi purposes, I opened a few guitar cases, then picked out a red-white-and-blue Gibson with a spangled strap. This shadow cast from behind my back—Clarence. "That the one you want?"

"Precisely." I held the guitar and made what I thought might even be an actual chord, gave it a strum. "Sublime, yeah? That make you proud to be an American?"

"Uh … sure. I mean, I guess."

Guitar neck gripped in one hand and Geiger in the other, I followed the old man back out onto the main stage. I checked the gauge on my reader: the needle steadily climbed.

It mounted in direct proximity to the corpse.

Son of a bitch if the killing weapon wasn't evidently secreted somewhere in the old bastard's eternity box.

Doc Jenkins and company were still passing a guitar, crooning original compositions. I handed over Jake's patriotic Gibson guitar to Doc. "There you go, as promised."

The songwriter's brow wrinkled. "Well, thanks kindly, Hector," Doc said, looking confused. "I mean, I guess..."

Bud spotted me then. He ordered a second drink, then drifted my way. I accepted the offered glass. "Not single malt," Bud said, "but the best blended they've got."

"Which is to say one wrong-headed step north of swill. *Still.*" I held up a hand. "But hold it for me for a second." I walked over toward Jake Gantry's coffin, watched the needle on the Geiger counter spike again.

Didn't need to go the distance as I watched that indicator surge toward the red, and I surely didn't want to risk poisoning my innards anymore than I maybe already had. So I retreated back to Bud. He handed me my drink and said, "What, that body giving you the creeps, Hec?"

I took a slug of the scotch, savoring the burn, then slung the strap of the Geiger counter over one shoulder. Gripping Bud's arm, I led him down off the stage and toward the back of the Ryman, way back to the cheap seats by the stained-glass windows that were holdovers from the structure's days as a proper house of worship—before it became the "Mother Church of Country Music."

Bud narrowed his brown eyes. "Lass, you look worried."

I parked my ass on the back of one of the old pews. I dropped the Geiger counter on the seat next to mine.

"The damn thing we're lookin' for is *right here*, Bud. Here in the Ryman. It's in that wicked cocksucker's coffin. If you have even faint notions of a family of your own someday, I'd urge you to stay away from that stage, here on out. The box of Jake's might shrink your balls. Find some damn gopher to freshen your future drinks, hear? Or better, don't drink the damn booze. I reckon it's tainted. God only knows what poison it's swimming with now."

Bud pushed his white Vaquero hat back on his head with two fingers and plopped down on the back of a seat facing me. "No joking? It's here in the Opry, Hec?"

"Thing seems to be in the goddamn coffin, like I said. Maybe stashed down there around about the son of a bitch's boots if they didn't take him off at the knees to make room for the thing."

"Your *sure* of that, Lass?"

"One hundred percent, Bud."

"How bad is it? Is it out of the lead case?"

"Still shielded, I think. I'm just being extra cagey 'cause I value my balls, if not my overall health." I looked down at my lap, despite myself. "Don't want any scary side-effects. I just don't trust Chuck and Company as far as I could throw him in his hundred-dollar suit and French cuffs shirt. *Never* trust a man who wears cufflinks, by the way, Bud, no more than you ever trust one who favors gin."

On that note, I drained what was left of my drink. "Why don't we get out of here, pal? Need to case next moves now that we've found this crazy goddamn weapon."

Bud nodded. "Where would we go?"

I said, "Might as well know now, Bud: I packed my stuff and threw it in the trunk of the Chevy. I'm not going back to that swanky dump. Stay on there if you want, but if you could give me a key to your place, I'll bunk there."

"I'll move out of Jake's mansion, too," Bud said. He made a face. "We both know I'm just in Logan's way. No other way to put it."

No doubt Bud *was* in the way... and *in that way*.

"Okay, then," I said. "While the women of the house are otherwise engaged, let's go back and fetch your stuff. We'll think out our strategy for this other along the way."

Bud said, "Okay... we—" I suddenly put a hand to Bud's chest.

Urgently, I asked, "Why in the damn coffin? Why put the damned canister in there and risk having it buried?"

The poet shrugged. I fished my pocket for coins. I passed Bud a fistful of change. "Please run to a gas station would you, Bud? Buy us a street map of Nashville?"

"Sure, Hec." Bud looked confused, but amiably compliant.

While Bud went in search of my roadmap, I found a payphone in a small compartment off the auditorium. Rick Corin the cop said, "What, you solve another case for me?"

"I may be on the way to doing that very thing," I said. "Have a question for you—and admittedly, it's going to sound queer enough."

"I can hardly wait, Lassiter."

I slipped out my notepad and pen. "I assume one of your boys is going to be riding a motorcycle or cruiser at the head of Jake Gantry's funeral procession?"

"One at the front, one at the back," he said.

"What's the itinerary on that?"

Corin sounded annoyed but rattled off the route from the Ryman to the bone yard.

I thanked him and hung up before he could press for an explanation for my question.

Bud dusted snow off his shoulders. His cheeks and nose were red from the cold and running through the icy rain. "Got your map right here, Hec."

"You're the best, Bud."

We unfolded the map and ferreted out the streets I'd written down.

"This is Jake Gantry's funeral procession route," I said as we found roads. Handing Bud my pen, I requested, "Trace it for me on the map, yeah, Bud?"

He did that as I recited road names.

Bud soon frowned.

I said, "Something stand out to you there, son? Somethin' about the combination of streets in that funeral procession route and a bomb in Jake's coffin give you pause, kid?"

"Yes," Bud said, gray-faced. "It really does, Lass."

The poet confirmed my worst suspicions: "This part along here?" He traced a bony finger along the map. He said, "This is an all-Negro neighborhood."

That made it clear enough.

Shaking my head I said, "Nah, Bud, if these bastards have their way, that's a crater, come mornin'."

28

Walking out of the Ryman we bumped into Logan, mounting its steps. This funny smile was pasted across the singer-songwriter's face. I dropped a hand on Logan's shoulder, stopping him mid-step. "What's goin' on, kid?"

"Great news, Hector! I just signed with Genevieve's agent!"

It came as a snarl. I begged, "You *chucklehead!* Please tell me you goddamn *didn't!*"

Logan said it, proud-like: "Just signed me a contract for representation, Hec. Enough of this negotiating contracts for myself. Enough of this handling my own bookings. Or you doing it for me. Forget all that. Got me a proper agent, now. Jonas Parker will see to all that so I can just work on writing and recording. 'Do what talent does,' as he puts it. I get to be an artist, now. Signed the contract on the back of Jonas' El Dorado. That is one sweet sled he's got. Get me my first real recording deal, I'm going to have a Caddy just like it."

Now I was seething. "You signed a damned agent's contract you didn't show to me first?" I shook my head. "Jesus Christ, this isn't something you do in a parking lot on a whim, goddamn it, boy. You get one shot to make a major-label debut in this business. You don't want it fouled up by some lousy, bottom-feeding agent."

"He's Genevieve's agent," he said again. "Major talent there."

"If she wasn't a looker, Gen would never have a recording contract," I said. "And kid, with her penchant for the bottle, and that mother of hers keeping a boot to her pretty backside, when she's thirty and all the hooch shows on that face and figure, her Cashbox and Billboard positions are going to fall like a goddamn rock. And you, Logan? You ain't pretty enough to be a slam dunk hit, kid. What you've got is all that girl lacks—real talent. But sadly, talent is no guarantee in itself. It ain't a meritocracy in this town. That's why you need the *right* agent. A smart shark with connections and a track record."

Logan winked at me. Fucking *winked*. "That's just it, Hec—that arrest thing, it's a great *hook*, Jonas said. We're gonna to play it up. Jo wants me to write some prison songs, a couple of murder ballads."

Bud looked away down the street. He said, "If you give me your keys, Lass, I'll warm up the Bel Air."

I tossed Bud the keys then squared off against Logan. "Let me see this so-called contract, Logan."

"Don't have a final copy on me yet."

"Yet you *signed* it anyway. Goddamn your stupidity you cow-simple fool."

Boy was belligerent now. "That's right. I surely did that. Sign, I mean. It's my career. My decision."

"You stupid young son of a bitch." I fished out a cigarette and fiddled with my Zippo. Not even a spark now. I cast my unlit cigarette into the snow and pocketed the spent lighter. "Kid, you're just about the most exasperating soul I've come across in fifty eight goddamn years on this planet of fools. What exactly the hell is a Jonas damn Parker? Who are his other clients?"

"Genevieve, like I said," Logan rattled off a half-dozen other names—not a one of the rest was familiar to me. Call it bitter vindication.

"So he's a shyster with a single viable client," I said. "Maybe two clients, presuming you have any success at all under his direction. But that's no foregone conclusion, kid. Damn it, anyway, Logan, you don't really want to market yourself as some sorry and pseudo ex-con, do you? Really? Do you *really* want to spend the rest of your life singing about San Quentin and running from the cops and rotting on death row? Because kid, it's going to make for a pretty soul-killing medley when you're thirty, forty... Hell, fifty, *if* you make it that far. One day you're going to be too old to be convincing singing those kinds of songs anymore. That's about the time you'll be relegated to road houses and the county fair circuit."

I squeezed his shoulder harder. "Listen hard to me Logan: Being a creative artist, it's not just about making a splash up front, kid. It's about growing a career as a musician. Same as it is for authors and painters. You've got to think about your long game. Look to the arc of the career, not just your first release with a major label. Everything, every step, has to be calculated. Cased and all the angles spotted. Creation is soulful. Making a living creating is a potentially soul-killing chess game. But it is *the* game, son, and we have to play it like pros. We have to play it to win."

Logan waved a hand. "Hector, it's done, got it? I'm happy, really thrilled, to have a proper agent. Besides—and no offense, old man—how can I seriously take your advice, given your attitude about your own so-called *career*? All this moaning and bitching across three states about people always confusing you with your books and characters. About them always expecting you to be some kind of particular and impossible-to-live-up-to man's man based on their readings of your books. Hell, you're the one always bellyaching about the scandal rags dropping your name. Always the one talking about chucking it all and going off under some alias to lay low. Do you *really* have the guts to think you're a good candidate for giving me career advice? From where I sit, hell, you're a goddamn warning."

That was more than a little like a kidney punch.

Kid really landed one on me.

Nevertheless, I managed a kind of smile, trying to come across friendly and helpful. "Look sonny, just introduce me to this Parker asshole. Maybe I can still get the contract adjusted in some favorable way. Maybe get a little back for you. And I'm willing to do it with a gun to that cocksucker's head. Because, well, I get the sense if I read that contract, I'll see this son of a bitch Parker owns you, kiddo, body and soul."

Logan brushed off my hand. "It's *done*. Jonas is already off to notarize the contract."

"Kid, that's another sorry sign this contract stinks to hell and gone. A notary is supposed to be present at the signing. He's supposed to be there to *witness* the contract being inked, not rubber stamp it for some shyster with an El Dorado after the fact."

Logan changed the subject on me. "Gotta get back inside to Gen. Where are you and Bud going? This shindig could go hours, yet, you know. Party is far from over."

Shindig? Party?

I said, "I've done my bit of respect paying at that wake for your girlfriend's rotting and evil ex, dumbass. One last thing: When do they plant old Jake?"

The kid's brow furrowed. "Bury him, you mean? Tomorrow morning, about ten. Again, where are you and Bud going?"

"Back to the Gantry place to fetch Bud's duds. We're movin' out. Hell, I already cleared out. Those ladies are the worst kind of news, both of 'em." I searched his face. "But I expect you'll be staying on, yeah?"

"Yep. I mean, I do mean to. Why are you leaving?" Logan hesitated, then said, "Does Donna know you're going?"

Figured then the kid knew about me and the damned mother. More the reason to flee.

"Donna will know when she gets home," I said flatly. "Sincerely? I think she's *extra* bad news, kid. Maybe the worst news for her own daughter. And this jury is still out, at least a little, on that girl you're courting. At best, GG's a sorry wreck, sonny. She desperately needs a shrink and a big body of water between her and her own wicked Mama Rose Lee in there if she's gonna see thirty with anything close to the face and figure she's riding to fame now. Hell, she needs that distance if she's gonna have spit's chance of making twenty-five."

Red-faced, Logan twisted the toe of his boot in the snow, said tightly, "How's about we meet for a drink tomorrow night, Hector? Before you leave town, I mean. Say 'see ya' over some good booze? End this on a better tone than we're headed for now?"

Well, that sounded like a full and hard dismissal to me.

I said, "So you're really staying on in this goddamn town then?"

"It's my plan. Jonas has got me a songwriting gig over at—"

"No!" I cut him off. "Now I *know* this cretin is no damn good, Logan," I said. "Do you know how those goddamn songwriter factories are run? Like a goddamn slave galley, that's how! They lock you in a room from 8 a.m. to 5 p.m. with some other songwriter who probably has a fraction of your talent, kid. They don't care who they partner you with, it's likely just some other sucker they tricked into signing a devil's contract. Despite all that, they expect you two to come out of that box of a room with at least two songs they can peddle at the end of every workday. They pay you chump change for those ditties and they hold royalty rights as their own and make all the real money. Depending on the songwriting factory this Jonas Parker just sold you to, you may actually have to wear a suit and even a fucking necktie while you write those goddamn middling songs for too-little *dinero*. It's the land of the man in the gray flannel suit you've sold yourself to, boy. Nothin' truly creative about any of that, not one lick."

Logan pressed his hands to his ears as if I was some goddamn harpy or siren to be shut out.

"We're *done* with this talk, Hector," he said, hands still pressed tight to his ears like a goddamn child. "You know where to find me if you still want that drink tomorrow. But no more talk about this or my agent if we meet for that drink. Got it, Hector?"

I smiled and shook my head. "Oh, I get it. And I ain't thirsty, not a bit. *Adios*, Logan. See you in the discount bins, kid."

29

Cursing goddamn Logan "Buddy" Loy Burke, I picked up a newspaper and ducked into my Bel Air.

Bud had presumed to take the wheel position again. That was just as well—I was spoiling for a fight after my angry exchange with goddamn Logan Burke. I felt like drawing someone else's blood and so wasn't a good candidate to drive among the civilized population.

I tried to get a cigarette going with my spent Zippo, then cursed and thrust it to the back of the glove compartment of the Bel Air when I failed to get anything close to a spark. I held out a hand, palm-up. "You still offering that loaner Zippo, Bud?"

Fiske smiled uncertainly and handed me his Zippo emblazoned with the quote from my long-ago novel, *Border Town*. "Keep it as long as you like. Hell, it's yours forever, now. You really okay, Lass?"

I spun the wheel on Bud's Zippo with a thumb—got instant blue-orange flame. I fired up a Pall Mall and said, "Bud, if a man of musical taste wanted to go to a Nashville bar, and if he wanted to spend a few hours hearing good music nobody else has heard yet, where exactly would that man go?"

Bud smiled and said, "So you want me to drop you at such a place while I go and clear us out from the Gantry place?"

"It's the strongest notion I have presently, Bud. Logan went and signed a management contract with Gen Gantry's agent a bit ago. I sense a catastrophic career mistake in that. So screw the stupid son of a bitch. Why should I care more for his career than he seems to? It's still a few hours until we have to joust with Prescott Bush. I just have a hankering to sit in a bar with good music somewhere, Bud. Have me a notion to listen to some fresh and edgy music and push certain things of moment far from my mind for a while."

Then I opened the local daily paper, found a photo of myself under some gossip banner: "Seen & Spotted." I showed Bud, said, "You were wondering how I was going to draw out that racist prison writer. Well, here it is, I guess. I sense a government plant in this gossip item."

Bud nodded sourly and nudged up the windshield wipers against the mounting sleet.

I tipped my head back against the seat and blew smoke toward the cracked passenger's side window. "Here's my vision of the minute, Bud. In no particular order, I aim to duck dumb-ass songwriters and fetching but poison widows who'll stop at nothing to turn a buck on their saucy daughters. I propose to dodge atomic apocalypse and racist songwriters and would-be jailhouse novelists. At least for a fleeting time. Make sense enough, buddy?"

Bud smiled and hung a left, palming the wheel. "All that makes perfect sense, Hec. I know a real good place, Lass. When do you want to me to pick you up?"

"Say six? And is there a drugstore close by where I can buy a legal pad? I feel like writing while I wallow in that good, unknown music."

"Sure. You drafting the next crime novel?"

"I say this exclusively to you, Bud: *No.* Aiming for something very different. I want to try my hand again at writing the novel I couldn't get my arms around back in twenty-four."

Bud shot me a look. "Seriously? You were in Paris back then, weren't you, Lass? Hemingway, Stein and Ford? The Lost Generation crowd?"

"That's right, Bud. And I wasn't a crime novelist then, not yet. Not even close. I was sweating blood trying to be a very different kind of writer. Now I think that I want to try hard again to be that author, Bud. I want to try to do that while there's still maybe a little time left me."

30

In a corner booth by a crackling hearth, I sat with my notebook, twenty-four hand-written pages into a novel that had no blood and not a single murder so far.

No duplicitous, pretty women, either. I wasn't going to venture into any of that tired, over-worked *noir* territory this trip to the well.

Hell, maybe I'd never, ever do that again, I told myself.

More—and more importantly—I *loved* what I was writing. I knew I could push this piece to its perfect, proper end and turn it over to some as-yet unmet and fresh literary agent who'd rally behind the new Mister Me and push hard to get his worthy manuscript published as a proper literary novel.

But maybe all that would at last have to happen under one of those pseudonyms I'd so long dodged.

A sexy, smoky-voiced singer-songwriter was the night's headliner at the bar Bud selected for me. She was brunette, pretty and slender, yet busty and very leggy. I have a type, sure: She was that type's sultry embodiment. The singer had flashing dark eyes and a penchant for perfectly twanged-up torch songs: very much my kind of country singer and woman.

Her repertoire included not a single tune I'd heard of, yet every song she sang reached me and I loved, *down deep*. The woman was clearly a songwriter to be reckoned with, a true and rare find these stingy days. She was someone I dearly hoped no Jonas Parker ever got his bloody talons into.

The barmaid was palpably annoyed with my water-only consumption, so I ordered a whiskey with water back; something I intended to nurse. In honest admiration, I asked the fetching singer-songwriter be sent any stipulated favorite drink when she reached the end of her first set.

I was bent low over my notebook, savoring the belly burn of my stingily sipped whiskey and mired deep in the country of my new novel when a shapely shadow fell across my notebook. The singer-songwriter smiled and hoisted a virgin glass. "I'm told I have you to thank for this, Mister."

"I was admiring your songwriting. Call it a less-than-worthy tribute to your righteous talent."

"You're a writer too," she said. "I mean, that looks like a manuscript to me. Is that a short story? A novel?"

"I am a novelist."

I instantly regretted confessing that.

The sultry singer-songwriter tugged out the chair across from me and sat down. She sipped her drink, teased savoring lips with tongue, then said, "Have I heard of you? Might I have read you?"

I wetted my lips and sipped my drink. "Sincerely doubt it," I said. "I sell books in the dozens, at best, probably. You, on the other hand, are excellent. Transcendent...And very earthy in your content. I admire your writing. What do I call you, Miss...?"

She presumed to help herself to one of my Pall Malls. She lit it with Bud's Zippo I'd dropped on top of the pack of smokes. She glanced at the inscription and smiled uncertainly. "*Hm.* I *dunno.* Anyway, I'm Brandy Sparks." She held up Bud's lighter and wrinkled her pretty, lightly freckled dappled nose, inspecting it. "This 'Hector Lassiter' person, is he you?"

"No. God in hell, *no.* That's just a callow quote I once stupidly admired as a kid when I couldn't get any traction on reality. Outgrew it long ago and fast chucked it aside as anything that matters. That Zippo's just a tool for a vice, now."

Somehow I got that out without choking on my own goddamn, half-lying tongue.

"Call me..." I reached for some *maybe* names, then settled impulsively on the wickedly personal familiar:

"Call me Beau. I am Beau Devlin."

I had no idea in the moment how that collision of charged handles would stick.

We shook hands. Brandy said, "Then I give you credit, Beau. Even writing your own stuff as intently you've been, you've *still* been an attentive audience. Maybe the only soul in the joint I believe truly listened to all my lyrics. Here's the thing I want you to know: Every night, I pick one person in the audience to sing to. *You're* my audience tonight. Is that an okay thing with you, Beau?"

Oh my God, but I was stricken, then and there, with a terrible passion for that woman.

"I'm humbled," I confessed. "Your songs are really wonderful. Stark and sublime. You're going to be huge in your time. You know that, don't you?"

She smiled. "You silver-tongued devil. From your lips to God's ear."

She blew some smoke and looked at the cigarette. "A filthy habit. But it adds husk to the voice, and so...?"

"Maybe not like you think." I dared to reach over and snub out her smoke. "Some novelists delude themselves the same way about booze or drugs. Convince themselves it opens up the mind. That's a delusion. If you're writing for eternity, you must write sober. And troubadours like you? They have to sing full-throated and pure."

"You really believe that, Beau?"

"All the way up. Never did buy the notion of altered states of mind firing worthy writing. Not for a second. Older I get, the *more* I believe that's so."

She eyed her dead cigarette. "And, so...?"

"And so you probably sound wonderful without those damned coffin nails."

"*Maybe*. What time do you have, Beau?"

I showed her my Timex's face—didn't want to put on my glasses so I could see the time myself. Vanity, again.

She smiled and said, "Next set starts too soon. Will you be around after I close, Beau?"

"I *wish*. Afraid I have to push on."

Part of me didn't want to go, of course. Not that I was all that worried about standing up Prescott Bush. But even now, that goddamn time bomb was ticking away at the feet of Jake Gantry's corpse, so far as I knew.

She smiled uncertainly. "I'll be here tomorrow. Well, all week, really. Think you might find your way back here tomorrow, Beau?"

"I really don't know, darlin'. Honestly? Probably *not*."

She smiled and finished off her drink, then reached across the table and turned my wrist so she could read my Timex again. "It's that time. *Please* give me a request, Beau."

I thought hard and fast about it, said, "Know a Mexican tune named *Cancion Mixteca*?"

That ditty perplexed her. "Can't say as I do. Try again?"

"Then how about something American but not so country? A real torch song. Say, *Where or When?*"

"Oh, I know that one. I love it. And I could maybe twang it up."

"That one, then, please."

"I sure hope you'll be back tomorrow night, Beau."

Smiling, I took her hand, kissed its back. "Break a leg, honey."

Hang around?

Sensed I could have … to some certain, again breathless end.

But that wasn't something I thought about for too long. Just couldn't convince myself it was an okay thing to run a game by a fellow creative writer on this dark night of the soul—couldn't bed some worthy writer while I was trucking under a half-assed and impulsive alias myself.

So when Brandy was deep into a second song, eyes closed and throwing some soulful rasp into her tune sans cigarettes, I closed my notebook and slipped out the front door. That was cowardly, in its way—let's agree upon that, up front.

I wandered a few doors down to a neighboring bar with half-an-hour left until Bud was scheduled to pick me up. The bartender shot me a look when I stalked toward the phone booth in the back, ordering no drink on the way.

I sat down in that booth, closed its folding door and slipped out my little black book.

By my calculation, it was late afternoon in Los Angeles.

My true love's elderly grandmother answered.

I asked for Alicia—the woman I'd fallen so hard for—*and lost*—last year, when Bud and I had first jousted with Prescott Bush.

Bud ... Bush.

And now here I was, reaching out to Alicia.

It was scenting of old home week.

My sentimental side, unbridled and given its head, was running wild and heedless, dragging along the rest of me for an unpredictable, probably doomed short ride.

That voice—a year and some weeks since I'd last seen her, last heard her stepping into me. Her silky, strong tones tore through me, down to bone.

Alicia Vicente, talking to me, again, across all those miles.

One word, but it bored to my core: "*Hola?*"

I still had a shirt that smelled of her. I had a single photo I'd stared at during too many a cold New Mexico night.

My voice sounded thin to me, too scared: "Alicia, it's Hector. I ... I thought I'd see how you are doing."

Hesitation, goddamn it.

The pause seemed to lag on, forever.

Then: "I'm fine ... I'm just fine. Where are you Héctor? Are you here in California?"

It sounded to me like maybe she hoped that was not the case.

"In Tennessee, actually. Guess who I ran into here in Nashville? Bud! Mr. Fiske came here to write an article on Johnny Cash. Bud is looking great and living clean, no cigarettes. He's well on his way to establishing himself as a songwriter, here. Isn't that great?"

I heard a sound, realized it was a baby crying.

Alicia had a *toddler* last I knew.

Now there was a baby? My stomach rolled. Surely it meant there was some other man, yes?

There was some rustling, some shushing of the child, then Alicia said, "Why are you calling me now, Héctor?"

That brought me up short.

I stumbled, then said, "Seeing Bud, maybe. Thinking long and hard about last year, something I do every day, frankly. I ... I felt like calling you tonight. I sorely miss you, darlin'. I miss you desperately. I do that all the time, really."

Alicia pressed harder: "And so ... what of that?"

"I've been thinkin' hard about you, darling. Thinking about *us* for a long time now."

I laughed nervously. "I mean, I truly do think about you every day. And every night. *A lot* at night. And I've been thinking about your daughter and even your grandmother."

Silence.

I'd never met Alicia's daughter, face to face. Never met her grandmother.

But it was *true* that they dogged my thoughts, *too*.

I pressed on, firmly: "You don't have to say anything, Alicia. I just want you to know that I'm utterly *done* with me."

There was a moment of silence, a terrible few seconds during which I thought that maybe she had hung up on me. Then she said, "What do you mean, you're *done* with yourself? You're not thinking of ... well, *hurting* yourself, are you, Héctor?"

I wet my lips, gathered my focus. "No, not *that*, not at *all*. It's not like you're thinking in that way. I'm just so *tired* of myself, honey. I'm just so damned tired of being this thing that's become *me*. I'm thinking maybe I'm just going to walk away from it all. Figuring I'm truly prepared to soon walk away from this sorry life of mine. I just don't want to live like this anymore, darlin'. Hell, I don't even want to write the books I've been writing, not anymore. All that dark and doom laden stuff is poisoning me inside.

Truth is, I'm sick past death of *Hector Lassiter*. Tired and bored with myself, literally beyond words."

More silence. Eventually, a deep sigh. Alicia said, "So what exactly are you saying, Héctor? I'm sorry, but I don't think I understand what you mean."

How could she understand? I was groping my way toward the future with each stumbling word I was putting to her. Hell, I wasn't certain where I was presently headed, not really.

"What I'm saying is that I'm thinkin' real hard about walking away from Hector Lassiter, I think. *Burying* him, so to speak. Maybe *forever*. I've started writing that different book we talked about last year on that beach in Venice, California. I'm really writing a *proper* novel. No murder, no killings to come between these covers. I want to publish it under some other name, I think. If I do that, if I change my way of living and put Hector Lassiter to rest, so to speak, I want—I *wonder* if you'll think of letting me back into your life. I'm going down to Cuba in a few days. You see, Marlene talked me into patching it up with Hem. Ernest and I started doing that on the phone a few weeks ago. So I'm going to Hem's place in Cuba to finish smoothing things over. Close out some old business. When that's done, I'm going to start that new quiet life. Once I'm into it, I'd like to visit you, Alicia. Maybe we could just share a quiet dinner, no strings, no promise of more?"

I could hear her breathing. I imagined how she might look at the other end of the line, the long thick black hair that nearly reached her waist... her skin the color of whisky. Her dark eyes that always seemed to see through me. She was probably twisting the phone cord in her slender fingers and biting that full lower lip, one saucy, long leg crossed over the other. She was in L.A. and so it was far warmer where she was. Maybe she would be wearing some sleeveless dress. I remembered kissing her bare shoulders; the tickle of the soft, dark hair against my lips as they grazed the down at the back of her neck.

The scent of her perfume was suddenly and vividly present in the phone booth with me.

After a long silence, Alicia said, "I really have to go now, Héctor. But... well, you go to Cuba and you do fix things with your friend, Papa. You keep writing that new novel. You take real care of yourself and please give my best to Bud."

Another long pause ensued; I respected the silence.

After a time, Alicia said, "Next year, when you're a few months into this new life you envision, if you really are settled into that new life, and if things are at last truly quiet..."

I held my breath, waiting for it...

"*If* you've *really* made this change, and if you find yourself in Los Angeles, then you have my number. Ask me to dinner again then, yes?"

It wasn't a closed door, thank God.

"You don't have to say anything back," I said. "I just need you to hear it. I love you, Alicia."

No hesitation, now. "I love you, too, Héctor. But that's never been the problem between us, you know."

I knew, at last.

"The problem is me," I said. "Always has been. So I'm aiming to fix that, *mi corazon*. We'll talk again in 1959. Please give a hug from me to your little girl."

"*Adios*, Héctor. Mind yourself well. *Vaya con Dios*."

"*Adios*, Alicia."

31

I was again standing in front of the bar where Bud had dropped me, well under the canopy to stay out of the falling snow, when the Bel Air rolled up out front. I gestured for Bud to join me.

"What's up, Lass?" He checked his watch, limping up to me. "Just have time to make it to our meeting with Bush if we get going right now."

"We will," I said. "Just meant to caution you again about talking too freely in my car—seems the sucker is bugged, again, by at least one foreign party, or maybe more. So regards the missing device, etc. we only say what we want people to know. Clear on that?"

Bud nodded. "Crystal."

I slapped his arm. "Good. So let's roll, Kato."

I swung into the passenger seat. It was toasty warm in the Chevy. I found some Roy Orbison and cranked him up: that voice of good old Roy's, like a soulful ghost. Let our clandestine listeners bask in *that*.

❧

We were sitting in a back booth of Mom's when two men in black suits wedged in alongside us. They were clearly government types. But they had a more conservative cut to their suits than the duds Chuck Easton's minions had sported. One of the black-clad men said, "I.D., please?"

I carefully reached for my wallet with two fingers. Bud did the same. For kicks I almost handed over Basil Sloan's Kentucky driver's license—his wallet still resided in my overcoat pocket. Not sure why I hadn't tossed it, yet. But I wasn't up to teasing these fellas who I figured for being stooges to Sen. Prescott Bush.

The men checked our driver licenses, and as they passed them back, the one across from me reached over and pulled back the flap of my sport's jacket to reveal the butt of my holstered Colt.

"Glad you're taking your safety seriously, sir," he said. He looked at Fiske. "And you?"

Bud said, "There's an automatic in my waistband, at my back."

"Good," the stranger said. "Okay, then. We're going to go get the senator."

They were gone about two minutes, then the two men returned with two more men in tow. The first, Senator Bush, was tallish, white-haired, and looked like the banker he once was.

The other man was unremarkable, a bit shorter than Sen. Bush.

I slid out of the booth and extended a hand. Prescott shook it first and said, "Hector Lassiter? We meet face-to-face at last."

"Senator."

Bud and Prescott shook hands then, Bud looking wary all the while. I offered a hand to the other man and said, "And you, sir?"

"This is Ernst," said Prescott, before the man could answer for himself. "Let's leave it at that for now, please."

I looked the senator, said, "But he's to be trusted, you're saying." I slid back into the booth alongside Bud. "That *is* the drift?"

The senator winked. "That's right, Hector. That's indeed the drift, as you say."

So we were already down to a first-name basis. Heady.

Ernst slid into the booth across the table from Bud and I, then Prescott followed him. Sniffing, the senator said, "Very quaint place."

As he looked around at all the framed and autographed photos of country crooners, Prescott's black-clad stooges commandeered a booth behind us.

"To the good, it's well off the tourist maps," I said. "At least for gun-toting foreign operatives of unknown Middle Eastern-origin. Those boys seem to be busy using their idle time to try and lay American women when they're not kidnapping writers and demanding gone-missing hydrogen bomb components."

Prescott arched an eyebrow. "I sense there's more behind that rant than your penchant for glib remarks, Hector."

"That's right," I said. "Not long after talking to you, some Middle East-types tried to kidnap me at gunpoint. He said his faction—whatever that is—is determined to lay hands on the *component* before the 'Jews' can maybe take possession."

Prescott and his guest exchanged portentous scowls.

"Many people are interested in getting this device, just like you warned me," I said. "Not so sure which desert hell hole these old boys who tried to get the drop on me call home, but..."

"The so-called device is indeed a very hot commodity," Prescott said. "No surprise in that, of course. This man— these *men*—who tried to kidnap you, what became of them?"

"The cohorts I gave the slip to. The man who tried to get the drop on me in my car I dropped down a sewer hole. Likely as not, he's asphyxiated by now. I doubt he could reach the manhole cover I closed over him, and if he did, he wouldn't have the leverage to lift it."

"Very resourceful." The senator almost smiled. "Tell me where you, *er*, deposited him. I'll have some men check, just in case he's still alive and can therefore be interrogated."

I did that. Prescott said, "I should learn to stop under-estimating you, Hector."

"You maybe should at that," I said.

Dottie wandered over then. She had one hand thrust down the pocket of her apron. I figured she was probably fingering her hatpin and sizing up the politician and his cohorts for potential to cause trouble. She probably didn't see many suits and ties in her place, not proper suits and neckties, anyway.

I said, "Whiskey sodas for Bud and I, darlin'. What wets your whistle, Pres'?"

The politician smiled frostily at Dottie and said, "Gin and tonic, please. Ernst?" The senator's mystery guest ordered a sherry.

Dottie made a face at that and I said, "Can you do that for Ernst, Dot?"

She gave me a funny look and said, "I think there might be some around. Maybe."

Dottie turned and went in search some bottle squirreled away somewhere. Once she left us, Prescott said, "Have you had any success?"

"I think I know where the device is now, although I still have to recover it," I said.

That admission resulted in another ominous glance between Prescott and Ernst.

Bud said, "Sir, you know who I am, but your friend here..."

I said, "Bud's right, your honor. Who's your buddy? What's his stake in all this?"

Prescott held a finger to his lips as Dottie returned with tray of drinks. She handed Bud and I our whiskeys and the politician his gin and tonic. She said, "Be right back." I watched as she ducked down behind the bar, pulled up a bottle and blew dust from it, triggering a coughing jag from one of her regulars. She opened the bottle, poured some in a glass and held it up to the light, this dubious look on her face. Dot returned to our table, placing the glass in front of Ernst.

She said to the stranger, "Be sure to drink more than just this one, hon', since I cracked the seal. All my time here, nobody's *ever* asked for that stuff, and I'm not sure how long it'll keep now that it's open."

The little man smiled and nodded; Dottie drifted off.

After a sip of my whiskey, I said, "I put it to you again, Prescott. What's your friend's stake in all this?"

"That's honestly up to you, Hector," Prescott said. "I'm hoping to appeal to the better angels of your nature. I'm offering you and Mr. Fiske a chance to leave a remarkable legacy. Tonight, I'm offering you a chance to shape history, to change the fate of a people."

32

I said, "Once again, who exactly are you, Ernst?"

"No, that is not the way we should begin," Prescott said. Bush sipped his gin and tonic. As I've remarked before, I've always distrusted gin drinkers. But in this case, I had this intuition about Bush, some gut instinct to cut him some slack for his dubious taste in hard liquor.

Prescott pointed a finger at his companion. "Tell them Ernst, tell them everything. I feel we can trust these two men, in this matter, at any rate."

Ah, Prescott: bastard was indeed still spoiling over the pig-in-a poke skull I'd sold him and a certain Yale fraternity last year. I stifled any expression that might be construed as gloating.

The stranger sipped some more of his sherry and twisted the glass nervously. Ernst said, "In 1949, an associate of mine, a Mr. Gimmel, began surveying the Negev Desert, seeking uranium."

Bud said to Ernst, "You—and this Gimmel—you're both Israelis, aren't you?"

I added, "And the uranium search in that damned desert—you're seeking components for your own atomic weapon?"

Before Ernst could answer, Prescott said, "You're both right. Israel's neighbors are saber rattling, Hector... Bud. *No*, that's putting it far too mildly. Israel's bordering countries have pledged nothing less than Israel's annihilation."

I took a deeper drink of my whiskey, savoring the burn. "These neighbors of your country, Ernst, do they conceivably have their own atomic weapons?"

"Not yet, and perhaps not for many years. Likely not for many decades, in most cases."

Nodding, I said, "How far has your own bomb project progressed?"

Ernst said, "For some years, we been working with those in France. In 1956, we had French assurance of their provision of an 18MWt heavy water reactor. Then there was... a complication."

"That Suez Canal flapdoodle," Prescott cut in, turning a lip. "In the wake of that 'crisis' and more attendant Soviet saber rattling—as well as French self-recrimination for reneging on the first promised reactor—France again pledged a reactor for Israel, this one a 24MWt reactor. Construction on the device commenced late last year."

Ernst put down his glass, smacking his lips after another quaff of his sherry. "We arranged to have the components of the reactor designated devices for a desalinization project to cover the true nature of our undertaking. We obtained the heavy water from Norway."

I said softly, "So soon your country *will* have its own bomb?"

Prescott and Ernst exchanged another glance. Ernst nodded, indicating Prescott had best answer my question. Bush said, "The French—by that, I mean damned de Gaulle (he said it like it was the foulest of obscenities he could muster)—is back-pedaling. Perhaps a bargaining ploy. But perhaps not. Charles is threatening to withhold the enriched uranium necessary to complete the first atomic device."

So there it was. It was clear to me what was intended now.

Bush was angling to have little old private citizen me turn over the recovered U.S. "component" to Ernst—off all the books, presumably—so Israel's first atomic weapon could be completed.

I took my time, lifting my glass to my mouth, aware of these three sets of eyes appraising me, measuring my reaction and guessing at what my decision might be. The whiskey still burned my belly and I realized it had been a while since my last meal.

Rather unnecessarily, pretending to buy myself some more time to weigh my options, I said, "You want me to give you our missing device, is that it Ernst?"

"We want you to gift Israel the *component*, yes," Prescott said. "Once the prototype is complete, through channels, various intelligence services will be permitted to learn Israel has a viable atomic weapon. Once one bomb is known to be completed and viable, there will be little point in de Gaulle or others denying Israel further enriched uranium deposits. More importantly, Hector, think of the difference it will make for a country and a long-persecuted people. A difference you—and your young friend—will have made possible against racists of the worst stripe."

Ernst searched my eyes. "Please, Mr. Lassiter, I beg you do this. It's not any exaggeration to say you will have provided my country, and my people, with a shield that will protect our sovereignty, perhaps for several generations to come."

I bit my lip and sighed. I glanced at Bud. Having long ago guessed at the young poet's politics, I had little doubt whose side of this wild proposition Bud was likely to favor. Bud didn't surprise me. He said, "Lass, it's not like our side doesn't have plenty of other bombs."

No, it wasn't like that, not at all.

Irresistibly, I thought of luckless Cassie Allegre. I'd once gotten tangled up in her quest for a supposedly game-changing weapon that would forever change a racial equation, or so she desperately believed.

But the so-called "Spear of Destiny" she and my acquaintance Orson Welles had sought remained a likely myth, to my mind. Fairytale Sunday school stuff and Bible Hokum.

Atom and hydrogen bombs?

All too real. All too game-changing.

Nodding slowly, I raised my glass again. I checked the other glasses, then signaled Dottie. She bustled over and checked Ernst's sherry glass. I said, "Set 'em up again, sweetheart. And make Ernst's a double. And do you have anything I can eat? Think I'm flirting with a diabetic coma, honey."

"I have chili," Dottie said. "Will that do?"

"Sold. And extra crackers and Tabasco sauce." I nodded at Bush. "While we wait for that, how about if just you and I take the air, Senator?"

Prescott nodded and rose. He signaled his stooges to remain behind. "I'll be fine," he told them, then, "I mean, you *did* confirm Mr. Lassiter is in fact armed?"

They nodded. "Then no worries," Bush said. "I trust Mr. Lassiter's reputation with a six-shooter."

We shrugged on our overcoats and edged out the front door into another snow flurry.

I lit a cigarette with Bud's Zippo and stamped my feet to keep warm. My hand was shaking a little from the low blood sugar. "This Easton, who is he really, Senator?"

Prescott paused, said, "Formerly, he was CIA. Now? Even I don't know. And that unsettles me, frankly. There's so much going on now that vexes me. Black budgeting—do you know the term, Hector?"

I shook my head. Prescott said, "It's hiding weapons or operational costs as unnamed tag-alongs to other federal expenditures. There are even intimations, or at least indications, of a kind of shadow government forming within our government proper. Ike warns we have nothing so much to fear as the industrial military complex, you know."

"You're starting to hurt my morale," I said. "You're toying with my cherished sense of forever striving to stay mellow, Senator. This is pretty unsettling stuff. I mean, if *you* can't learn who Easton is, what the hell?"

"Precisely why I caution you from turning that device over to him, Hector. Lord knows what would become of the infernal thing from there."

"This is *really* demoralizing me."

Prescott gave me a faint smile. "Why should I be the only one?" He put a hand on my shoulder. "Hector, if you know where this device is, and can recover it without Easton or other parties stepping in and taking it from you...?" His eyes searched mine.

"Like I said, I *have* found it. I'm certain of that. Well, about ninety-nine percent certainty on that count."

"Where is it?"

"Don't worry. I've all but decided to do what you propose. It's just a question of me recovering the damned thing in a few hours."

Bush smiled and pressed his hand harder against my shoulder. "If you need assistance..."

"It not like that," I said. "It's in a funny place and it's going to take some finesse to get at it. But I can do it. What I need is for you to stay in immediate hailing distance. Maybe run interference for me the next few hours with any resources you can bring to bear. Help me shake any tails, to lose the likes of Easton and his minions. Help me slip foreign nationals. That kind of thing."

"I can do that, certainly."

"Oh, and one more thing. My Bel Air is bugged and probably riddled with tracking devices from God knows how many competing interests. It would be real favor if you had someone who could see to that."

I figured in doing that, Bush would see to installing some devices of his own, but those I was prepared to accept. Hell, he or his cronies had done same thing to my car the previous year. I needed someone to have my back, and I was short on better prospects than Prescott Bush. There was just no good alternative: I was forced to trust the blue-blooded son of a bitch.

Prescott smiled thinly. "Albert in there—the taller one—is qualified to do what you ask."

I handed over the keys to my car. "It's the turquoise, fifty-seven Bel Air parked out back, just across from the Ryman. New Mexico plates. But you probably already know that."

Bush said, "Do you have a notepad I might borrow, Hector? A pen?"

"I am a writer." I handed him both. The politician scrawled down something, passed it to me. "The number where I can be reached. It's a secure line. That's to use in case this other device doesn't work or you exceed its range."

He handed me another radio, a different color and model than Chuck's. "When you have the device...you know."

"I'll radio or call you, with all haste," I said. "This thing truly scares the hell out of me. I'm not looking to babysit it for long, believe that."

The senator nodded. He said, "Not many men are afforded the opportunity to leave a legacy like the one you're granting these people, Mr. Lassiter. It's a secret legacy of course. One you'll never receive public credit for, true. But you'll know, and Mr. Fiske will know."

I smiled and shrugged. "I've already got a loud reputation and a too-big public profile. Have my measure of celebrity for what that's worth, which hasn't proven to be much, in the end. So I'm not lookin' for any credit, Senator. Like you say, it's enough I'll know. Enough Bud and I will know."

"You really should let me put some men with you in this recovery effort," Prescott said. "I promise, they'll be discrete and follow your instructions."

"Sorry, no. A crowd scene won't do. It's nowhere you'd expect and, as I told you, it's going to take some special flavor of finesse. Besides, as you don't know exactly who or what Easton represents, or what resources are behind him, there's a certain risk to you, isn't there, in exposure for assisting me?"

"Perhaps," Prescott said. "But, given the stakes, I'm prepared to run that risk."

Old Prescott really was coming across as the idealist, this trip to the well.

And Easton? An enigma. So I was still hewing to that old "Devil you know" angle until I had firmer footing. "Just leave it to me. I'll get this done, then we'll talk delivery."

Prescott rubbed his hands quickly up and down his arms. "How soon until you have the device?"

"With luck, before dawn. So not too long at all."

"We should get back inside. It's terribly cold."

Clapping his arm, I said, "We should do that."

I held the door for the senator, expecting he expected it of me.

Bud looked up as he saw us approach, said, "We're still on?"

"Still," I said.

Bud punched air.

Ernst reached out and took my hand, started pumping it. "Mr. Lassiter, what you are doing—"

"Please," I said, freeing my hand, "you'll get me all choked up, pal."

"There are some more details to work out," Bush said.

I pointed at Bud. "Tell the rest to Bud and he'll fill me in. I've got some thinking to do while I have my chili." I squeezed Bud's arm, then patted it. "Meet back up with you here in a couple of hours, okay? Just need some time alone to think. To plot."

33

I was idling at a red light when two big men stepped in front of my presumably freshly unbugged Bel Air. They started a pushing match with each other. Profanities, more shoving. The traffic light turned green, but big and belligerent as they were, I was loath to hit the horn.

I was about to back up and get some distance to pull around them when the passenger side door of my Chevy swung open and a man slid in beside me. He slammed the door behind him and waved the two men in front of my car off.

It was my prison-writer protégé.

Frank Robbins said, "It's been a while, old friend. Now *drive*, teacher."

I gave Nashville's number one racist a once-over:

His thick, sandy hair was cut and butch-waxed into a flattop you could rest drinks on. He was just a shade over six-feet tall and had the kind of muscle mass that only years spent in prison, passing time working out in the yard and doing countless pushups in a cell to fight boredom, can put on a man who has fearsome focus. He wore a black leather jacket over a black Polo shirt; black pants and shoes. I could just see tattoos on his neck above the collar line of his knit shirt.

I said, "Has indeed been a while. Hell, long enough for a lot to have changed on your end." I got my Chevy in gear, as ordered. A black sedan with a lot of heads silhouetted inside slid in behind us as we tooled through downtown Nashville. "I've been looking for your novel. By the way, am I calling you Frank or Jasper this evening?"

"You don't have to call me anything, Hec," he said. "If I remember rightly, you were the one to point out to one of those other guys back at Quentin he didn't have to drop a character name into every line of dialogue in a two-way conversation. Trust the reader's imagination and your ability to give each character a unique voice to make it clear who's doing the talking, you said. That said, when I read you, you seem to have an aversion to personal pronouns."

"I believe I did say all that. But that was for writers ready for the high-board, like you are. Or like you seemed to me at the time. What happened, pal? You should be writing gritty novels about life on the inside, not playing Junior Hitler here in Hillbilly Heaven."

"Hard to gain traction as a jailbird. So I came southeast and started over." He looked around, then smiled at me. "Turns out I really like snow."

I almost said, *Because it's white?*

"I'm still writing, you know," he said. "It's so hard to break through. I've got the start of a great novel, but I'm having trouble with the ending. Maybe you could help me with the finish."

I shrugged. "Maybe I might have helped with that, back when. Would have tried to if you stayed focused on the task and stayed clean. But this stuff you're fomenting here? What the hell?"

"This isn't anything new, Hector. You spent so much time focusing on me as a writer you could bring before the world of letters, you never really looked at the man in front of you. Quentin is a powder keg, split right down racial lines. The niggers are organizing within the prison system, this thing they actually dare to call Black Power. Well, us in the Bluebirds, we're organized *already*. So we started up spreading our thing out to other prisons out west. As our guys go out, get arrested and get sent back into other prisons, our Aryan gospel spreads. It's a very strong bond between us. That's our motto, *Blood in, blood out.*"

"What does that mean?" I had a sense but I wanted to hear him say it—figured I wanted him to make me hate him that much more, to firm my resolve for whatever bloody thing he might drive me to try and do to him and to his, *soon*, I hoped.

He smiled. "You have to make a kill to get in to the Brotherhood...*blood*. And to leave, you have to give blood—but *your own*. Once you're in, the only way out is by dying."

I said, "So you came out of Quentin bent on starting a race war on the outside? Jesus, the precious time I wasted on you."

"Hardly that much time at all, Hector. And hardly a waste for me. Writing skills are potent political skills. Communication and connection is a valuable—even a priceless—talent. I owe you, a lot, for helping me hone my writing skills...improve my vocabulary and speaking abilities." He shrugged. "As to the rest, it's who I am and always have been. You wrote it yourself, in one of your supposed *novels*: the older we get, the more we just become the person we always were."

I reached for a cigarette and he quickly reached under his coat. Now I knew he could easily outdraw me. I shook my head. "Just goin' for my lighter, honest."

I slowly, carefully pulled out Bud's Zippo and my Pall Malls and got one started. He took an offered cigarette and I reached over and lit him up with the Zippo. Blowing smoke, I said, "You could have been a contender, I think. Right in the ring there with Algren and some of the other gritty new boys."

"I haven't given up on any of that," he said. "In fact, what I'm doing is toward the end of protecting what you do, in a very real way. Writing fiction is still what I mean to do someday, Hec. I mean, in the end. Last New Year's Eve, a man came to me. He's a Federal guy, I think. He's connected to government in some way. FBI? CIA? *Something*. Anyway, he's a novelist, too. He writes thrillers. Donovan pointed out to me how the coloreds are corrupting what we do."

Frank pointed at himself and then at me. Company I surely didn't want to be in. He said, "These colored writers and poets are undermining the Western Literary tradition. Stirring up the coloreds here in the south and in the cities with their writings. Bastards like Ralph Ellison, Du Bois and Langston Hughes, and the like. So, Donovan gave me the germ of a plan. Viewed in certain light, I guess you could say what I'm doing here I do with the tacit support of the Feds."

"God knows I was a sorry mess in 1957," I said thickly, "but that I could misjudge you *this* badly shakes me to my foundations, you sorry son of a bitch."

He shrugged, looked really sad. He said, "Guess I chose poorly, too. Signs are, you're working with some other arm of the government, trying to undermine my work here. I like you, Hector. I'd hate like hell to hurt you. You don't really have a dog in this hunt. So why don't you go back down to New Mexico and write another terrific novel for me to savor and love?"

I stubbed my cigarette out in the ashtray with my right hand. I moved into my position for quick draw of my Colt from under my overcoat and sports jacket's flaps. I was fast running out of options. Frank watched me do that … I'd never pull on him fast enough.

I said, "If the government boys who came my way aren't gas-lighting me, you're actually angling to blow up most of this city and kill Christ only knows how many people to further your twisted aims." I smiled, and said, all false bravado, "I brought you into the literary world, cocksucker. I'm prepared to take you out of it, too."

He just shook his head, a sad smile on his face. "Hec, how deeply are you in with these government shills?"

"All the way up," I said. "This car's bugged. Everything you've said to me is probably on wire recorder somewhere for your trial, assuming you're taken alive. And we're being followed by more than yours."

Convinced I'd never outdraw the bastard in a straight showdown, I slammed on the brakes, only then reaching for my Colt.

Cars converged on us from all angles. The black sedan with Frank's cronies nearly plowed into the back of my Bel Air.

Snarling, my former student said, "I'll fucking kill you now, Hector, I swear it."

He rolled out of my still skidding sideways Chevy. The bastard rolled up over the curb and onto the sidewalk then half-ran, half-limped to the black sedan behind me as the bullets began flying.

The sedan backed up fast, botching a bootleg turn and instead slamming into a row of parked cars. Its dangling front fender kicking up sparks as it grazed the pavement, the sedan tore off in the direction we'd come.

All my government tails peeled off in pursuit.

Left alone, shaking in the legs, I shook loose and lit another cigarette. I checked my Chevy to make sure she hadn't caught a slug or been struck by that tailing sedan. When I got back in my still immaculate Bel Air, my hotline to Easton was crackling. I said into the gizmo, "You better tell me you got him, Chuck."

This pause, then a soft, "We didn't get him." Easton hesitated, said, "Maybe we should meet right now, Hector. Talk next moves. Figure how to draw him back to you."

"No way, Chuck. I'm bringing this thing to a head, tonight. Going to wrap this thing up like my life depends on it, because now it clearly does."

I switched off the radio and slung it under the passenger seat.

34

Bud reached for the handle of my Bel Air. "Not yet, Bud. Over here." I led him across to the steps of the Ryman. "Figure when Prescott had my car combed for gizmos, he quite likely took the liberty of installing a few of his own," I said. "Hell, I'd be disappointed in him—and my own assessment of the son of a bitch—if he *didn't* do all that."

"Probably a safe bet, Lass." Bud nodded at the auditorium behind us. "So we do this, now?"

"With the audience we probably have lurking on rooftops and in the shadows right now? No, Bud, we most certainly don't do that thing."

He scowled. "So what *do* we do?"

"First, in case they have a night watchmen or we trip some alarm, we need some fancy togs that will cover our breaking into the Ryman. Figure we need some glittery props. And we need to shake those tails we likely have. So let's run down an alley or two and find a goddamn taxi or maybe even three."

In another alley a couple of blocks from the costume shop we'd broken into, Bud and I shivered in our skivvies as we put on the country-and-western suits—authentic, spangled Nudie duds we'd stolen. I slipped on a black jacket with satin piping and shiny silver rhinestones. Sucker wasn't cut quite loose enough to accommodate my Colt's shoulder holster, but there wasn't time during the commission of our smash-and-grab to be terribly choosy about tailoring. I slipped on a black cowboy hat and tugged my pant leg out of the top of my boot where it had snagged.

"Hate like hell to do this to Nudie," I said, "but given the cause…"

Bud slipped on his stolen jacket—sharkskin silver with big blue rhinestone musical notes over each tit—then plunked on a gray cowboy hat. I reached over and tightened up his silver steer's head bolero tie. He smiled and shook his head. "Damn, Lass, we look like the Sons of the Pioneers."

"And that's exactly the point, Bud. In case we got caught by the law, or others, we say we're performers who forgot to fetch our guitars before the place shutdown. We'll claim we found the Ryman's door unlocked and, well, you get the drift."

"We should have a band name," Bud said.

"You work on that poet." I pointed across the street at a white Nash Rambler. "While you do that, I'm going to hotwire that sled over there," I said. "I like that extra length, to keep that damned radioactive device as far from us as we can until we can turn it over to Bush and company."

"What's the rest of the plan before we do that?"

"We'll call Logan once we get that car going. Pry him off Gen Gantry and demand a last favor from the daffy son of a bitch. I'm going to have Logan pick up my Bel Air.

Spare key's in a magnetic box in the rear right wheel well. I'll give Logan some instructions and tips for shaking tails. Doubt even he'll be able to screw up the task once I give him the drill. While he's doing all that, we'll break into the Ryman, steal that goddamn contraption and toss it in the back of the Rambler. Then we haul ass to meet Logan. Once we move the thing to my car, we'll make a swift run to rendezvous with Prescott. Get that damned thing in his hands. Hopefully we'll be left alone once we're known to be shed of the thing."

It took me about four minutes to hotwire the Rambler. Jimmy Hanrahan, who'd taught me the dubious art of such chicanery, would not have been impressed.

After, as Bud sat in our idling, soon-to-be-stolen sled, I called Logan and shamed him into picking up my car.

Driving back to the Ryman Auditorium, Bud asked, "When you waved that Geiger gizmo over the coffin, it didn't slide into the kill zone, did it, Hec? I mean, the thing is still safe to handle?"

"Safe as it can be," I said. "It's still in its protective canister, it would seem. That said, I don't want to tarry around the goddamn thing. Hell, I maybe still have some notions about siring a brood of my own down the road."

Bud dropped his hat on the seat between us. He said, "Given the rumors about Prescott and Skull and Bones and Bush personally stealing Geronimo's head, maybe we should have asked him along for this coffin robbing gig."

I smiled and shook my head. "Yeah, that's a thought... But I'm hoping to avoid any actual decapitations this trip to the well, Bud. And evil as he was, I'd hate to see even Jake's skull squirreled away in the Skull and Bone's trophy cabinet."

Bud nodded and tipped his head back against the seat. "Have to say, I'm a little surprised by your going for Prescott's pitch. Pleasantly surprised. Like Easton said, whatever else you might or might not be, you've always been the patriotic sort. Figured you for returning its property to the U.S. government."

"Bush *is* the U.S. government." I sighed and palmed right. "Or at least he is, in part. Like you said, Bud, it isn't as if our side doesn't have plenty more of these goddamn bombs. More than enough to kill the entire sorry planet many times over, I reckon."

I hesitated, then put it out there. "And there's the sorry issue of my ego. I've gotten to thinking hard about legacies, lately. I mean, beyond leaving a bookcase full of novels that might go out of print any second. Particularly given the sorry state of the publishing industry these years. Been thinking about having no kids since losing Dolores. This is an opportunity to play kingmaker on a scale far beyond my wildest imaginings. Hell, how many crime writers and poets get a shot at shifting the balance of power across a continent? And Christ knows, I do love helping a worthy underdog come out on top."

Now Bud had this silly, fond grin on his face. In his *True Magazine* profile of me the previous year, he'd tried to make me out to be some kind of Dos Passos-like crusader-as-novelist, a social activist or the like.

The real me? *Never* such a political animal, not a bit.

And truth be told, I didn't view what I was committed to now as a "political" move.

No, it was more like what I'd told Bud, a balancing of the scales in favor of a persecuted people.

It was also a gesture for many of my lost ones—for Cassie... For my poor Duff, and for Marie, the little Jewish girl that Duff and Jimmy and I had risked so much to save during the last war. Marie was alive, sure, but still living in a kind of hiding in northeastern Ohio, years and years after Hitler had died in his bunker.

This was a big fat stick in the eye of just such bloodthirsty zealots.

How on earth could I do otherwise and ever face a mirror?

35

We were three blocks from the Ryman. The Rambler was just starting to get warm, slow to get cozy because of that extended interior compartment. Bud said, "Where'd you learn to hotwire a car, anyway, Lass?"

"Crime writer, remember, Bud? The shady tricks of the trade. Got to know it to write it correctly." I arched an eyebrow. "Right?"

Bud nodded. "Not with your imagination. Stealing these outfits, stealing a car: we're in really deep if we get caught. I mean, I don't have a lot of confidence Prescott will step in to pull our asses out of this fire if we're caught in the act."

"No, he'll more than likely disavow all knowledge of us and our nefarious undertakings on his behalf, the goddamn politician. I think that's a safe enough bet," I said.

"So what next, Lass?"

"More crime-writer stuff, I guess you'd call it. I'm going to pick the lock on the Ryman's front door. Then we're going to hustle up to that coffin, pop the pins on the bottom lid and grab that damn lead-lined canister. We'll sling it in the back of the Rambler and make tracks, just like I said."

Bud nodded, said, "Sure, but once it's in Prescott's hands? What's next for you?" Bud had this funny smile on his face. "Hell, what's next for *me*? I mean, honestly, what do you do, and where do you go, after you've just averted atomic Armageddon?"

"For my part, I get out of this Godforsaken town with all due speed," I said, smiling. "I'm going to drive down to the Keys, stash my car at my old house down there and fly over to Cuba." I hesitated. "Marlene finally guilted me into patching things up with Hem. Ernest and I spent some time on the phone a few weeks back. I'm going down to Cuba to stay at Hem's place for a few days and finish burying the hatchet. And also try to close out some related old, unfinished business while I'm down there."

That sparked Bud's interest. "What kind of old business?"

"Stuff going back to about circa thirty-five. To thirty-seven and forty-seven, too." I waved a hand. "Just bloody old loose ends, Bud. There always seem to be loose ends. Scores to settle. Fiends to put firmly down at last. Older I get, the less I find I can bear to leave things unfinished."

Took about two minutes for me to pop the front door locks on the Ryman. Perhaps even Jimmy Hanrahan would have been impressed by that proficiency—it isn't the easy thing you see in movies, picking locks.

We slid in fast, then closed and re-locked the doors behind us.

Bud and I thumbed on flashlights. I said, "Keep the beam trained to the floor, Bud—remember all those damned stained-glass windows behind us. Be damned embarrassing to get caught for breaking and entering, but even worse being caught doing that in these crazy country singer suits. That could hurt my wonderful goddamn public image you've helped enhance with your recent *True* article, bless your heart."

Bud played along with my gallows humor, taking the edge off some of the tension from our break-in: "Thought you were ready to put Hector Lassiter to rest for a while?"

"I wasn't kidding, Bud. But I do have my pride. I don't want to send Hector Lassiter off as some kind of a sorry joke or punch drunk idiot. So I aim to see we don't get caught tonight. Who are we, by the way? What name did you come up with for us to cover these crazy threads?"

"The Jellico Mountain Boys. You're Calhoun Rogers, I'm Tyrell Denton."

"Guess from that group moniker we're some sort of a Bluegrass act?"

"Yep. High-Lonesome," Bud said.

Indeed.

We followed the downward-directed flashlight beams to the stage, mounted the steps and cagily approached the coffin. Some lazy or vengeful bastard had left the upper portion of the lid open so old Jake was left to gather dust overnight.

On the other hand, it did make it easier for me to spring the bottom portion of the coffin lid. I tipped the remainder of the lid up, felt it lock into upright position, and searched around Jake's boots with my flashlight: *nada*.

Bud said, "In retrospect, guess maybe we should have brought your Geiger gizmo, Lass. Just to be sure it's still here, I mean. What if they already took the thing away?"

"Nah," I said. "I'm betting against that. I still think they mean to detonate the damned thing in that neighborhood you described for me. Now, help me get this asshole's feet out of the way, won't you, Bud?"

We put down our flashlights, angled at the box. Bud grunted as he took hold of the dead crooner's knees; I grabbed Jake by the boots. Sucker was stiff as a statue. We wrestled Jake up off the bottom of the coffin and angled him so his boot heels rested on the side of his box. I thumped around with my flashlight on the coffin's bottom until I found what sounded like a hollow space.

I slit the lining along the edge of the box's bottom with a pocketknife and pulled it back. I removed a square cutaway-cum-lid to reveal the lead container stashed in a hollow compartment underneath.

It took both hands to lift the damned thing—sucker was heavy as hell. Bud helped me wrestle it from the box, then replaced the lid over the hiding space and smoothed out the silk lining, tucking it back into the crevice at the coffin's bottom. We maneuvered old Jake back into position and closed the bottom of his casket.

"Christ only knows what the pallbearers would have made of that," I said. "I mean the bottom of the coffin being so much heavier than the top. It's almost like having an extra Jake or two wadded up there at one end."

Bud pointed at the lead container on the floor at our feet. "There's nothing rigged to the thing to explode it," he said. "Shouldn't there be dynamite or something like that? Some kind of timer?"

"I wish I could say I'm surprised, Bud, but that hidden compartment is a good bit bigger than it needs to be to contain just the device. I think the bomb-maker is due here yet tonight. Bastards probably didn't want to run the risk of accidentally blowing up the Ryman and all the country musicians in town along with it. They don't want to annihilate *that* particular brand of Nashvillian—you know, *white*. So I figure they're going to rig the bomb tonight. More's the reason for us get out of here, *muy pronto*, Bud."

We shoved our flashlights down into our pants pockets, dipped low together and took either end of the lead box in our hands. I said, "Remember to lift with your knees, Bud. You get a hernia lifting this thing, I swear to God I'll put you down."

"Somebody's going to be real angry in a bit," Bud said, rising with me. He began walking backward up the aisle to the front door as I guided him best I could in the near dark. Huffing as much as I was, Bud said, "Maybe we should put that other lead box Chuck Easton gave you in the coffin to fool them."

"Wouldn't fool 'em long enough to make it worth the risk coming back," I said. "Think about this—and it is a chilling notion, to be sure. To rig that bomb, some poor son of a bitch, or more likely several of them, are going to need to open up that lead container and risk fatal radiation poisoning and terrible burns to wire it to the secondary explosives and detonator, or timer. That's a textbook suicide mission, Bud. Probably for the bastard who drives the hearse, too, though he might just be some hapless mortuary worker. A doomed patsy."

"God, you're right about the ones who'd have to set the explosive," Bud said, looking a little sick. "Can you imagine doing that to yourself, actually sacrificing yourself, all for..." Words failed the poet.

So I said it for him. "All because you hate some other race that much? So much you'd kill in the name of your alleged faith? That's why I warm to giving that particular country this goddamn deadly thing we're breaking our backs with now."

We reached the doors with our load.

The Ryman's door knobs were turning.

Bud's eyes widened. I took the thing in both hands and nodded him to the other side of the door. I pressed back against the wall on the near side of the door. The lock gave and the doors opened.

Bud and I hugged the shadows inside, holding our breath as nearly a dozen black-clad strangers filed in quickly and closed the doors behind them.

Once inside, several of the men broke out flashlights. As Bud and I had done, they pointed them at the floor, quickly making their way to the stage.

We couldn't open the front doors of the Ryman to escape with them inside now—not without letting in light from the streetlamps and a brisk wind that would alert the bastards to our leaving. We surely couldn't hope to out run them, not lugging the lead box we were mightily straining to carry while simply walking slowly.

I waited until they were almost on stage, then signaled Bud to help me with the box. I whispered, "Make your way along the back row there, Bud. We'll crouch down in the far corner and wait them out. Once they see the thing is gone, they'll likely leave fast."

We crab-walked with our weighty load behind the seats until we reached the last seat in the last row, cloaked in shadows, then ducked low.

The click of the coffin lid being raised echoed in the hall, followed by some other noises and low murmurs as they moved Jake's corpse, going about it a little less carefully than Bud and I had done.

There were some jiggling beams from flashlights, then one of them uttered a single, harsh, "Fuck!"

Then, "It's goddamn gone!"

More urgent whispers ensued. Something that sounded like, "At least let's put the TNT in, wipe out as many of them as we can tomorrow morning."

I checked the glow-in-the-dark hands on my watch, measuring their progress. After fifteen minutes, still cursing, the men filed back out the front door of the Ryman. Men? Maybe not all of 'em. One's silhouette, one up front, looked distinctly feminine, fetchingly curvy.

Bud said, "How long until we follow 'em out?"

"We don't, poet. Let's go out the back way just to be extra safe. Just in case they left behind anyone to watch the front doors. Once we're out back, I'll bring the Rambler around and pick you up."

"After, I want us to find a pay phone," Bud said.

"What for?"

"To warn the cops there's dynamite in Jake's coffin. We can't let them blow *anyone* up. Not one person, Lass."

"Of course we can't. Right, Bud. We certainly can't let 'em do that."

36

Bud turned up the car heater. I was at the wheel again. The songwriter-poet was watching storefronts whip by behind the flurries. I said, "Did you get Corin directly?"

"A flunky, but he took me seriously, I think. Said he'd get word to Corin and then head over to the Ryman immediately."

"After the question I put to Corin about the funeral procession route, he'll take it seriously enough. He'll also probably come looking for me. More's the reason to show this town my back, and just as fast as I can."

Bud said, "Where are we going to meet Logan?"

"Not too far from here," I said. "Just have to hope the kid followed my instructions to the letter."

"You're hard on Logan, you know, Hec? Maybe riding him too fierce."

I shook my head. "Not hard enough, I'd say. Not after that crazy management contract he signed with Gen Gantry's agent. I do scent shyster. Kid might as well have flushed his career down the toilet. I suspect this agent of his, this Jonas Parker, now owns Logan, body and soul. Logan's got all this raw real talent, despite all his other shortcomings. Hate to see him trip himself up out of the gates."

"Sounds like he's made his own choice, Lass. Not much you can do now." Bud checked the rearview mirror on his side; checked over his shoulder. "Seems we also have the road to ourselves."

"Seems so," I agreed. "Or maybe Prescott's boys are just better at shadowing. "I find it hard to believe someone isn't trailing us, one way or another."

"And Logan, really think he can lose spies in that Chevy of yours?"

"If Prescott's boys really stripped the Bel Air of gizmos? Maybe. Assuming Logan follows all the instructions I gave him for shaking tails. Though I expect Prescott's own boys will stay on Logan's caboose easy enough. But as we're allied with them for better or worse, it's no harm."

This noise in my overcoat pocket. I dug out Chuck Easton's radio. Bud said, "Going to answer?"

"Think I best do that very thing," I said, "though I'm strongly tempted to toss the bitch out the window."

"What do you think he'd do if you just shut him out now, Lass? Think he'd really call down trouble on you? Maybe the Internal Revenue Service?"

"God forbid, Bud. Now you're scaring me in brand new ways. The IRS scare the living hell out of me."

"So, you're going to answer him?"

"Yeah, but not on the first try," I said. "I suppose I want to feel at least a little courted, Bud."

The poet smiled. "Such a tease..."

Five minutes passed and the radio buzzed again. I pulled curbside and pressed the button. "Chuck?"

A pause. "Hector? You've been out of pocket for a while. I was worried. Where are you? I tried you a few minutes ago."

"Must have been in a tunnel."

"Where are you *right now*, Hector?"

I thought of Bud's name for our country act. "Headed back from the outskirts. Hill country. Bud and I were chasing these racist sons of bitches who have the canister, and dodging Middle Eastern types in the bargain." A painful pause for effect. "Sorry to say the news isn't good, old pal. Well, maybe it could be worse, actually. But only a little."

Chuck sounded half-skeptical, half-invigorated. "What's happened? Tell me everything."

"There wasn't time to call as this all got rolling, Chuck," I said, "I'm damned sorry for that. But things began moving too fast for any reaching out. Real blood and thunder stuff rained down. Short form: The device was to be hidden in Jake Gantry's coffin. These crazy bastards meant to blow up a colored neighborhood along the funeral cortège's route, come the mornin'. Bud and I tumbled to the plan and raced to the Ryman, where they were in the act of rigging the bomb. Had us a ruckus that turned into a crossfire when these foreign nationals stepped into the fray.

"Anyway, a car chase ensued out to the hinterlands. I actually got separated from my Bel Air in the early going, I'm afraid. And soon enough, well, sorry to say, we were well out of radio range."

"Where's the device Hector? Did these people lose you and Fiske out there in the sticks somewhere?" That deduction of Chuck's pissed me off, even if all this was a crazy lie.

"Nah, we ran 'em to ground okay, Chuck." I winked at Bud. He just shook his head, looking more than a tad nervous.

Chuck said, "And the device?"

"Lost to all, Chuck, no fears on that front. We got 'em cornered in some caverns there up in the higher ranges. When they saw they were outgunned, one of the Klansmen, or whatever they call themselves, tossed the radioactive bitch down some abyss. Tourist plaque posted there claims the hole he pitched it down is same as bottomless. Either way, it's gone, gone, gone, Chuck. Suppose it might as well be sunk down there in all that quicksand off Tybee Island, after all. Same fate, really."

Chuck sounded unhappy enough at the prospect the canister was unrecoverable. He said, "And these so-called Klansmen? These foreign nationals? Where are they now? Where do I find—"

"They did some real damage to one another," I said, cutting in. "It really just remained for Bud and I to pick off the stragglers either side and pitch 'em down the hole with the rest. Less to explain later, agreed? Cavern pit's deep enough that I don't think we have to worry about tourists complaining about any funny odors, come the spring thaw."

"These caverns, Hector, where exactly are they?"

Bud shot me a look like maybe I trapped myself.

I hadn't: Over a breakfast along the road with Logan, I'd spent a good bit of time browsing over Tennessee tourism brochures, Rock City, Ruby Falls and various "lost caverns" and the like.

"It's that tourist place about thirty minutes outside the city, like I said. Hit any gas station in town here and pick up a brochure, you'll find the place, Chuck. But it's a big, deep, fucking hole, old pal. A real Hell-mouth, as I view it. Try as you might, I think that wicked ore has gone right back to its origins. Lost to some deep and fearsome pit at the earth's core where it probably should have stayed in the first place."

Another long pause. Chuck said, "Hector, I want to believe all this, I do, but, well, you disappearing for so long, and your car...?"

He trailed off then. Figured it was because he was about to say something about the tracers on my Bel Air having gone dead on him, but then I wasn't supposed to know that he'd bugged my Chevy. I figured Chuck remembered that too, even as he began working his jaws on the subject.

After a time, he said, "You're *sure* it went down that cavern's hole?"

"Watched the lead box go over the side myself, buddy. Container was a bit bigger than the one you gave me. And loads heavier. The poor bastard who pitched it down the hole could barely manage the thing by himself. Sucker must have weighed a ton."

"Very heavy," Chuck confirmed. "Yes, it weights quite a lot."

"You'll be wanting your Geiger gizmo back," I said, sounding reluctant. Fact is, I really was: I hated to lose my bootleg tunes I'd recorded. "Is there someplace I could drop it for you?"

"Uh, hold onto it, if you like," Easton said. "I mean, it's still a top-flight tape recorder. Call it a gift. Maybe you can use it for dictation for one of your novels."

Figured old Chuck was going to head back to Washington or wherever he reported, pronto. I'd be glad to see *his* back. I said, "I'm goddamn sorry, Chuck. Bud and I both are... sorry as hell. Sure wish I could have done a better job for you and Uncle Sam. But like I said, events overtook us. They simply overtook all of us. Swamped us. Goddamn it."

Couldn't tell from his tone if Chuck really bought it. After a time he said, "At least it's safe from foreign hands, Hector. Thanks again for all you tried to do to help."

I tossed the radio on the seat between us. Bud said, "Think he really believed you? Because I'm skeptical he did."

"Me too, I think. But then I am the cynical sort by nature. Is the glass half-full, or half-empty? Either way I look at it, if the stuff in the glass is any good at all, it's not enough."

37

The rendezvous place I'd picked for our meeting with Logan—juxtaposed with Bud and my own country crooner's garb—made for a strange enough scene.

But it being night and snowy, it seemed to me the most private place to meet would be another tourist trap, another place I'd plucked from my time spent reading tourism brochures.

In 1897, to celebrate the Tennessee Centennial, the festival organizers decided to build a full-size replica of the unspoiled Greek Parthenon as part of the celebration. God only knows who had that crazy epiphany. God only knows how they then succeeded in actualizing the crazy son of a bitch.

That relic, and other jaw-dropping copies of famous structures, were built out of temporary materials—stuff calculated to remain standing just long enough to see the festival through to its end.

But Nashville soon enough fell in love with its Greek temple and wouldn't let it be torn down. In the 1920s, city fathers dipped into the Nashville coffers and funded an eleven-year effort to construct its ailing Parthenon in permanent form.

Tonight the wind was sending the snow squalling around Nashville's *permanent* Parthenon's fat, old soaring Greek columns.

Bud, holding his hands to the heater vents, said, "All this time in Nashville and I didn't even know this was here. Weird."

It was surely strange enough: this outsized, pale Greek Temple with enormous Doric columns and statuary, squatting square in the heart of Hillbilly Heaven, the centerpiece of Centennial Park, just a few miles up the road west of Music Row.

I checked my watch, growled, "We'll give Logan another ten minutes to get here before I'll officially start worrying, I think."

Bud tried to make conversation. "So, you and Hemingway have already talked you said? It went okay? Even cordial?"

"Chummy enough," I said. "Better than I might have expected after so many years apart from poor old Hem. Good enough to wangle an unsought invite down to that crazy island he calls home."

Bud nodded. "And so, after you get back from Cuba, you're really going to try living your life as someone other than yourself?"

"Mean to try it on, at least." I hesitated, then put it out there. "Called Alicia earlier to tell her what I was thinking about—this new life, I mean."

That genuinely surprised Bud. "And what did Alicia say to that?"

"Said to call her after I'm a few months into this new life. We may have dinner, then."

The young poet smiled, looking more than surprised. His finger was quickly up in my face. "Hector, if you screw this up, I swear to God..."

"Don't jinx me, Bud. Please."

I could see the glow of headlights coming up over the snowy rise.

Showtime.

A deep breath drawn as I turned off the Rambler's lights. I didn't want to turn off the engine for fear of not being able to replicate my job hotwiring our stolen ride in the Nashville Parthenon's ground's gloom.

"That your Bel Air, Lass?"

"I think so," I said. "But sit tight a minute, just to be sure."

My Bel Air ambled up to about fifty yards off the nose of the Rambler. Logan climbed out of the Chevy and waved at us. "Now we go," I told Bud.

We stepped out into the swirling snow, backlit in my Bel Air's headlights. "You could have parked closer, you know," I called out to Logan. "Don't want to lug this load we have any farther than we have to. Why don't you pull the Chevy up closer, okay?"

I turned my collar up against the chilly wind and Bud and I held onto our cowboy hats' brims. I expected some crack from Logan about our country-and-western togs. When he held his tongue, I started to get this undefined but undeniable sinking feeling.

With a single unfinished sentence, Logan justified my worst fears: "I am *so* sorry..."

The passenger side door swung open then and some fella who had been crouched down slid out with a shotgun. He pointed the shotgun between Bud and I. The Bel Air's back doors opened and another stranger climbed out hoisting a second shotgun.

The last one struggled out of the backseat with some effort.

The third man leaned back in to fetch a pair of crutches. No stranger that one, of course: Basil Sloan.

38

Basil limped up behind his new hired guns, smiling with that missing front tooth.

"How'd this come to be, you're asking yourself, ain'tcha, Lassiter?" He had a slight whistle when he talked now, a lisp because of that chomper I'd cost him.

"Guess I am at that," I said.

A gap-toothed smile: "Famous man like you, well, you attending that Gantry sendoff, pictures of you and some woman—a pretty blonde—turned up in *The Nashville Banner*."

Damn it to hell: so many flashbulbs going off in the palace full of country music stars, it never struck me I might be photographed, let alone have my mug *again* stuck in the damn evening newspaper.

Goddamn my outsized reputation for tripping me up, yet again.

Basil smiled. "Decided I'd have the boys drive me by the Ryman on the outside chance you might still be hanging around. Didn't see you, but what I did see was your Bel Air with those New Mexico plates. *My* Bel Air, I mean. So we just sat out there waiting and watching, until this boy Logan showed up. He tried to be clever, circling blocks and doubling back and the like. Too bad for him, and you, that my new boy Travis here is former-Nashville *poe-leece*... He knows all the tricks for shaking tails, and better, for maintaining them. We made our move at a traffic light. Travis snuck up and got the drop on your boy singer. Price he pays for not lockin' the doors."

I clucked my tongue and nodded at Travis. He had been the first man out of my Chevy with a shotgun. "You must break Rick Corin's heart, Travis."

Travis said, "That cocksucker. I never did like Corin, that ramrod-straight and righteous son of a bitch."

Basil narrowed his eyes. "Enough of that, Tray. So, I'm asking myself now what is the idea of you two dressed up like Hank Williams and Ernest Tubb?" He gestured at Bud and I in our spangled Nudie suits. "And then hauling the other crooner up here in your car to meet outside of this goddamn screwball building?" Basil ended with a head feint at the Parthenon. "Just what's goin' on here? This all seems like crazy business."

I weighed options, assessed angles.

Bud was good in a brawl and willing to put a man down for keeps. I knew that from bloody past experience. My poet would back my play, regardless how reckless it might be.

But Logan simply wasn't battle worthy.

Basil wasn't much of a threat in and of himself, not in his present state with a shot-through hand and both feet perforated as they were.

But snaggle-toothed Basil's two hired hands—one an ex-cop with a double-barreled now pointed at my gut— well, with them in the mix, we clearly weren't going to fight our way out of this pinch with any prospect of coming out on top.

No, I was going to have to finagle us out of this mess, if that was even remotely possible.

I smoothed a hand over my Nudie jacket, hoping it might obscure the bulge of my Colt in the event I got a chance to put the sucker into play. "They took up a collection at old Jake's wake," I said. "Money for a pet cause of Jake's, the NCLC."

Basil's lip curled. "Well, that colored-lovin' son of a bitch. Now I'm well glad he's croaked."

I shrugged. "Logan was in charge of seeing to the collection cans. So Logan stowed the gelt away in the Ryman. Bud and Logan and I decided *we* could maybe make better use of that money. So Bud and I dressed this way to sneak back into the Ryman to try and steal the offering jar. That's the reason we're in the Rambler—it's stolen too, if you must know. Just couldn't risk having my Bel Air seen fleeing the scene of a crime." A crooked smile. "I do have my pride."

Basil grunted. "Then where's the damn money you stole, Lassiter?"

"Not so fast," I said. "It's hidden, and squirreled away pretty well, at that. Let's make a deal, buddy. What *is* there? That sum will more than make up for what I owe you, I think even you'll agree that's so. Plenty for doctor's costs, even a good dentist to give you back your winning smile. It'll make up for all that, *and* leave enough to see you well through for a long ass spell back there in Bluegrass Country. It'll do all that and you'll still have what you need to pay these husky new boys of yours for their threatened mayhem, Basil old pal."

"I take the money and you three walk, is that really the offer?" Basil asked.

"That is," I said, "the offer." A hopeful smile. "So what say you?"

"Maybe," Basil allowed. "Maybe we could do that. But first I want to see this money. Need to see for myself how much jack there really is."

I sighed, trying to look at once dejected, but as if I might still be foolishly, hell, *desperately*, holding out just a little hope Basil might yet let us walk. "It's stowed in the back of the Rambler," I said. "In a big old metal box back there."

Basil grinned, spat and jerked his head at his stooges. "You call that fucking hidden?" He set off on crutches along with his unnamed flunky. That left Travis, the ex-cop, standing guard on the three of us. Travis half-turned and ordered Logan to move alongside Bud and I.

Logan gave me a hard look as he moved my way. Travis was focusing on me for the moment. He rightly figured me for the biggest risk, it seemed.

But I could see Logan's brain working in his naked facial expressions. He'd finally found a pair, but he'd tardily done so, and at the very *worst* of times, as was becoming typical of the boy.

Yep, I just *knew* Logan was going to rush Travis. I doubted he could close the distance in time to avoid a shotgun blast, particularly because the fool would probably start his charge with some stupid war whoop to telegraph his intentions.

I was just starting to shake my head *no* at the songwriter when things went from bad to worse.

This voice called across the distance: Basil shouted, "Send that skinny one Lassiter calls Bud over here to stand with us. We'll do that just in case this Lassiter decides to pull somethin' more. I feel better having his boy close by me. At very least, it'll keep the scrappy old son of a bitch docile."

Poor Bud shot me this sick look.

Goddamn me, but I'd been too-clever-by-half.

Travis motioned with his shotgun, said, "Shake a leg, Scarecrow. Move it along now, ya hear?"

At that moment, *I* was thinking about bellowing and then rushing Travis, despite the fact it was clearly suicide. But better I die a fast and bloody death than have young Bud exposed to all that radioactive ore Basil was about to unseal.

Bud, probably sensing my intent, started walking—walking *real* slow, playing up his very real limp—before Logan or I could do anything bloody and reckless. They seemed to be having some trouble with lock on the box. I heard a couple of shots, then Basil said, "There, *that* got the son of a bitch!"

I almost closed my eyes: I simply couldn't bear to see Bud getting closer to the wagon's tailgate and what awaited him there when the box's contents were laid bare.

Bud was maybe half way to the Rambler when Basil began screaming.

Then Travis' head exploded from a single, perfect gunshot.

39

The screams coming from Basil and his cohort were horrible, not like the screams of men, or even women. Their cries sounded inhuman—truly animal.

This choked voice that must have been Basil's because of the slight lisp from his missing tooth, but guttural and pained now, begged, "Close it, oh, for Christ's sake, close it now! Oh God! *Please*... put it away!"

It was just as I heard that heavy box's lid drop closed that Travis' face disappeared in a pink and red cloud from a gunshot to his head.

I flinched as I felt a second and wholly unnecessary bullet fired at Travis whistle close by my cheek. The shots had come from *behind* the dead ex-cop—somewhere down the hill from the Parthenon.

Several black-clad men strode over the darkened horizon soon enough. Prescott Bush and Ernst brought up the rear. Didn't require much in the way of deductive powers to tumble to the realization that Prescott's boys had successfully tracked Logan to us.

Good enough thing Bush did that, as it turned out.

I waved at Prescott, then tromped through the ankle-deep snow to the back of the Rambler, stepping wide until I could confirm the lead box's lid was indeed closed tight.

Basil and his cohort lay there, both evidently blinded, judging by the strange burns and blisters on their faces and hands; their burned and bleeding lips and gums.

Neither was holding a gun; neither was looking in my direction.

I said softly, *"Holy Jesus."*

Basil choked out, "Lassiter? Is that you? I don't know what you did, but I'll surely *kill* you for this. I swear I'm going to kill you, slow and bloody."

I backed away then, not sure how much radiation Basil and his dying stooge might be putting off, all on their own. As I moved away from them I called back, "Afraid it's simply too late for any of that, Basil, old pal. Fear I already killed *you*."

Prescott Bush nodded and clapped my arm. "The others are dead?"

"They will be soon enough," I said. "They opened the lead box—and quickly closed it—but not in time to save themselves. Not sure what can be done for them. They're a mess."

"Not much at all can be done for them I fear," Ernst said, looking ashen and a little nauseous. "Even the possibility of simply making them comfortable isn't really an option now. Kinder perhaps to shoot them, if I might be so candid."

Candid. Yeah.

I watched Prescott to see if he'd actually issue that bloody kill order.

Meeting my gaze, the senator said, "Rest assured that we have special teams that handle these sorts of things,

Hector—I mean matters dealing with radiation poisoning and such. Accidents do happen, even in laboratory settings, despite all our best and most energetic efforts to safeguard our people. I'll see a crew is sent up here to handle all this. They'll do all that can be done for those two."

Nodding, I said, "I hope fifty yards away from that open box—and having its lid and most of a car between the thing and a person—is enough to avoid any health issues for me and my boys."

Ernst nodded. "The box was open only for a second, yes? At that distance you should be safe enough."

Bud said, "And at thirty yards?"

Ernst squeezed his arm. "We'll run some tests if you wish, but I'm sure you'll be fine."

Poor Fiske didn't look terribly reassured.

Prescott said, "The box is in that vehicle then?" He pointed at the Rambler.

"That's right," I said. "But the lid, though down, *is* still unsecured."

Prescott nodded, then pulled a radio from his pocket. He pressed a button and said, "Send in the recovery unit." The senator winked and said to me, "Just a few minutes and they'll be here. They have radiation suits. They'll re-secure the device's container and then it and Ernst will leave here by helicopter. There's a special plane waiting for them in Kentucky." He beamed. "All in all, a good showing tonight! Lassiter, you're okay, after all!"

No response was appropriate for that bit of palpable disingenuousness.

Ernst, the little man from Israel with a still-unknown last name, then hugged Bud and I and kissed us both on either cheek. He said, "My friends, what you have done?

There simply aren't sufficient words to express my gratitude. Nor the gratitude of my people and my homeland."

Logan finally found his voice then. "What the *fuck* is going on here?" He looked Bud and I up and down, then said at last, "And why in God's name are you two dressed like Jake Gantry?"

I was about to answer the crooner when the next shot rang out.

One of the Senator's praetorian guards fell face first into the snow, turning it red. Another agent took a slug in the gut, losing enough meat out the hole in his back to look a goner, too.

The rest of us hauled ass up the steps of the Parthenon, hugging the backsides of those soaring concrete columns, and scrambling for hidden or holstered guns.

40

Prescott and Ernst were pressed up behind the pillar to my right. The senator had snatched his dead minion's gun before scrambling up the temple's steps. Ernst, too, had a gun, some automatic he must have had hidden somewhere.

Bud and Logan crouched behind the pillar to my left. Bud tugged up his pant's leg and fished around in the cuff of his boot. He handed Logan a .38. Logan took the pistol, holding it awkwardly. I could only hope he wouldn't shoot me, or himself, by accident. Logan said again, "What the hell is going on here, Bud? Hector?"

I drew my Colt and took a quick look around the pillar. I saw maybe a dozen men moving out there in the dark some distance from my Bel Air. What looked like four more reinforcements crept up behind the first dozen.

Christ: My underarms were damp, my mouth dry.

It was starting to look like the Alamo.

Prescott said, "Who are these damned people, Lassiter?"

"Search me," I said. "Figured you might know. Either way, there's at least sixteen of 'em out there."

Prescott's remaining men—one with a perforated wing—hid behind other pillars.

The numbers surely weren't on our side. Prescott said, "The container is still out there between us and them. That *won't* do!"

Prescott pulled out his radio and said to whoever was on the other end, "When you get here, anything out there away from the temple is a target. You're authorized to use any necessary force to secure the *object*."

I shot Prescott a look, said, "If your boys shoot up my Chevy, I swear to Christ, I will—"

The Senator rolled his eyes. "These are professionals. They don't waste bullets. One shot, one kill."

I bit my lip and flinched as a bullet nicked my pillar. "What if those fellas out there in the snow banks are *also* professionals, Senator? Maybe it's Easton and company skulking out there. It's not like we know if he *is* still government, or not. And if he *is*, it'd be damned embarrassing if different factions of the federal government had themselves a Tennessee shootout, wouldn't it?"

"If it *is* Easton," Prescott said, "it's something we'll sort out later. Particularly as they fired on us first. They've killed at least one of mine, so far. Perhaps two."

A few more bullets ricocheted off my pillar. I thought about what Bush had said, replied, "In that spirit, then..." I leaned around and squeezed off a couple of shots. Two men fell.

This voice snarling from out there in the dark: "Hector! Do you hear me, Hector? Stop this shooting *right now!*"

It was certainly a woman's voice: I tried to place it. She yelled again, "Hector? I mean it—you all stop your shooting, or we'll kill your friend."

Kill your friend?

I looked at Bud and Logan, still safe behind their pillar at my side. Prescott raised an eyebrow and scowled at me.

He snarled, "Who is that woman out there? And who is this friend she's threatening?"

"I'm asking myself the same things," I said, confused.

The senator said, "You'd better figure this out damned fast, because in a few minutes, anyone out there will be cut down by aerial fire, Mr. Lassiter."

I hollered back, "Lady, what the hell are you *talking* about? Who the hell *are* you?"

There was scorn in the woman's voice now. "Have you already forgotten the sauna the other night, and what we did there? The fine time we shared? And your friend? You've already forgotten dear Esther? Take a look out here. We'll hold our fire so you can see—I promise nobody will shoot."

Esther? Goddamn it to hell!

Prescott said, "Don't fall for it, Hector! They could have a marksman with a scope."

"Thanks for that happy thought, pal."

I eased around the pillar.

A woman wearing a ski mask and black jacket and slacks stood with another man, also masked. Between them, they held wide-eyed Esther, two guns pressed to her head.

I couldn't see her face, but the tight black clothes she was wearing—and Esther being hostage—made it just as clear to me as her crack about us screwing in the sauna. It was Donna Perkins, sure enough.

"Turns out I *do* know the woman they're holding hostage," I said to Prescott Bush.

"And it sounds as if you know the other one, too," Bush said.

Biblically. Yes. But now I was spoiling to rain down some Old Testament-style vengeance on Donna.

I said to Bush, "Get your people on the radio again, Senator. Tell 'em to hold their fire a couple minutes?"

Prescott bit this lip. "I can. Hell, with all this shooting, we'll have the whole Nashville police department falling down around us at any moment. But Hector, if it comes down to losing you and a single hostage, or that device out there in the back of that heap, you know what I'll decide."

"Hell, I'd *agree* with you doing that very thing, given the stakes. Just please give me a couple of extra minutes, yes?"

As Prescott reluctantly raised his airborne *compadres* on the radio, I said to Logan, "The Bel Air's keys, kid—I need 'em, now."

Logan dipped a hand in his pocket. He tossed me my car keys.

I pocketed them and slid my Colt down my waistband at the back, covering it with my rhinestone-studded jacket. I yelled out to Donna, "What do you want? What do you want in return for letting Esther go?"

Donna yelled back, "You well know what we want, Hector. Give it back to us and she'll be released."

I said to Prescott, "Here's my play: I've got a spare lead container given me by Chuck Easton. It's stowed in the trunk of my Chevy. I'll try to pass it off to this bunch as the real thing. Not like they're apt to open it now and risk radiation poisoning confirming it's legit, not under the gun as they are, right? Yeah. So, *after* they take the dummy box, I'm going to grab their hostage, throw her in my Chevy and get the Bel Air up behind this Greek gewgaw, so your boys can turn the grounds out there into a killing jar for those monsters."

"But they might take you hostage too," Prescott said.

"They do that, and I'll see a few go down before your boys finish the job. This is the plan we have, Senator. Now,

I'm heading down there. I'm just frittering away the extra time you bought me jawing like this."

Bud said, "Hector..."

I smiled at the poet. "Gotta do it, Bud. We both know that. Hell, it might even come off *just dandy*."

Bud looked dubious, even a little sick.

I yelled to Donna, "I'm coming out now." I slipped around the pillar, holding open my Nudie suit jacket to show my empty shoulder holster. I dropped off the ledge of the temple and began walking slowly down the sloped mound. The headlights were still on in my Chevy and cast a long shadow behind me as I walked down the hill, hands high above my head.

As I was halfway to my car, Donna said, "What's with those crazy togs, Tex?"

"Dressed for a date—some flashy dame with no racist homicidal urges," I said. "What is this about? You've got a money machine in your daughter and inherited mansion. You're set for life at this rate. Why are you wallowing in all this murderous shit?"

Donna shrugged. "Chubby Checker and Fats Domino are well out-charting my girl. This is an investment in the future—putting that dark genie back in the bottle."

Jesus. How to argue with logic like that? I didn't even try.

Esther looked pretty bad. I was afraid she might stroke out or have a coronary at any second. I said, "You take it easy there now, Esther, you hear? I swear to you, we'll have this behind us lickety-split. Gonna get you home to family, safe and sound before you know it." She didn't look encouraged.

I said, "Might as well take the silly mask off Donna. Those government-types up the hill know all about you now. They also know all about your ties to this racist cabal of Old Jake's."

"Not sure I believe you," Donna said. "And if those Feds all die here tonight? What's it to me, then?"

I shook my head. "So, all this time, you and Jake and your racist band were in this together. Gen told me you have training as a nurse. What'd you do? Spike one of Jake's cocktails during some racist soiree? Why'd *Jake* have to die? Was he foot-dragging on this business about detonating that radioactive weapon here in his favorite town, or was he talking about writing Gen out of his will?"

"Bit of both, if it really matters," Donna said. "And of course it really doesn't. I just didn't foresee my daughter becoming a suspect in Jake's murder. Only reason I let you into the house was I figured—soundly based on your reputation and infamous tomcat urges for younger women— that you could help exonerate her, and probably pretty quickly... just to show off and try and get a little jailbait ass, maybe. What I didn't figure on was you looking for the weapon, too. When that crazy machine of yours went off in the Ryman, I figured out right there you were working for the government and what you were looking for. Now, where's the box, Tex?"

A man walked up behind Donna. He was also masked, but I knew that build, surely knew that voice. "I told you I'm going to kill you, Hector." Frank wrapped an arm around Donna's waist. He pointed a gun at me with his other hand.

"You two are an item?" I curled my lip. "Jesus... I think I need some medical testing, pronto."

Enough jawing: those killer helicopters would be here soon, raining down certain death from above. I carefully reached into my pants pocket for my keys and dangled them. "You let Esther get in my car. While she does that, the rest of you can come with me around to the trunk of the Chevy and I'll give you your goddamn killer box. It's going to take at least two of us to wrestle it out of there—tellin' you now. As I guess you already know, it's a heavy damn bastard."

I smiled, said, "Hell, figure it weighs about the same as all those long and heavy chains you're going to drag behind you in hell for all time, Donna...You too, *Frank.*"

"That almost hurts, after all we've shared," Donna said. "And I expect we'll have plenty of time together down there in Hades, if half the stories I hear about you are true. You're surely no angel, Hector."

I gave a shaggy chuckle. "Maybe a dark one. And, as you've attested, stories tend to collect around me, sugar. Some of 'em are even true. But a lot of them aren't. And, whatever my sins, I'm at least contrite. Now, how'd you find us out here? You somehow manage to follow Logan, too?"

"A bartender at Mom's is on the dole to me," Donna said. "Gives me tidbits of gossip. Shares the names of promising songwriters I might recruit. My friend the bartender spotted you and the Senator having your little chat. So I deduced you were working with Bush to recover the weapon. I had Bush followed from Mom's. Then we followed Bush and his men *up* here. I really don't think the senator expected to be followed. What's the cliché? Pride goeth before a fall?"

I said, "You were *truly* fixing to blow that thing up in that neighborhood and kill all those poor folks? Jesus Christ, but you're the sorriest piece of work I've ever come across, and that's covering some very mean ground, woman."

"*Still* mean to do that." Donna shoved Esther at me. I caught the old woman in my arms, steadied her, and wrapped an arm around her shoulders. "You both lead us to the Chevy," Frank said. "No tricks because we're aiming at your heads."

I said softly to Esther, "When we get around back of the car, duck to the ground on the passenger's side."

Donna said, "What did you say to her? What are you two talking about, Hector?"

"I asked if you hurt her. And I asked what you did to her on the drive over here, you twisted bitch." I half-expected a pistol-whipping across the back of the head for that one. But Donna held her temper well enough. She was in control, at least for the wicked moment, and well knew it.

I inserted the key in the Bel Air's trunk lock and twisted; noticed my hand was shaking. Goddamn nerves. Goddamn weakness that comes with age, I lashed myself.

If I lived through this night, I really must embrace this idea of leaving me behind, I told myself.

Frank motioned me away from my car with a gun. "Step back Hector. For all I know, you have a machine gun loaded and waiting in that trunk."

"If only it was so this one night." I took a few steps back from my car, pulling Esther along with me, positioning her so I could shove her alongside my car for protection when I started the gunfight.

Donna's stooge thrust his gun down his waistband and lifted the trunk lid. He struggled with the heavy lead box. Donna said, "*You* help him, Hector. That's not a request."

I nodded bitterly and set to the task with both hands.

Smiling at Frank, I said, "By the way, I've decided to help you with that finish to your story after all. Despite my deep disappointment in you, I mean to supply you with your story's ending."

He gave me this funny look, then, pure acid, quipped, "Mighty white of you, given things, Hec."

As we got the lead box up and out of the trunk bed, I worked up the extra leverage to push the heavy box hard at Donna's man. The weight of the thing overwhelmed the man, tied up both his hands and set him tumbling backward on heels as he fought the weight of the load.

Then I drew my Colt and shot Frank between the eyes.

Hoping he hadn't already gone too far away to still hear me, I said, "There you go, old pal—*the end.*"

Her minion stumbled back into Donna as he still struggled with the weight of the lead box bearing back on him. He fouled seething Donna's return shot at me. Turning my Colt on Donna, I yelled, "Go now, Esther!"

A couple more men were running up to assist Donna, who was now on her back, her legs pinned under her flunky who was flat on *his* back with the lead box sitting squarely on his chest.

I put a bullet between the trapped, masked man's eyes, figuring to further pin Donna down under his corpse.

That got the bullets flying every which way again.

People freshly screaming and shouting more orders.

A bullet whipped by my face and I turned, already cocking. I shot at the two masked men running toward me to assist Donna.

One of them toppled, then the other fell—that one taken out by a shot that came from somewhere behind me.

As I turned to see who had assisted me, I saw that Donna was now up from under the corpse, pointing her gun at my face.

"Drop the six-gun, Tex."

Feeling like a dead man standing, I lowered her hammer and slung my beloved Colt in the trunk of my Chevy. "Are you *really* going to shoot me, Donna? I mean, after the *fine time* in the sauna and all?"

Donna flinched then. I flinched too: she pulled the trigger on me, but her single shot went very wide of mark, somewhere well over my head. I snatched up my Colt and was about to point it at Donna's heart.

But she staggered; fell to her knees. Her gun arm hung limply at her side. Her other hand groped between her breasts. She raised her hand to look at it. Something glistened there on her fingers—something I took for blood.

Dark as it was, and Donna being dressed all in black, I couldn't really be sure.

Her hand trembled once, then she fell face first across the empty lead box resting on the dead man's chest.

Something rustled in the bushes behind me. I drew down on Bud and Logan—nearly shot the latter through before I recognized them.

Bud said, "Sorry, couldn't risk you going this one solo lobo, Lass. I got the one over there. Logan got this one."

Bud pointed his smoking gun at Donna's body. "We really need to move, Lass"

Sure. But I was still focused on dead Donna, bleeding out there at our feet.

Well, well: Logan had *finally* come through in the clutch.

Characteristically, he'd picked the most dicey of times to find his spine.

Kid looked pretty shaken up. Logan said, "Who was that who I…"—he seemed on the verge of puking, ended with—"…*you know?*"

Logan was checking out Donna's ass, the shape of her thighs in the form-fitting black slacks. I watched it hit him, then. His voice was funny as he asked me, "Is that a *woman* I just shot?"

"Barely," I said. "Rest assured that you did good, Logan. She was about to kill me. So I owe you, son, large. I—"

There was this chopping sound in the air now, Prescott's helicopters arriving.

There were more shots coming from behind the remaining members of Donna's band.

The Brotherhoods' still-standing troopers were caught in a looming three-way crossfire now between Prescott and company up in the temple, the new, unknown faction firing into their flanks, and in any second, all those killing shots that would rain down on us from above.

I grabbed Esther's arm and hustled her into the passenger seat of the Chevy.

Bud and Logan squeezed into the open trunk to lay down any required covering fire behind us.

I got the Chevy's engine fired up and dropped the hammer, tearing up the hill toward that crazy building, Senator Bush, and safety.

As I gripped the wheel, I acknowledged to myself, *Alicia would be appalled.*

41

The rest of the gun battle, if it could really even be called that, didn't last too much longer past the helicopters' arrival.

At some point, there was enough of a rout to embolden one of the big helicopters to loft down there close by the Rambler.

Men in funny, head-to-toe, white suits and masks ran out and grabbed the lead box from the back of the Rambler. I heard a couple more shots when they got there and before they left with the box—probably signaling the mercy killings of Basil Sloan and his radiation-poisoned *confrere*.

Call 'em "handled." And, given what I'd seen, "mercy killing" was an apt euphemism for what they'd been dealt.

Once the box with the uranium was safely on board the helicopter, Prescott and his remaining men and Ernst made a dash for the helicopter. A few of Prescott's stooges gathered up their own dead.

Senator Prescott Bush leapt into the chopper—the bastard didn't even say good-bye or thank-you. Hell, he didn't even wave.

As the helicopter rose above the Greek temple, the last of the gunfire ceased. I saw a familiar figure coming my way: a glowering Chuck Easton and a few of his black-clad flunkies.

Chuck said, "We still have all those listening devices at the Gantry place. We heard Donna Perkins laying out her plans for tonight's attempted recovery. All this time, we never knew she was part of this conspiracy, let alone a kind of point man, if you will." Chuck shot me a mean look then, his demeanor turning on a dime. "And I thought you said that the weapon was in a pit some place in the hills, Lassiter!"

I shrugged, lighting up a cigarette with Bud's Zippo. "I seemed to have erred, there, Chuck. Your empty lead box is out there, somewhere, under the body of the dead woman. You can have that back."

Chuck squeezed my arm. He snarled, "Where's the *component*, Hector?"

I shrugged off his hand and pointed at the helicopter high overhead now. "Up there, old pal. The *component* is on its way to the state of Israel, where it can maybe do more good than here. Least ways, that's the story I've chosen to believe."

Cursing, Chuck threw down his gun, then kicked the tire of my Bel Air. "Goddamn it! *We* wanted to be the ones to give the damned thing to the Jews!"

I watched him fulminate, watched him kick tires again, still ranting.

Jesus Christ.

Shaking my head, I held down the front seat of my Chevy for Logan and Bud to slide in back. I helped Esther into the front passenger's seat again.

I took a last look at all the bodies strewn around the phony Parthenon and shook my head. I said to Easton,

"With all this shooting and noise, even the obviously lacking local cops will find their way up here, eventually. Probably sooner rather than later. You best get cracking on a cover story, pal. One of the top cops in town here, fella named Rick Corin, he's the take-no-prisoner's type. But not quite like you and certain Senators seem to take no prisoners."

I gestured a last time at the bodies strewn around us in the bloodstained snow ... *la neige rouge.*

Getting the Bel Air in gear, I rolled her fast out of Centennial Park and headed back east toward Music Row. Tardy cruisers, party lights twirling, were coming the other way, splashing the snowy streets with red and blue light.

Esther gave me directions to her home, then sat in silence, staring out the passenger window. She was probably wondering whether she'd still have a job come the morning.

Driving back into downtown Nashville after we'd dropped Esther, Logan said, "*Now*, will somebody please tell me what the hell this was tonight? What the hell just happened?"

He set his focus on me: "Hector, what *was* all this?"

I shrugged. "Answers you're surely owed. But not quite yet."

42

I drove Bud and Logan to Bud's favored bar. Over a pitcher of Margaritas, I explained it all to Logan, the kid's brow furrowing deeper as I unfurled my dark tale.

Logan handled the stuff about the atomic bomb stuff far better than Bud had. Instead, he said, "Donna Perkins was really a part of all this?"

"*Was* is the operative word, kid," I said. "She's back there among the dead."

Logan got this sick look: "God, that woman I shot, it wasn't ... *you know?*"

Bud watched me then. I went for the kind lie:

"*I* shot Donna," I said. "That scheming murderous bitch. The world is better shed of her. Her daughter, too. That group was positively lousy with bent women. The one you killed—and saved me and Esther by doing it, don't you ever forget that, son—*that* bitch you put down was some other seriously nasty piece of work. But Gen's going to be more alone than ever, now. I don't see much of a bright future for that one as things stand. Her mother seemed to run the whole show for that little gal. Even arranged that crazy marriage to Jake."

"She'll have *me*," Logan said. "*I'll* see to Gen."

Christ. Of course he would try. I sighed. "You're really staying on here in town then, kid?"

"That's right," Logan said. "I should get to Gen now, you know. Need to let her hear things from me before some cop, or reporter gets to her first."

"Probably so," I said. "You should be there to comfort her. But don't tell Gen about the bomb or anything else if you want a shot at a life with her, kid. You just stand by and be ready to pick up the pieces after some suit or badge breaks the news to her about her mother and what she was tied up in. Remember what a lousy liar you are and keep these secrets, Logan. Open your mouth, ever, and you'll be in so far over your head you'll never find sunlight again. Listen to me at least this once, won't you, son?"

"I understand," Logan said. "I'll do as you say. Promise."

Shifting around in the booth, I dug out my roll and skidded off some bills and wadded them into Logan's hand. "For the taxi fare home." Logan and I shook hands. I said, "And just watch your back with Jonas Parker, kid, please. I still scent real trouble from that sorry sucker."

Logan shook Bud's hand and then was gone. Just like Prescott. I hadn't even rated a simple and perfunctory last good-bye from Logan. It was almost like I wasn't even here, anymore.

Well...

Bud said, "So what now, Lass? You start that drive down south come morning?"

"That's right, Bud. But I think I want to do that *tonight.* I'm finished with this town for a good while. Hell, maybe forever. And who knows whether Chuck might change his mind and come after me. Or maybe he might tip Corin to some other stuff we've been party to tonight. Old Chuck strikes me as the vindictive sort. I'd at least like to get across the state line—safely in another jurisdiction—before I sack out for the night."

Bud nodded. "That all makes sense."

He fiddled with his glass. "How about I ride shotgun a ways, Lass? I think you're right about getting out of town for at least a few days, to let the heat die down."

I smiled. I suddenly had me this sentimental, match-maker notion tugging at my heartstrings, even if it would take me a ways in the wrong direction.

"Absolutely," I said.

43

That little diner was still bound in snow when we rolled up to her about one in the morning.

Raylene, the pretty young girl-next-door waitress, gave me a double take, then she smiled and said, "You bring your singer friend along, too?"

She gestured at the booth where Logan's autographed record sleeve remained tacked to the wall.

I shook my head, "Sorry, darlin', but the crooner's otherwise engaged. Brought along a different writer friend. He's a poet and songwriter. *The real thing*. Far better company." I introduced her to Bud.

The poet had gifted me a chapbook of his newest poems. I handed it to Raylene so Bud could autograph it for her. "Singers come and go, sugar. Authors and poets *endure*."

As Bud and Raylene chatted, I drifted over to the jukebox, browsed the songs. I found something that wasn't country, a cover of *Where or When*, putting me in mind of this other thing that awaited me much further down south. Those "loose ends" I'd told Bud about—old and clinging ghosts who refused to release their hold.

Open books, screaming to be closed out.

And I thought inevitably of Hem. How *would* that Cuban reunion go?

At least it would be warmer in Cuba; sultry winds and rum drinks and the steady pound of the sea against that bloody island's shore. Cuba ... my first love's last stop.

I glanced over at the counter. Bud already had beaming Raylene's hands gripped tight in both of his. They were laughing at something. The poet had grown up on me, for sure.

Lingering by the jukebox, I waited until Raylene was drawn away to serve another customer.

I took a stool next to Bud and said, "Think I'm going to get rolling, kid. Don't feel at all tired and I want to put some more miles in my mirror before dawn. See if I can't at least outrun more of this damned snow."

I foisted over some bills to Bud. "For a room if you choose to stay on a few days. And for that fare back to Nashville." I nodded at Raylene. "She's a real good kid, Bud. Comes from poor, working-class stock, but she's authentic, I think. Got a good heart and an old soul. And pretty, too. Don't you dare break her heart, kid."

"I like her already," Bud said. "May just stay on here those few days."

I clapped Bud's back and rose. "Send me another copy of those poems to New Mexico, won't you, son? I really do want to read 'em. I *do*."

"Promise." Bud hesitated. "So what's it going to be, Hec? Any ideas about this new persona you're flirting with?"

"Not too firmly, not yet." I smiled. "I've still got to be Hector Lassiter down there in Florida and in Cuba with Hem. But between here and there?" I pulled out Basil's wallet, thumbed through various I.D. cards inside. I flashed one Bud's way.

"Maybe I'll see if I can't put a nicer shine on this late son of a bitch's name on the drive down to the Sunshine State. Call it practice for my second act."

Bud stood and hugged me hard. I patted his back, feeling a bit awkward. I squeezed his arm. Reaching for my pocket I said, "Almost forgot to give you your Zippo back."

"You can mail it to me," Bud said. "Or just keep it, please. Anyway, may be some cigarettes to be smoked between here and the Florida panhandle, you know, Lass?"

Indeed.

As I was slipping out the door, Raylene called to me, "I don't think I ever got your last name, Mister." She smiled sheepishly. "And I think I forgot your first name."

I gave her a last smile. "Doesn't matter a lick anymore, darlin'. You just watch over Bud there for me. And see if you can't get some food in him. Lad needs more meat on his bones, don't you think?"

In the light of the diner's flickering red road sign, I warmed up my Bel Air and fiddled with the radio, thinking more of Hem, more of those loose ends I meant to tie off in Cuba, but mostly thinking of Alicia.

After transferring all my cash to the late Basil Sloan's wallet, I shoved my billfold with all my real identification cards into the glove compartment alongside my exhausted old Zippo and unloaded Colt.

After some time and a lot of static, I found a good radio signal—more Roy Orbison.

Getting the Bel Air in gear, I got her rolling through the dirty snow and mounded slush. I pointed my Chevy south.

I drove all night.

APOSIOPESIS

Excerpt from the *El Paso Herald Post*, dated November 1, 1967:
MYSTERY AUTHOR HECTOR LASSITER FOUND DEAD IN BIZARRE MURDER/SUICIDE

Excerpt from the *El Paso Herald Post*, November 1, 1970
AUTHOR'S GRAVE ROBBED AND CORPSE MUTILATED
Hector Lassiter's head stolen

Excerpt from the *Nashville Tennessean*, November 18, 1972
NOIR POET ESKIN "BUD" FISKE DECLARED LEGALLY DEAD
Missing poet presumed posthumous following disappearance two years ago

Excerpt from the *Nashville Banner*, December 12, 1975
LONGTIME COUNTRY SWEETHEARTS SPLIT
Gen Gantry divorces Logan "Buddy" Burke, citing irreconcilable differences

Excerpt from *Crimespree Magazine*, September/October
2007:

NEW BOOK PROMISES TO CAST DOUBT ON VENERABLE CRIME NOVELIST'S ALLEGED MURDER

**Controversial theory alleges far-reaching conspiracy in
Lassiter 'death'**

A new biography by journalist Marcus French promises to
blow the lid off—

APOCHRYPHA

THE LAST INTERVIEW

REDUX

The end of all our exploring will be to arrive where we started and know the place for the first time.

—T.S. Eliot

OAHU, HAWAII
FEBRUARY, 2008

The old man sat at a picnic table in the shade of an umbrella, sipping a mojito and reading the paper. Rush Limbaugh was wrapping it up on the radio, lamenting the sorry remains of the GOP presidential field.

The Democrats, with their cut-and-run strategies, scared the old man even more.

But hell, it looked like they were actually going to field a black candidate for president. The old man could hardly believe he'd lived to see even the prospect of that happening. Too bad it had to be *this* particular man. The old man scented a disaster in the offing, a presidential debacle that could ultimately serve only to elevate the reputations of sorry old Warren G. Harding and Jimmy "Malaise" Carter.

The old man turned off the radio and switched over to a CD mix: Tom Russell singing *Tramps & Hawkers, Gulf Coast Highway... Chocolate Cigarettes*. Some favorite tunes from Tom Waits, David Olney and Bruce Springsteen.

The old man wore khaki slacks and leather sandals and a white guyabera shirt. His thick white hair was brushed straight back and fell longish at the nape of his deeply wrinkled, suntanned neck. The wind from the ocean whipped over the terrace's edge, carrying the sound of the waves breaking on the craggy rocks far below.

The old man lit another cigarette with a battered, much-repaired Zippo and shook his head at the newspaper. More suicide bombings on the Gaza strip; Israeli leaders warning Iran was maybe a year away from having the bomb, too. Israel had previously taken unilateral action against Iran's nuclear program, launching an air strike with conventional weapons that destroyed a reactor under construction there, embodying one of the old man's own favored axioms when he was in his storied, intrepid prime: "Retaliate first."

Question and supposition now was whether the Israelis would launch a *second* aerial assault to thwart Iran's growing nuclear ambitions.

The world the old man found himself living in now was not remotely the one he'd envisioned. Both sides were intractable, some on the one side perhaps truly crazed, just blood-simple as all hell. Suicidal nihilists in yoke to a bent-ass interpretation of dubious-in-the-first-place dogma.

And certainly he'd never live long enough to see how it would all sort itself out in the Middle East, if it ever did sort itself out in some still-far-distant day.

Live to see it? As if:

The old man *had* to die sometime.

Good genes and crazy voodoo curses aside, there *had* to be an end, and soon, didn't there?

Hank Williams himself wrote that troubling tune: *I'll Never Get Out of this World Alive.*

Nobody *gets out of the world alive...*

Hell, the old man had passed his own most optimistic sell-by date *decades ago.*

He'd thwarted every actuarial table wicked old life could throw at him. The old man still had all his own teeth, for Christ's sake. He still knocked out two thousand words a day, much of it quite good, when his sometimes untrustworthy back granted him blessed, sufficient time in the old leather safari writing chair.

Despite a sea of booze and warehouse of coffin nails, in spite of his erratic blood sugar and Christ only knew how many other flavors of physical and emotional self-abuse, the old man had buried a couple of dozen doctors and surgeons, so far.

Sometimes the old man actually let himself wonder if he had the capacity to die.

He had *endured*. He was now truly what he never expected to be: The Last Man Standing.

The old man had at last become what a long-gone friend had described as "the presumptive, sad and sorry son of a bitch condemned to cut off the lights and pull down the shades on the 20th Century. An indomitable, magnificent warrior-bard, too tough to ever die."

Oh, he'd get around to dying, in time, the old man was sure of that, down deep.

Everyone owed God a death, after all. That was one of Hem's favorite lines, taken from the Bard. But despite his age, no clear end was yet in sight for the old man.

A shadow fell across the table. He hadn't heard her coming. Not that his hearing was so dimmed with age he mightn't have heard her approach, but with the whipping of the coastal wind across his compound's grounds, it was hard to hear much other than that low roar.

And then there was his music: Carmencita leaned over and kissed his bronzed cheek, switching off the CD player on Springsteen's *Girls in Their Summer Clothes*.

Now over fifty, Carm was still pretty; still the eye-pleasing echo of her beautiful Mexican mother.

"He's here now," she said. "Do you want Fernando to sit with you two?"

"*Non*, but *gracias*, darling."

She set down the bag she had carried out with her and reached in and fished out the black eye patch and a small plastic case. "You want me to see to these, Papa?"

The old man smiled and winked. "You know I've never quite gotten the hang of it."

She finished and stepped back, surveying her work. Carmencita squinted her pale blue eyes and adjusted the strap on the eye patch and said, "There. That is good, I think."

The old man reached into the bag and stood and took what remained there and shoved it down the waistband of his pants, at his back, pulling the Cuban shirt's tails down over it and carefully sitting down again. "Your brother saw to preparing it?"

"Fernando said it is quite ready."

The old man shifted around so it didn't dig into his back and said, "Then see the boy out. Oh, and another mojito would help the cause. That, and whatever the boy wants to drink."

"*Sí*, Papa. Good luck."

A bittersweet smile: "To us all."

The young author followed Carmencita out across the terrace, the wind pushing around the young man's sandy hair.

The interviewer was slender, less than six-feet tall. But then tallish writers, like actors, had always seemed a rarity in the old man's experience. Whether fiction or nonfiction scribes, most of them seemed to top out under six-feet. Maybe some kind of Napoleon-complex coaxed all those words from the shorter of them?

Carmencita said, "This is Marcus French, Papa."

The young writer was a career biographer specializing in thick tomes about the lives of the "great dead crime writers."

His oeuvre included volumes on Hammett, Chandler and Cain. Woolrich, Goodis and Lassiter. The usual suspects. The old man had read worse books about all those. Marcus got it *nearly* right: but old Marcus maybe wasn't so sharp at catching the nuances, at detecting the layers. But then so few were, really.

Marcus thrust out a hand and said, "It's my honor, sir."

Still sitting, the old man took the young man's offered hand and shook. A firm grip on his side.

The old man held up his other hand to block the sun from his brown left eye. "You'll pardon me if I don't stand," the old man said. "At my age, you try to ration movement."

"You look very fit for a man of your age, sir."

"You're too kind," the old man said coolly. "And please, quit calling me *sir*. We're just folks here, Marcus. Call me Beau."

The young man smiled and pulled out a chair. "Beau Devlin. *Right.*" The interviewer smiled and thanked Carmencita as she sat a bottle of Keoki beer down in front of him. She placed a mojito next to the old man's right hand. Carmencita and the old man exchanged a glance as they noticed how the young writer narrowed his eyes at the mojito.

Old habits: they died hard.

The old man thought he should have asked for some other type of drink. Maybe some kind of *gin* cocktail: *that* could have set this egghead's head spinning.

The reporter opened a canvas knapsack and pulled out a digital recorder. He said, "Do you mind?"

"I don't mind, not at all," the old man said. "But with this wind you're not going to have anything intelligible on there later, I'll wager."

The reporter pulled out a microphone with a small clip attached. He plugged one end into the recorder and said, "Mind if I pin this to your shirt collar? It won't catch my questions, but it will hear your answers, even over this wind."

The old man shrugged. "Why not?"

Marcus did that and slid back into his seat. He took another sip of his Hawaiian beer. "Despite some of our testier exchanges, I really appreciate you agreeing to meet with me at last."

"Like I had a choice? After all your crazy and ranting threats? 'Testy' doesn't quite cover the way you've come at me, sonny. Not close."

The old man waved a hand. "Letting you come out here, to talk to me now? I'm just trying to save you from embarrassing yourself, kiddo." He paused, "I think you need help. I frankly think you're delusional. I'm Beau Devlin, semi-retired author, not that other writer you insist I am."

That got the boy's back up. He said, "I'm confident I'm right, sir."

The old man sighed deeply and sipped his mojito. He squinted out at the ocean with his single brown eye. He thought he could see a whale out there on the horizon, maybe even a pod of them. He pointed, said, "Whales, see 'em?"

The young man twisted around in his chair and took a look. "But not *white* whales."

"No," the old man said, his voice growing hard. "Blue."

Marcus said, "On that note—whales and so forth, metaphors, allusions and double meanings—it was all there in your novels and short stories you know. The *clues*, I mean. They crept in whether you wrote in first- or in third-person. Even when you wrote under an alias. They were always there for any really close reader to find, despite all your efforts at obfuscation. Under all that careful planning and the meticulous dodges. All the precautions and all your false trails. Despite all the help you had from so many quarters, you betrayed yourself with your own words. Like all fiction writers, you bury your true and deepest secrets—all your obsessions—there in your works of so-called fiction. Nothing isn't real. Nothing is really made up. It's there for people like me to find if they look, that's all. That's all it takes. It's all about attention to detail, for readers and writers."

"Confusing persona and personality is a very old and dangerous trap for readers and especially for literary critics." The old man pulled out a cigarette and lit it with a disposable Bic lighter. "My name is Beau Devlin, son. I don't write *crime fiction*. This theory of yours? It's just flat-out crazy, kid."

The biographer smiled meanly, his gaze focused on the eye patch. "Oh, I trust my instincts. I trust them enough to go to press with my book. And I'm not confusing persona and personality."

The old man just shook his head. "But you're *so* wrong." He sighed. "Just to indulge you a moment, you understand: What was the first supposed *clue*, kid?"

Marcus brushed the hair back from his eyes where the wind had blown it. "The thing that *really* got me started?

It was while I was writing the first Lassiter biography. I was reading the collaborative novel, not *The Big Comb-over*, but the second Lassiter-Fiske 'co-creation,' *Head Games*. Just a small little thing that slipped by in book three, chapter five of that novel. Something a sharp-eyed editor might be expected to catch."

The young nonfiction writer sipped more beer and lit his own cigarette with the plastic lighter. It was a filtered cigarette.

The old man thought, *Lightweight.*

Marcus blew smoke out both nostrils and said, "In *Head Games*, it's 1970, and the *character* Bud Fiske is on the run, stowed away in a boxcar on a train bound west into Mexico. He's escaping with the *character* Hector Lassiter's severed head originally stolen by Skull and Bones. As readers, we've been left to question the condition of Bud's mind. Bud's been having ongoing conversations with the skull and so forth. Even supposedly collaborating on a manuscript with the head. Presumably that manuscript results in the very book we're reading..."

The old man shrugged, arching an inquiring, salt-and-pepper brow over his exposed eye. "It's just a work of fiction, kid. A simple *story*. But keep going, old son. You're this far out on that crazy limb. Might as well saw it off, kiddo. 'Dig that crazy grave,' as the old mystery hack wrote so many moons ago."

"As the chapter closes, the skull, Lassiter's skull, is singing—or rather humming—a song," Marcus said. "A tune called *Cancion Mixteca*. It's a song that has become very important to Lassiter throughout the narrative of *Head Games*. A tune that crops up in scenes when he with his young Mexican love, a woman named Alicia. It comes up again when he is alone with Marlene Dietrich. And then yet another time when he is among strangers in a VFW hall. But never *ever* is it a song Hector mentions or hears in the presence of *Bud Fiske*. So how could Bud know the title to the tune if he's merely hallucinating all of that?"

"God preserve all authors—even all the goddamn lamentable *crime writers* I've never met—from 'close readers' like yourself," the old man said, blowing his own trail of smoke out the side of his mouth. "You're right, kiddo, some editor should have caught that mistake—that clear continuity error."

The biographer said, "Oh, I don't think it was a mistake, not at all, sir. I've read *everything* that's carries the byline 'Hector Lassiter' or 'Eskin Bud Fiske' and at least five or more times. It's not the kind of oversight either author makes. They're both too meticulous. Both are too controlling of the text. They don't make those kinds of mistakes. Neither writer is casual about words, or nuance. There simply are no accidents in the Lassiter and Fiske narratives."

"So what is it, sonny? I mean, from your crazy little literary scholar's perspective?"

"A clue, or a signal, unconscious or otherwise," Marcus said, smiling. "It could be viewed as a literary affectation. Say, establishing the narrators of *Head Games*, whether it be Lassiter, or Fiske, or *both*, as, you know—*unreliable*. The only other way Fiske could be hearing that song from Lassiter's skull would be if Lassiter is indeed a ghost at the end of the novel, as some have had it. Or, as I said, if there was deliberate effort to undermine the validity of the text."

"You're getting way too longhaired here for me, boy," the old man said. "You're actually makin' my head hurt. It's clearly a simple writing mistake on the part of these two long-dead authors."

Marcus just smiled and shook his head. "And like *I said*, that was the *first* thing that tipped me things weren't as they were being presented in Lassiter's novels. It set me to digging *deeper*. All those historical facts and real people underpinning Lassiter's narratives—especially the latter ones? A reader just starts to take it all for gospel *fiction* as the books accumulate on him or her.

"But like it was written in 'The Last Interview,' the short story that first purported to establish the facts of Hector Lassiter's alleged death, La Mesilla was a *backwater*, and Hector Lassiter was by far its most famous resident. A famous man with lots of key friends and favors owed. Hector Lassiter was a man who could easily enough make things happen in a place like that one. He was a famous local hero who could make people bend rules and laws for him. Even plant self-penned stories in newspapers, say. Make elected officials lie about medical conditions and lost legs and to vouch for staged crime scenes. A man with enough money to buy off a soon-to-be-ex fifth wife. Enough money to keep Hannah Lassiter happy and silent about his true fate."

Marcus smiled meanly. "Gets *better*, you devious old trickster. 'Beau Devlin'? Hector Lassiter's maternal grandfather was a man named '*Beau* Stryder'. His first wife was this foxy raven-haired bisexual babe named 'Brinke *Devlin*' who once faked her own death in Paris, setting up a kind of template for Lassiter himself, later, I'll argue. Still want to lie to me, *Beau*?"

The old man frowned and snubbed out his cigarette. He sipped some more of his mojito. Despite the wind, his shirt was starting to stick to his back in places. He dragged a hairy forearm across his damp forehead. "Coincidence."

The biographer smiled and said, "Further evidence: The 'man who lived what he wrote and wrote what he lived' could do a lot of clever things, but he couldn't make Andrew Nagel, his supposed junkie interviewer and eventual slayer a living, breathing man. Not even with the help of his co-conspirator Bud Fiske. There was no such man as Nagel, and I'm not relying on any work of fiction for that name. I'm standing on the 1967 obituaries and crime scene reports regarding Hector Lassiter's 'actual shooting'. I mean the public records files down in New Mexico."

"So you think this Hector Lassiter's death was a put-up job," the old man said. "Some kind of fake out?"

"You know I do," Marcus said. "Hector Lassiter was dead tired of shouldering his larger-than-life public persona. This macho monster his audience embraced. He somehow found himself in another unhappy marriage. Poor bastard was still carrying a torch for this Mexican beauty, Alicia who he'd met and lost in 1957. Hector Lassiter was tired to the bones of his picaresque life and legend and literary output getting all twisted up and feeding on one another in crazy, dangerous ways that took too much from him. I think Lassiter just wanted to sit back and ride out his last years in quiet, writing very different kinds of books. Dark books, in their way, but not crime fiction of the ilk associated with Hector Lassiter."

The old man reached behind his back with one arm, pressing at the base of his spine and wincing like his back bothered him. "So what do you plan to do, sonny? Write some goddamn sequel to your Lassiter biography and set out this whacked theory of yours? Try and describe what form this Hector Lassiter's life took after this supposed death-and-resurrection gambit you've come up with in that fevered and crazy brain of yours?"

"If it stopped there, I might do just that thing," Marcus said. "But as you've gathered, I'm still collecting details about what form Hector Lassiter's life assumed after his so-called *death*." The biographer scooted back his chair and looked under the table.

"You've got two feet, old man," he said. "Both clearly real."

The old man smiled, measuring his interviewer again. *"That's right,"* he said. "Two feet, two *hands*." A mocking smile. "Also got ten toes and ten fingers. Down to one peeper—a car accident, blinded by the sun around Big Sur back in eighty-eight. Bastards took my driver's license from me after that. I—"

It happened quickly then; old as he was, some thing's had been stripped from the man, reflexes being prime among those.

Marcus reached across the table and snatched off the old man's black eye patch.

The old man's revealed right eye was the palest blue and full of fury.

"You really shouldn't have done that, son," the old man said.

His interviewer, grinning now, said, "Yeah! Fuckin' *yeah!* I fucking knew it all along!"

Spittle flew as the biographer jabbed his fingers at the old man's exposed blue eye. The interviewer snarled, "One-hundred-and-eight-years-old and *still here!* Still *alive! Yes!*" Marcus punched air twice. "The alleged amputated leg, the fake murder by 'Nagel' all the way back in sixty-seven ... Pretending all these years to be long dead? All a dodge! *Fuckin'-A!*"

The biographer sat back in his chair, shaking his head, this silly goddamn grin on his face as he looked at the eye patch clutched in his hand. "As you're not David Bowie, I'm guessing that left eye's darker shade is the result of a special contact lens, Mr. Hector Mason Lassiter." He smiled and shook his head. "Alive! Still *alive!* You clever, crazy magnificent bastard!"

The old man thought:

Alive, yes.

And dangerous.

Still plenty dangerous, you goddamn prying young fool.

The old man leaned over and cupped a hand to his eye and blinked out the colored contact lens. He blinked a few times more and then looked at Marcus with blazing, pale blue eyes, eyes paler, even, than his pretty daughter Carmencita's arresting blue eyes.

The interviewer had never seen anything like them— brutally frank eyes, but *pained*... the eyes of artist that had seen and suffered much. More, maybe, than almost any other set of eyes left on earth—just owning to simple time itself.

"By what right do you do this, Marcus?" The old man leveled a finger at his interviewer. "What right do you have to out me, now? I chose to walk away from that other life a long goddamn time ago, boy. Long, long before you ever drew air. You have no right to try and drag me back to that discarded life. I've moved on from those books, far from that sorry wreck of an existence. You have no right to try to take my present life from me. I've tried, God knows, to impress that upon your agent, and by extension, on you. For God's sake, you let this be. *Please* do that."

Marcus waved a hand, said, "*Please* back at you, old man. None of that is my fucking problem. I have a right to practice my trade, just like you did all those years ago. The fact is, you created this situation for yourself with your lies and ploys, old man. You conned your own fans—your most loyal readers. *I'm* not the villain here. Not at all. *You* are the villain. Aren't you ashamed of yourself, Hector? Hiding all these years behind those other books and by-lines? Pretending to be this Beau Devlin?"

The old man shook his head. "Jesus Christ, I wrote books plenty of people have enjoyed, since. I made up stories for them and they kindly paid me for the privilege. End of story. I don't owe them any more than that, and the man in those earlier books isn't me, not *really*. Hell, he never was the real me. You're just scenting some big book contract and a maybe movie deal, boy. We both know that's so. This has *nothing* to do with anything other than your own greed, Marcus. I built *my* career on my *talent*. You're trying to build yours on my back. You're angling to make a name for yourself, standing on my goddamn chest. And worse, you're doing that at my family's expense. That last, especially, simply cannot stand, boy."

The kid got a finger up in the ancient author's face. It was all the old man could do to keep from grabbing that finger and bending it back toward the boy's wrist until it snapped. That all would have been easy enough to bring off, despite his advanced age.

Marcus snarled, "*Fuck* you, old man! Not like you're apt to be around long enough to regret anything I do regarding your story. And, hell, how many shots does a guy like me get at a big one like this? You're the ultimate genre *get!* And whatever my own thoughts and motives, your readers have a right to know the truth about you, Lassiter. On that note, the only crime writer with a murkier *end* than yours is Eskin Fiske. Where is the real Bud Fiske, Mr. Lassiter? I've tried to find leads, but..."

The old man said, "In 1958, Bud and I got tied up with a little mess involving—"

"I've read the so-called *novel,*" Marcus said sharply.

Hector narrowed his eyes, all but decided. "Bud was much closer than me when we were exposed to the contents of that infernal lead box back in Nashville. It took a few years, but the resulting cancer ate poor Bud alive and fast once it took its hold. By the time the doctors tumbled to what Bud was ailing from, it was all *through* him. At least it was a quick end for Bud, thank God."

"Is that another *story,* Mr. Lassiter? Another *tale?* Another fucking lie?"

Another fucking lie?

The old man frowned: What, he should give up his best, still-living friend to satisfy this young egocentric cocksucker of a self-declared biographer? It would be a cold day in hell.

Marcus said, "I think Fiske is alive, too. I mean to find him, Hector. That quest will be the sequel to my book about finding you still alive."

"You're firm on that one. No alternative?"

"That's right. I am firm."

"Final answer?"

"It is."

Well, so be it, the old man thought.

The old man smiled. "Well, I've always been *a tale-teller,* Marcus. You, above all others, should know that, or presume that you do. Seeing as you're my unofficial biographer. And, kid, we're avowedly *not* on a first-name basis, not from your end. Hell, you're no friend of mine. You're not even a savvy reader of my stuff. I sense the really good stuff *confuses* you. Based on my reading of your book about me, I have to say you missed all my best effects. You seem sadly at sea. Far out of your depth."

Hector Lassiter dipped his left hand into his shirt pocket and pulled out his battered old Zippo. He lit an unfiltered Pall Mall. He placed the lighter on the table between them. Marcus squinted his eyes. The lighter still bore the words:

One True Sentence.

The rest had nearly been rubbed off through use.

"Come on kid," Hector said. "As you're a fellow writer, I mean. Step up to the plate, old pal. You of all people know how this game is played. You start me a true sentence, and I'll finish it for you, sharp and good, little man."

Marcus tried to smile but it came across as more of a sneer. "Yeah, well fuck you and your condescension, you evil old cocksucker. I remember that scene from your story, *The Last Interview*. You having fictional Andrew Nagel play this game with your doppelganger just before Andy got shot to death. Sorry, but I'm not playing your wicked game. And anyway, you're not exactly that old man in your story, right? You just said so yourself."

A smile. "Why don't you tell me what I am, French? You *critic*. You're the so-called Hector Lassiter expert. Where does the line between fact and fiction fall in our shared *here and now*, scholar? Answer like your sorry life depends on it, 'cause if I *am* the man in my books, well, maybe your life really does hinge on your answer." The old man leaned in close. "You can't have it both ways, kid."

Hector waved at the surrounding, wind-whipped grounds. "Call this the lion's den."

Now his interviewer was starting to sweat. "This isn't funny."

"On just that much, we agree," the old man said, his voice raw. "It never has been. *Andrew Nagel*. There's a name that takes me back. Sometimes—more for some than others—life indeed imitates art. In my *art* Andrew Nagel was an unworthy biographer come to harass a tired and dying writer in cynical, self-motivated ways. Yet repugnant as I tried to make him, Andrew Nagel wasn't within spitting distance of the sorry son of a bitch you are, French. I'm asking you—*beggin'* you, boy—let this bad idea of yours go. Find something else to write about, for God's sake. Pick some other writer who'll actually appreciate your attentions. Hell, I'll even suggest some names. Push on and forget me and you can still walk away from here. You can do that vertical and published."

The journalist shook his head. "Fuck you, Lassiter! This is my golden ticket. My jackpot. You only get one shot like this, and you're mine. So, I guess it just sucks to be you, huh?"

The old man sighed. "Marcus, you really don't know what you're risking now."

The journalist crossed his arms. "For years you've stalled and dodged and you've jerked my chain, old man. I'm *done* being screwed over and played by you. It's not my fucking problem you've been found out. It's not my fucking problem what becomes of you once my book is out there. Or the film that will surely follow. You just aren't my problem in the end."

The old man bit his lip. "*Not* your problem? You really ought to rethink that, boy. From where I sit—and I'm warning you now, for a *last* time—I can still be plenty problem for you. The final problem, to coin a *genre* phrase."

"So try to sue me," Marcus said. "I'll have enough money soon to fight you and your estate until your children are dust."

Marcus slumped back in his chair, grinning. "To hell with you, geezer. Honest to God—you really think you'll even be north of the dirt by the time my book is in galley this fall? At your age? Get real! You'll be fertilizer before my book is an ARC. You'll be worm shit before my lay-down date."

His eyes flaring, surprising even himself, Marcus let fly, the back of his hand striking the old man on the jaw. The novelist glared back at Marcus as he wiped blood from his lip. He stared at his own bronzed and bloody hand—it was strangely steady, despite his age.

"That tears it," the old man said.

The kid was wide-eyed but still standing firm: "Don't even think about it, Lassiter. Take a shot at me, and you'll just break what's left of your old hand." Marcus fished a cigarette from a soft pack. His hand shook. "Face it. You're screwed, old man. Screwed and long past being a threat. Spin it anyway you want. Sure, let's even put it your way: I *am* going to build a career on your shoulders. I'm going to savor doing that after the past couple of years you've cost me on my book."

The biographer stretched a hand out for the antique Zippo, eyes off the old man as he reached for the lighter. "One true sentence," he read scornfully.

Still looking at the Zippo, Marcus said, "Okay, here's one for you and you don't even have to finish it: Your story is mine to tell, and what happens to you, to your wife and to your *adult* children afterward, that doesn't matter a thing to me. None of that is my problem."

Hector sighed. "That was two sentences, boy. And neither of 'em rises to the standard of truth."

Now he had decided. The old man cocked on the draw. "You seem settled in your mind. And so I am, now. It's *adios*, French. *Vaya con dios.*"

The interviewer looked up from the battered old Zippo. His smile dimmed as he saw the long-barreled Colt pointed between his eyes.

"I'm sorry," Hector said, "truly, I am, Marcus, but I've haven't lived this long in the shadows to have some damned unwanted and unworthy biographer wreck my chosen present life. I tried to warn you off, Marcus, old kid. I tried *so hard* to do that, and for *a very* long time..."

There were no neighbors and the wind covered the sound of the single shot.

Fernando walked out of the house after, his own gun hanging unfired at his side. Carmencita's twin gestured at the dead man with his gun. "Sorry, Papa. I *would* have done it, you know. Happily."

"Old habits and vices," Hector said. "So no, son, this was my sorry thing to do." The old man massaged his wrist where it hurt from the recoil of the ancient Peacemaker. It had been a long time since he'd pulled her trigger. The old Colt had more kick than he remembered.

"This will stop it?" Fernando's younger brother was walking toward them. Joaquin was taller than his brother, much closer to Hector's height and an uncanny echo of the younger Hector.

"Bud is seeing to Marcus's bottom-feeding literary agent," Hector said.

The old man shook his head. No. *Bud*—that wasn't right, not anymore.

Fiske had stopped being "Bud" not long after Hector had chucked his own identity.

Bud, too, had become tired of his burdensome public persona. Since late seventy-two, or so, Bud had been going by Raoul.

"Another old friend is seeing to Marcus's notes and computers," Hector said. "And still *another* crime writer, a younger acquaintance of mine who shares an editor with Marcus, he'll see to cooling *her* jets. Nothing too hard in store for that editor. My boy Chris has got a silver tongue and Lyon is colder and craftier even than me, in some scary ways. So, yes, this will stop it. Stop *this* sorry mess at any rate."

Fernando said, "Leave me and Joaquin to see to this, Papa." He nodded at the dead biographer.

The old man stood up and stretched and squeezed his son's shoulder hard, unable to look back at Marcus's sightless eyes.

Damn the goddamn nosey fool. The would-be biographer had been a pain in the old man's ass going on three years, snarling threats, issuing ultimatums. Goddamn Marcus French anyway for making Hector do such a thing to him.

"Thank you both," the old man said to his eldest son, sick to his stomach at what he'd left to clean up.

The old man walked across the terrace and made his way down some winding tile steps to another, smaller terrace, lower and closer to the ocean—the end of a thousand roads, many of which still bore no names.

Hector clutched at the railing and tipped his head back, savoring the wind in his hair and across his bronzed face; whipping at his shirt and pants' legs.

Feeling the sun against his eyelids, the old man's mind turned back to all his lost and most-loved ones: to Brinke and Duff; to Hallie, Hannah and Dolores. To Hem, Orson and Jimmy and so many others who'd gone ahead of him.

A soft hand squeezed the old man's shoulder. A honeyed voice said, "What do you see, out there on the horizon?"

White gulls hovered overhead. The sea was the color of carnival glass. A ship rode the waves far out there. The shadows grew longer.

She could hear his smile in his voice. "I had my eyes closed, actually. Just imagining."

A writer to the end, the woman thought.

His wife said, "So many years of peace, and now *this*. If this loco young man figured it out, there could be others, Héctor. Perhaps even worse ones than this."

The old man smiled. "Then, given my age, they best get a leg up, darlin'. Hell, even I won't keep forever. Young fool was right about that much."

He kissed Alicia's forehead and pulled her close. Alicia said, "What would all those readers of Héctor Lassiter's think if they knew the truth?"

The ancient crime writer—the last of the *Black Mask* writers, the last of the great pulp authors and last of the Lost Generation; *the last man standing*—smiled and shrugged, watching more whales venturing far out to the horizon. The moon was above them, suddenly, pale and swollen in the distance.

That ship was drawing closer.

After a time, Hector said, "Hell, I really don't know. Not sure I even truly care. *Head Games, heh!* It was a good and elegiac enough ending I gave *Hector* in that book, don't you think, darlin'? Wasn't that a good death for *that* Hector Lassiter? Let's leave them with that one, don't you think?"

Alicia smiled and brushed the eternally unruly comma of white hair from over her husband's right eye.

She said, "Oh, I don't know. Think what legends might rise up around you if you indeed returned to the world now. What if Héctor Lassiter, believed posthumous for *decades*, suddenly triumphantly came back from the dead? What might happen *then*?"

It was *almost* tempting to the old man.

It would be so simple: Just call a press conference and step back into that limelight he left in the fall of 1967.

The media would go *berserk*.

All his works would surely come back in print, like that ... sell like icy lemonade in hell.

Hector Lassiter had at last outlived all of his enemies. He was sure of exactly that much.

In the time left him—whether it be days, or months, or even years, Hector could bask in past glories and one of the greatest benign literary hoaxes of all time.

Salinger disappeared into darkness.

Hector's best and accidental writing mentor, Ambrose Bierce, had disappeared, period.

But Hector Lassiter could return from the void as no other mysterious author ever could.

His beloved last wife was right: it would surely feed his loopy, larger-than-life legend.

Maybe Alicia really could read his mind. He often suspected she could do just that. He kissed her cheek, and pulled her closer.

She smiled and kissed him again. Alicia said softly, "When legend becomes fact ... ?"

"Print the legend," Hector Lassiter whispered back.

THE END

ACKNOWLEDGEMENTS

Special thanks to Debbie, Madeleine and Yeats McDonald. It would have been impossible without your love and support to have followed Hector Lassiter's journey to its end.

Also to Svetlana Pironko, Michael O'Brien and to my former editors, Alison (Janssen) Dasho and John Schoenfelder.

Thanks also to Madeira James and Jen Forbus for all their continuing work on my website, and to Recorded Books' Tom Stechschulte, forever the "voice" of Hector Lassiter.

I'm also deeply indebted to all the independent book-shops and mystery specialty stores and booksellers who have taken the Hector Lassiter series to their hearts over the years and urged the novels on their customers, as well as to librarians who've recommended the Lassiter novels to their patrons. The latter do the Lord's true literary work.

Very special thanks to all of the singer-songwriters and musicians who contributed memories, stories and reminiscences that inform this novel.

I'm particularly grateful to Katy Moffat, who, over a long lunch in a snowbound German Village restaurant a few years back shared stories of Nashville and songwriting;

of the challenges of the songwriter's life and so many wonderfully rich, musician's life-on-the-road war stories that helped me craft this novel. Katy's cover of *You Don't Know Me* played countless times during the composition of this last book, becoming a kind of anthem for Hector Lassiter's ultimate journey in the novel.

I'm also deeply indebted to Tom Russell, Michael Martin, Katy Moffat, Andrew Hardin, Gretchen Peters and Barry Walsh for allowing me to sit in on various sound checks over the years, and for putting up with all of my questions regarding their craft.

I owe a very special thank you to Mr. Alec Wightman, impresario of Zeppelin Productions in Columbus, Ohio, and a Trustee of the Rock and Roll Hall of Fame, for arranging interviews and affording me access to the above-mentioned musicians. This book would not be what it was without his special and deeply appreciated support.

Also, a tip of the Stetson to the good people of Nashville; to the fine folks at Tootsies and Ernest Tubb's Record Shop and to all the dreamers and buskers who still enliven Music Row. This novel was substantially written and polished in the bars and backrooms of Nashville performance halls while taking in the very music it celebrates.

Lastly, thank-you to all the loyal readers of the Hector Lassiter series.

Though some standalone novel or short story about Hector might someday find its way into print—we never say *never*, after all—Hector Lassiter's larger and definitive tale officially ends *here*, as it was always intended to.

The last secret of the Hector Lassiter series of secret histories is that the main story has always been about Hector

Lassiter, the author and man, and of Hector's highly idio-syncratic creative journey as a writer.

I thank you so much for sharing Mr. Lassiter's long and often winding road.

Vaya con dios.

THREE CHORDS & THE TRUTH
Reader Discussion Questions
*(Spoiler caution: The following presumes reading of
not just this novel, but the other books in the
Hector Lassiter series!)*

1. The novel incorporates a quote by T.S. Eliot: "The end of all our exploring will be to arrive where we started and know the place for the first time." The novel brings Hector full circle back to the era of *Head Games* and the first Lassiter piece of fiction, the short story "The Last Interview." Were you surprised how the author chose to end the Lassiter series?

2. This novel resurrects many old faces from *Head Games*. Were there any you were particularly pleased to see return? Did any catch you off guard?

3. Hector spent most of his life up to the 1960s constructing his legend and stature as a writer and public personality. Were you surprised he came to rue that persona over the arc of the series?

4. Why do you think the author chose to end the series in Nashville, against the backdrop of the country music scene?

5. Race plays a central role in this novel. How has racial discrimination manifested itself in prior Lassiter novels, and how do those depictions inform this last book?

6. The Lassiter series turns on little known or under-reported historical events. Had you heard of the Tybee hydrogen bomb incident before reading of it in this novel?

7. Do you believe, as some others do, that the dumped hydrogen bomb—presumably still resting somewhere off the Carolina coast—still possesses its nuclear trigger?

8. Hector faked his death and walked away from his former life, reinventing himself as a writer in the fall of 1967. Do you support his decision to do that? Do you agree with Hector's last, ill-fated interviewer's assertion that the will of the readers should trump that of the author?

9. In the series' original, abbreviated publication sequence, *Head Games* appeared first, apparently ending with Hector's death. Befitting its title, *Head Games* was soon after revealed to be a narrative by a calculating Hector who was intent upon essentially writing his own obituary. The actual series ends with Hector, very old, yet still very much alive. Do you favor that ending, or the one that Hector devised for himself in *Head Games*?

10. Did the ending of this novel—and of the series—satisfy you? Would you have concluded Hector's saga differently? If so, how?

11. In the end, it's implied that *all* of the Hector Lassiter novels are the product of Hector's own mind and hand. As he is known as "the man who lives what he writes and writes what he lives," what do you think that implies about the validity of the tales you've been reading? Does the implication Hector perhaps shaped the novels toward some calculated end change your regard for them in any way? How does that idea affect your view of their author?

ABOUT THE AUTHOR

Craig McDonald is an award-winning author and journalist. The Hector Lassiter series has been published to international acclaim in numerous languages. McDonald's debut novel was nominated for Edgar, Anthony and Gumshoe awards in the U.S. and the 2011 Sélection du prix polar Saint-Maur en Poche in France.

The Lassiter series has been enthusiastically endorsed by a who's who of crime fiction authors including: Michael Connelly, Laura Lippmann, Daniel Woodrell, James Crumley, James Sallis, Diana Gabaldon, and Ken Bruen, among many others.

Craig McDonald is also the author of two highly praised non-fiction volumes on the subject of mystery and crime fiction writing, *Art in the Blood* and *Rogue Males*, nominated for the Macavity Award.

To learn more about Craig, visit www.craigmcdonaldbooks.com and www.betimesbooks.com

Follow Craig McDonald on Twitter @HectorLassiter and on FaceBook: https://www.facebook.com/craigmcdonald novelist

CPSIA information can be obtained
at www.ICGtesting.com
Printed in the USA
LVOW10s2310060317
526354LV00001B/188/P

9 780993 433115